One True

THEORY

of

LOVE

"A gorgeously authentic voice."
—Kavita Daswani, Author of *Salaam, Paris*

"Every mother, every daughter, and anyone who's ever been in love should read this book! Grab the tissues. It's a triumphant tearjerker!"

—*New York Times* bestselling author
Vicki Lewis Thompson

"Evocative, poignant, and truly lovely. Laura Fitzgerald gives us a glimpse of a culture that's terrifyingly different—and yet heartbreakingly the same as our own."

—Alesia Holliday, author of
Seven Ways to Lose Your Lover

"A fun, romantic, and thought-provoking debut novel from a promising author." —*Booklist*

"A gorgeously authentic voice. Fitzgerald's narrative is infused with wit, warmth, and compassion. If you like cross-cultural books, you won't want to put this down."

—Kavita Daswani, author of *Salaam, Paris*
and *For Matrimonial Purposes*

"In this winning debut, Fitzgerald has crafted the powerful story of one woman's courage to look beyond the life she has been given—*Veil of Roses* is a poignant and uplifting novel full of charm, wit, and grace."

—Beth Kendrick, author of *Fashionably Late*
and *Newlyweds*

continued...

"Watching Tami find her voice through such small comforts as being able to sit alone in a house, walk to school unescorted, or buy lingerie with her sister will leave readers rooting for her." —*Publishers Weekly*

"After picking up *Veil of Roses*, I did everything one-handed for two days, I was so unwilling to put it down! Charming and heartbreaking and hopeful and funny, this is the rare book that completely transports the reader. Laura Fitzgerald is an amazing talent."

—Lani Diane Rich, author of
A Little Ray of Sunshine

"Poignant and warm, *Veil of Roses* is a story about having hope, finding love, and embracing freedom. I loved it."

—Whitney Gaskell, author of
Testing Kate

One True
THEORY
of
LOVE

LAURA FITZGERALD

NEW AMERICAN LIBRARY

New American Library
Published by New American Library, a division of
Penguin Group (USA) Inc., 375 Hudson Street,
New York, New York 10014, USA
Penguin Group (Canada), 90 Eglinton Avenue East, Suite 700, Toronto,
Ontario M4P 2Y3, Canada (a division of Pearson Penguin Canada Inc.)
Penguin Books Ltd., 80 Strand, London WC2R 0RL, England
Penguin Ireland, 25 St. Stephen's Green, Dublin 2,
Ireland (a division of Penguin Books Ltd.)
Penguin Group (Australia), 250 Camberwell Road, Camberwell, Victoria 3124,
Australia (a division of Pearson Australia Group Pty. Ltd.)
Penguin Books India Pvt. Ltd., 11 Community Centre, Panchsheel Park,
New Delhi - 110 017, India
Penguin Group (NZ), 67 Apollo Drive, Rosedale, North Shore 0632,
New Zealand (a division of Pearson New Zealand Ltd.)
Penguin Books (South Africa) (Pty.) Ltd., 24 Sturdee Avenue,
Rosebank, Johannesburg 2196, South Africa

Penguin Books Ltd., Registered Offices:
80 Strand, London WC2R 0RL, England

First published by New American Library,
a division of Penguin Group (USA) Inc.

First Printing, February 2009
10 9 8 7 6 5 4 3 2 1

 REGISTERED TRADEMARK—MARCA REGISTRADA

LIBRARY OF CONGRESS CATALOGING-IN-PUBLICATION DATA

Fitzgerald, Laura, 1967–
One true theory of love / Laura Fitzgerald.
p. cm.
ISBN 978-0-451-22588-7
1. Single mothers—Fiction. 2. Kindergarten teachers—Fiction. 3. Iranian Americans—Fiction. I. Title.
PS3606.I8836064 2009
813'.6—dc22   2008044957

Set in Adobe Garamond • Designed by Alissa Amell

Printed in the United States of America

This book is dedicated to my children, Carly and Luke,
and to the adults they will one day be.

ACKNOWLEDGMENTS

Writing a book can be a long, lonely journey. Mine wasn't. I'd like to thank the following people, whose efforts and involvement made the process both challenging and fun:

My first thanks go to Ellen Edwards at NAL, for her editorial tenacity, sharp eye, and open mind as the story changed and grew . . . and changed again, and again . . . and again. I am also appreciative of: Becky Vinter, Monica Benalcazar, Kara Welsh, and Claire Zion. Thank you to Jennifer Bernard and the other publicists working with Craig Burke; to Rick Pascocello and his team in advertising and promotion; to Sharon Gamboa, Don Rieck, Norman Lidofsky and his entire sales team; and to Trish Weyenberg and all the sales representatives in the field.

Thank you to Stephanie Rostan, my very trusted agent at Levine Greenberg Literary Agency, and to the rest of the Levine Greenberg team, especially Monika Verma, Beth Fisher, Melissa Rowland, and Miek Coccia.

I am profoundly grateful to Ross Browne at The Editorial Department for his editorial support throughout the extensive writing and editing process. His high standards, good sense, and laid-back persistence made this an immeasurably better book.

My friends and family continue to offer meaningful support and cheerleading on a daily basis. Thank you all. Extra special appreciation this time around goes to: Bill and Maureen, my parents, for hosting me when I'm in Milwaukee and spreading the word about me when I'm not; Julie Ore-Giron, who pounds the miles alongside me and is an excellent brainstorming partner, as well as generous with her time and enthusiasm in reading draft after draft; Lisa Dew, for a lifetime of friendship; Sherry Martin and Todd Martin, for ongoing friendship and support; Robin Brande, for being my writing-pal confidante; Annette Everlove, for legal advice and inspired feedback; Daisy Lebron, for sharing some of her toughest life lessons; Colleen Geurts, for sharing her single-mom rules for dating; Austin Hodge, founder of the lovely tea shop Seven Cups, for the tea lesson; Renni Browne, for her presubmission editing; Peggy Bommersbach, for her friendship and for sharing what it's like to be a young person in an old woman's body; to the women in my book club, for being great examples of how to live rich.

I so appreciate the readers and bloggers and book clubs who contacted me after reading my first novel, *Veil of Roses,* and shared their thoughts and invited me into their worlds. Please stay in touch! A special thanks to Liz Broomfield and a hang-tough to Stephanie Coleman-Chan.

Finally—saving the best for last: I thank Carly and Luke (poets and writers, both) for being such truly excellent individuals. I thank Farhad for—well, simply for everything. (I have kept a list. . . .)

*I*t's easy to look at men and think they're idiots. They watch their
ESPN and sneak their Playboys and for no good reason at all
refuse to ask for directions. It's easy to think there's just not a heck
of a lot of depth in men as a species.

I've got this theory. It's about Adam and Eve and how things really
went down that day in the Garden of Eden. I think the newness of
the relationship was wearing off and Eve, being a woman, had an
unquenchable need for them to COMMUNICATE about their
FEELINGS, which of course Adam, being a man, simply would not,
could not, do. And then the serpent slithered along, representing our
not-best selves, and whispered to Eve, "Keep poking him. Threaten
to eat from the Tree of Knowledge if he won't talk to you."

It seemed like a good idea at the time, but when Eve made the
threat, Adam shrugged it off, barely acknowledging he'd heard her.
Maybe he just said, "Go ahead, dear, if it'll make you happy,"
thinking whatever she was yakking about going and doing would
at least get her off his case for a while.

Being a man, he didn't consider how much was really at stake.
Which, of course, was everything.

Meg Clark stood and waited in front of her twenty-three kindergartners at Foundation Elementary School on Tucson's

south side. It was the last ten minutes of the school day, and at this hour they were ABC'd out and ring-around-the-rosy pooped. The time might have been better spent with them resting on their mats. But Meg always took this moment, because to her it was the one that mattered most.

She began and ended the day with song, and now, a few weeks into the new school year, her students knew that when she clapped and announced afternoon-circle time, they were to push the small-person tables and chairs out of the way and gather in a standing circle for one last time that day.

They'd already sung "Down on the Banks of the Hanky Panky" and jumped like bullfrogs from one imaginary lily pad to another. They'd done "Head, Shoulders, Knees, and Toes," and they were almost through their last song when Meg put out both arms like a school crossing guard and said, "Okay, stop!"

Her students came to a kids' version of a standstill. Meg waited as they collectively squirmed, tilting forward on their anticipatory toes. Scanning the circle, she looked at each in turn. There was Antonio, with his grin so big she wanted to scoop him up and smother him with hugs. There were Rachel and Emma and Max and Dylan and Taylor and Kira and Isaac and Remi and Ryan and Morgan and Katherine and Isabelle and Carly and Luke—all of them, with their beautiful, soulful eyes. In a school that was ninety-five percent Latino, most were dark-featured, the opposite of Meg, but at this point in their young lives, being the opposite of Meg didn't matter. They accepted her fully with their untainted hearts.

Under her guidance, they'd put their right feet in and pulled them back out. They'd put their right feet back in and shaken them—extravagantly—all about. They'd done the hokey pokey and they'd turned themselves around, one body part at a time.

And then at Meg's direction, they paused. It was important to her that this next part—in which they'd leap, with their whole selves, into the center of the circle—be momentous. And so she waited.

And waited.

And waited.

She waited for Marita, her sole nonsquirmer. With her long black braids, her love-me eyes, and her worried brow, Marita watched Meg's every move with a quiet intensity, as if afraid Meg might disappear should she for one moment let down her guard. Wariness preempted her enthusiasm until next to her, Lucas—goofy Lucas—wiggled her arm and whispered to her. Only then did she smile, and only then did Meg continue.

"Is everybody ready?" she said.

"Yes!" they shouted.

"It doesn't sound like you're ready," Meg teased. "Are you *really* ready?"

"Yeeeessss!" Marita said it along the others. "We're *ready*, Miss Meg, we're READY!"

We're ready. Those were the magic words. Really, Meg saw that as her only job—to help them be ready. For life, for love, and for everything in between.

She liked to fantasize that one day, when her students had grown up to be doctors to the dying and mothers to the drug-addicted and wives who'd been heartlessly shown the door, they'd think back to the last ten minutes of their kindergarten days, when their spirits still soared.

She hoped they'd remember how she dressed for them in polka-dot skirts and dangly earrings and how she tried to impart to them in a meaningful way the best piece of advice they were likely to receive in the entirety of their lives: that when life turned, as it invariably would—when it seemed nearly impossible to summon the courage to go on—there was only one best thing to do.

"All right, then." Meg beamed at her students. "And a one, and a two, and a one, two, three—let's do it!"

It was an imperfect circle into which they jumped, but that was okay. Life was imperfect, too. Together they did what they were supposed to, with joy and without hesitation: they put their whole selves in.

Lucas was the last student to leave that day. "Hey," Meg said. "Your shirt's on backward."

Lucas shrugged and grinned. "I know."

Meg grinned back. They had this same exchange almost every day. Lucas seemed genetically opposed to matching socks and shirts worn face-forward. "Thanks for getting Marita smiling there in circle time," she said. "What'd you say to her?"

Lucas shrugged again. "I told her if she didn't put her whole self in, I'd push her whole self in and tickle her whole self. See ya, Miss Meg."

"See ya, Lucas." Meg watched him go, then lingered in her classroom doorway and waited for her son, Henry, a fourth-grader at Foundation, to come tramping down the hall toward her, happily burdened with a backpack so heavy he had no business carrying it.

It was Friday, three o'clock—the weekend. They would officially mark it in a few minutes as Meg backed Coop, their lipstick red Mini Cooper, out of the school parking lot and tooted the horn—zipping off into the imaginary sunset, mother and son breaking free.

"Hey, Mom!" Henry called. "Guess what!"

As always when she saw Henry for the first time after any length of absence, Meg was momentarily rendered awestruck by the messy blond-haired beauty that was her son.

"What?" she said.

"No tienes cojones!"

Henry was nine, and he seemed to learn a new insult daily from his classmates (aka *fellow hoodlums*). And each day, he shared it with Meg and eagerly awaited her response. But what was she supposed to say? *No tienes cojones. You've got no balls.*

"Lovely," Meg said. "Just lovely. And it's even anatomically correct. But really—must you be so crude?"

"Yes, Mom. I must."

Meg rolled her eyes. He could be such a Henry. "Hey, Henry, guess what?"

"What, Mom?"

"If you say it again, there will be consequences." To show she meant it, Meg raised her eyebrows in a strict-mom maneuver before going back inside her classroom. While she lined up the desks and tucked in the chairs, Henry flipped off and on and off again the lights to her classroom.

"I got a hundred on my spelling test," he said.

"Henry, that's awesome."

"A-w-e-s-o-m-e," he said.

"Very good, smarty-pants. Are you ready?"

Henry flipped the lights off for the last time and Meg closed her classroom door behind them. With a practiced flourish, they burst through the school's front doors into the triple-digit September sauna-of-a-day, where the sun immediately assaulted them. Any day now, it would be biking weather, roller-skating weather, walk-outside-without-cursing weather. Any damn day.

But that day, the heat was just plain rude. While Henry fumbled in his backpack for his baseball cap, Meg scrambled in her purse for her sunglasses. Once properly outfitted, they nodded at each other and grinned. They would not be thwarted.

"Onward!" Henry cried.

"Onward!" Meg agreed. This was their battle cry, the motto of their lives. Henry was her guy—a kid who was loved and knew it, a kid who loved back with an enthusiasm Meg hoped would never dim.

"Can we get Harry Potter Number Two for movie night?" Henry asked as they buckled themselves into Coop.

"Henry, really." Meg turned and lowered her sunglasses so he could see her mock-scolding eyes. "Haven't you had enough of Harry Potter?"

He grinned at her. "Never."

Meg shook her head. Every week at Casa Video, she suggested alternatives, but Henry said no to the Brady Bunch series, no to the *Cheaper by the Dozen*s, no to *Home Alone*. It had recently occurred to Meg that he wasn't interested in any movie involving the proverbial big, happy family. Which was probably a good thing, since one wasn't in the cards for him.

"If you pick the movie, then I get to pick the ice cream,"

she said. This was another aspect of their Friday nights, one pint of Ben and Jerry's, shared in Meg's queen-sized bed while watching their movie.

"Deal," said Henry. "Are you going to pick Chunky Monkey?"

"You'll just have to wait and see." Meg tooted her horn as they zipped out of the school parking lot, moving onward, always onward. She did, in fact, have a hankering for Chunky Monkey.

Not to mention, because it went without saying, she lived to make Henry happy.

Men aren't idiots. They just like us to think they are because it gets them out of doing so many things they don't want to do. Like grocery shopping. Or cleaning out the garage. Or telling us how they really feel.

The problem is, when a man acts like a simpleton over an extended period of time, he sort of . . . becomes one. Until one day he remembers: hey, there's a real and complex person inside this shallow shell I show the world—and she's not honoring that!

This is what we often refer to as a midlife crisis, although it can happen at any age, and to any man.

The Golden Arms apartment complex on Country Club Road and East Fifth Street had two qualities that made it nearly impossible for Meg to consider moving.

First, it was one of the few places in central Tucson where she could afford a decent two-bedroom. Second, it was a twenty-minute drive from Meg's parents' house in the foothills. Since Meg's mother largely kept her world to a five-minute radius, this extra fifteen-minute distance meant one thing to Meg: freedom from Clarabelle.

Which was why she was taken aback when Clarabelle suddenly appeared at her kitchen window with a cheery *ha-loooo* as Meg was washing up that night's macaroni-and-cheese dishes. Not only was she taken aback—she was concerned. Clarabelle had just retired from her administrative-support position at the University of Arizona after thirty-five years and suddenly had lots of extra time on her hands. Meg worried regularly just exactly what that might mean to her, personally.

"Mom! Hi! What are you doing here?" Her mother's appearance threatened the very essence, the very unchanging routine, of Friday-night movie night. Unbidden, Meg's mind flashed on an image of Clarabelle crawling into bed with her and Henry.

Nope, that wasn't going to happen. Movie night was precious and Meg firmly believed in protecting that which was precious.

"I was just passing by!" Her mother's smile was breezily carefree, but Meg knew better. Clarabelle was a full-on hurricane. "I thought I'd pop in and say hello. It's been a while since I've seen the two of you."

"We saw you five days ago, Mom." Meg turned off the water spigot and reached for a towel to dry her hands. She met Clarabelle at the door. "At Amy's. Like we do every Sunday, remember?"

Amy was Meg's younger sister and the organizer of the family. A bit controlling, she hosted a family brunch every Sunday and all the major holidays, and if you wanted to bring a dish, you had to clear it through her first.

"I've got something for you." Clarabelle came right in, set her big purse on the dining room table, and rummaged through it. Meg loved bright colors thrown together, reminiscent of

Mexico or what she imagined Mexico would be like if she could ever afford to travel there, and decorated her apartment accordingly in reds, yellows, oranges, and turquoise. Clarabelle, in black, was like death in a field of flowers.

"I knew I'd forget if I waited." She pulled a newspaper clipping out of her purse and handed it to Meg. "Here. It's called 'Dogs: A Lonely Boy's Best Friend.' I thought you might find it interesting."

One. Meg took a deep breath.

"Well, gee. Thanks," she said. "That'll come in handy, seeing how there's a no-pets-allowed policy here."

Which her mother perfectly well knew.

"You might buy a house one day," Clarabelle said. "Lord knows you should be able to afford it, seeing as you didn't pay rent when you lived with us."

Two, Meg thought. She'd moved in with them after the Jonathan thing happened and stayed until Henry started kindergarten at Foundation, at which time they moved into the Golden Arms apartment complex. (The *Jonathan thing* being: My lovely wife of three years, you're pregnant? Well, congratulations, and I guess I should mention that all those times I told you I was studying? Well, I've actually been screwing my study partner. Yeah, and, um, I'm moving with her to New York City after law school . . . but congratulations on the pregnancy! I know you've always wanted to be a mom. . . . Jerk! Asshole! Complete asshole jerk!)

"I offered to pay rent," Meg said. "You said, *Don't be ridiculous.* I remember the exact conversation."

"You were in the middle of having a nervous breakdown,"

Clarabelle said. "We thought asking you to pay rent might put you over the edge, but we hoped you were saving your money to buy a house."

"That wasn't part of the deal," Meg said. "Besides, I love my apartment. My entire social life revolves around it. Not to mention, Violet's here. Henry wouldn't want to live anywhere else. With Violet for a best friend, Henry doesn't need a dog."

Without even deigning to glance at it, Meg slipped the article into her kitchen junk drawer on top of the last obnoxious one her mother had given her: "Mothering the Fatherless Boy."

Clarabelle put her hands on her judgmental hips. "Where is my grandson, anyway?"

"He's down at the pool," Meg said.

"*Alone?* You let your nine-year-old son go swimming *alone?*"

Three. Gloves off.

"Yes, Mom," Meg said. "And I gave him matches and lighter fluid to play with, too. What do you think? You think I don't know how to take care of my son?" She allowed herself to use a *back off, lady* tone, knowing from past experience that her mother would not, in fact, back off, but it was either start giving as good as she got or start turning to over-the-counter pharmaceuticals anytime she spoke with her mother. Talking back was cheaper.

"The whole Loop Group's down there," Meg said, adding, "And he's not swimming, anyway. Last I heard, he's building a spaceship."

"Loop Group," Clarabelle muttered.

Yes, Mom. The Loop Group. Meg and Henry called the trio of tenants who gathered each night down by the pool the Loop Group, because they were . . . well, loopy. Harley, Crazy Kat and Opera Bob—all three were certifiably quirky, but they were also decent and funny and reliably *there*. Meg considered them family, only refreshingly minus the baggage.

"How are you ever going to get a date if you hang out with those . . . those *people* all the time?" Clarabelle said.

Four, five, six, seven, and eight.

"Come on," Meg said. "How many times do we have to discuss this? I don't *want* to date. I've made a Conscious Decision not to. I'm happy with my life exactly like it is. Plus, there's Henry to consider."

"You can't let a child determine how you live your life," Clarabelle said.

"I certainly can," Meg said. "To me, that's what being a good mom's all about."

"You would think that." Clarabelle made a show of licking her lips. "I'm a bit thirsty. What do you have to drink?"

Meg felt her blood boil. *I'm a bit thirsty.* What the hell kind of comment was that? It was a sticking-around kind of comment—that was what it was.

"Would you like a glass of water before you go?" Meg said.

"Do you have anything *else*?"

"I have wine," Meg said. "But I don't think you'd like it."

"Wine would be lovely." Clarabelle followed Meg into the narrow galley kitchen, which was entirely too small for them both. When Meg pulled a half-full bottle of wine from the refrigerator, Clarabelle grabbed it and examined its label. "What's *this*?"

Meg took it back. "It's Two Buck Chuck. From Trader Joe's."

"Two Buck Chuck." Clarabelle's tone was doubtful.

"It's either water or a juice box or Two Buck Chuck or the boxed wine I got from Target, and I know you'd drop dead before you'd drink *that*."

Clarabelle shuddered. "Boxed wine. Ewww!"

Meg laughed. Her mother was nothing if not predictable. She, herself, a Target Girl through and through, loved boxed wine, the petite syrah in particular. *Life's easier without the cork* was another fitting life motto for her.

She poured a glass for each of them and handed Clarabelle hers. "What's Dad up to tonight?"

"Oh, who knows?" Her mother's tone was harried, which in itself was not unusual. Nor was the fact that her sip of wine was more like a swig. But her hands were shaking. That wasn't normal.

Meg stared at her for a long moment, waiting for her to continue. "What's going on?" she said finally. "Where's Dad?"

Clarabelle waved off her questions. "Oh, he's at The Loft seeing some French film. He's on a foreign-film kick lately."

She turned from Meg and took a spot in the armchair by the window, Meg's special chair, relegating Meg to the couch. "You're not, I take it?" Meg asked.

"You know how I hate subtitles."

"I know how you hate everything Dad likes." Meg put her feet on the coffee table and thought how she needed to paint her toenails soon, and then she pondered whether now was the time to say something to her mother about *it*. She decided yes, it was. It was Friday night, date night for other single women, and it wasn't as if she wanted to be on a date, but drinking cheap wine with her grumpy mother? Things couldn't get *all* that much more unpleasant. This was as good a time as any.

"Mom, I have a question for you."

"Well?" Clarabelle said. "Are you planning to ask it anytime soon?"

Aaargh! Meg felt her left eye twitch.

Her mother noticed, too. "Oh, for God's sake. What?" she snapped. "What are you upset about now?"

"You're being snippy."

"If you've got a question, just ask it," Clarabelle said. "You don't need to announce that you've got one."

But Meg had practiced. *Mom, I have a question for you.* That was how she was going to start. But why bother? A good mother-daughter chat required the benevolent involvement of both mother and daughter, and Meg felt rather alone in the effort.

"You know what?" she said. "Never mind."

"You want to know if I'm going to leave your father."

"No! God, no!" Meg had planned to ask her mother how happy she was on a scale of one to ten, but she realized Clarabelle's question had the potential to get them from point A to point B all that much sooner, which could only be a good thing. "It's just . . . you've got a lot of life ahead of you, especially now that you're retired. You're only fifty-eight. I think you *should* spend some time figuring out what you want the next twenty years of your life to look like."

Clarabelle harrumphed. "What's wrong with my life now?"

Gee . . . how to say it gently?

"I just know that for me, if I was your age and had the house paid off and had a nice pension like you do, I'd *do* something," Meg said. "Indulge myself, somehow."

The first thing Meg would do if she had time and money was take piano lessons. She'd always wanted to, even as a kid. She had an admittedly absurd fantasy of playing blues piano at a bar in New Orleans' French Quarter. She'd have long red fingernails that clicked when she played and her hair would be superlong and sexy, as opposed to shoulder-length and lazy. Sometimes she even imagined herself singing. She knew she'd never take things *that* far—she had an abominably bad voice— but she *would* take piano lessons once this mother-of-a-young-son phase ended.

"Indulge myself," Clarabelle repeated. "You sound just like your father and all his talk about do-overs and second chances."

"Well, he's a smart man," Meg said, although she knew Clarabelle hadn't meant it as a compliment.

Sure enough, she harrumphed again. "He's yakking about wanting to see the art museums of Paris. Of living on the Left Bank and taking up painting. Does that sound very smart to you?"

Fun, yes.

Like her father? No.

"Can't you just see Dad with one of those little black artist berets!" Meg laughed at the image.

"No," Clarabelle said. "I can't."

Meg's laughter faded. Her mother could be such a killjoy. "Why can't you just encourage him for a change?"

"Encourage him," Clarabelle scoffed. "For thirty-five years, I asked him to take me dancing and did he ever? No. Not even once."

"But what did he ever do that was so awful?" Meg said.

Clarabelle looked at her pointedly. "He stopped thinking I was someone special."

There were times when I thought I'd rather die than live one day of my life without Jonathan Clark in it. This was before he left me, ostensibly for another woman.

I was fifteen when I met him. He was my first love. My first lover, too, although we didn't call it that back then. We called it going all the way. *I sometimes used to bite his lower lip during our coupling, determined to draw blood. I'd clutch his hair in fistfuls. Jut my hipbone hard against his — anything to cause him physical pain. That's how much I loved him.*

I was twenty-three when we got married. He was accepted to New York University law school but came back to Tucson to attend law school at the University of Arizona because that's where I was. That became part of our truth — that he'd given up his beloved New York City for me.

I was twenty-six when he left me. Twenty-seven when I gave birth to Henry. So much of my life, even now, is defined by how old I was when X, Y, or Z happened with, to, or because of Jonathan Clark.

Henry was Meg's coffee shop guy. Most Saturday mornings, they went to LuLu's Café because LuLu served the best coffee in town from the best local roasters, Adventure Coffee Roast-ing, and she made the world's best scones. Meg always got a cheddar-and-green-chile scone, while Henry always got choco-late chip.

For whatever odd Tucson reason, LuLu's was almost always empty, even though it was a quaint little shop right on Broad-way. They usually had their pick of tables, and they almost always chose the same one by the window. But that day, some-one was at it, so Henry claimed the table across the aisle and noisily began to set up their chess game.

"Hey," Meg said. "Let's sit somewhere else so we don't bother this guy."

The man at the other table was working on his laptop, wrinkling his forehead in cute concentration. At Meg's words, he looked up. She could tell he didn't really see her at first as *her*—as Meg Clark—but rather just as some random person to whom he needed to respond. But then his eyes sparked and he came alive, momentarily back from the dreaded land of laptops in coffee shops.

"Please." He gestured for her to take the table. "You won't bother me at all. I'm just catching up on my e-mail."

Goodness, he had lovely eyes. They were George Clooney eyes, and Meg *loved* George Clooney, *especially* his eyes.

"Are you sure?" Meg said. "You looked engrossed."

"I'm sure," he said. "I'm just dealing with administrative stuff—one of my least favorite ways to spend a Saturday morn-ing. Don't give me another thought."

Yeah, right. With those eyes?

"My son can be excitable sometimes," she warned, "especially when he gets his you-know-what kicked in chess, which is what's about to happen."

The man with the George Clooney eyes had a lovely laugh. "I always enjoy a good you-know-what kicking."

Hoo-rah.

Meg loved good repartee and so she smiled at the man broadly. "If you're sure."

"I'm sure." His eyes lingered on hers for a moment before he turned back to his computer. It was at most a half-second linger. Surely, it was involuntary and without thought on his part, and surely, it meant nothing. Still, Meg felt a little jolt the likes of which she hadn't felt in quite some time. Was there a connection, maybe? Attraction? Even, perhaps, that long-dormant sensation of l-u-s-t lust lust lust?

She and Henry were in a happy place. Meg wasn't looking to date. But that didn't mean she didn't find men attractive. Plus, she'd been celibate for a couple years, ever since her few nights with Ben-the-artist-passing-through, in whom she'd indulged while her parents took Henry to Disneyland. Meg knew a gaze was just a gaze and that she shouldn't read anything into it, but she could tell the man was forcing himself not to look back up at her. And she liked that she had that effect on him. She liked it very much.

She plopped into the chair across from Henry. "Okay, sport," she said, "you're going down." Out of the corner of her eye, she saw the man smile.

In short order, Henry trounced her and made his typical big show of victory. When Meg saw the man watching with amusement, she shrugged at him. She hadn't let Henry win but she didn't mind losing. How could she, when it made him so happy? "He's got some big ol' strategy," she said. "I just play."

"Nothing wrong with just playing," the man said.

"Uh, *duh*," Henry said. "There is when you lose."

"He's a wee bit competitive," Meg said.

"I can tell," the man said.

His *eyes*. The . . . *something* in them—the delight, the sparkle, the . . . *something* . . . made Meg's heart beat fast. This time when his eyes lingered on hers, it was deliberate. And so was her return gaze.

"Yo, Mama," Henry said, breaking in. "Another game?"

"Sure," Meg said. "Let me get a refill on my coffee first, though. Want your scone now?"

Henry nodded. Meg glanced over her shoulder to see if the man was watching her as she walked away. He was, rendering Meg quite conscious of her size-six ass until she turned the corner and her posterior was out of his line of vision. Whew. She breathed easy again.

Meg handed her empty coffee mug back to LuLu. "Henry's ready for his scone."

"Ay," LuLu said. "Fresh from the oven, mamacita. *¿Y tu?* Are you ready for yours?"

"I'm going to skip it today." Not only did Meg not want to eat in front of the handsome stranger in her midst, she didn't want any leftover scone particles in her teeth because of the turnoff implications.

Oh, man, Meg. Get a grip. This was the problem with celibacy. One little look from an attractive man threw your pheromones out of whack.

This was not good.

In fact, it was the opposite of good.

Which made it bad, although admittedly fun.

The man had abandoned his laptop and stood in the aisle, helping Henry set up the chessboard. Her danger alert at full throttle, Meg came to a dead stop at the sight.

"Your son challenged me," he said. "I told him I'd be happy to play a match if it's okay with you."

"I suppose that's fine," Meg said, relieved he'd recognized the need to clear it with her. Nonetheless, her voice came out weak.

The man sensed her edginess, and while shifting farther back from their table and thus Henry, he searched her eyes, trying to figure out what was going through her mind. But it wasn't her mind that was the problem—it was her body. Every nerve ending was on fire, and the way he looked at her just compounded the problem.

"I hope I didn't overstep my bounds." He took a step toward her. "I should introduce myself. I'm Ahmed. Ahmed Bourhani."

What Meg heard was, *I've been waiting for you all my life.* She heard it smooth, like butter. The problem was, he hadn't said it. She just felt it, and it rattled her to the core.

When he extended his hand, Meg was so flustered she spilled coffee on her wrist and then winced, which caused her to spill even more. "Shit," she said.

"Sorry. That was stupid of me. I should have realized you had your hands full. Here." Ahmed took the mug from her, leaving her with only the scone in her left hand. "You okay?"

"You're not allowed to use the word *shit*," Henry reminded her.

"I know," Meg said. "I'm very sorry."

Ahmed put Meg's coffee on the table and turned back to her. "Let's try again." He held out his hand a second time. "Hi. I'm Ahmed."

"I'm Meg." From the delight that sprung to his eyes when their hands touched, Meg could tell he'd felt the same spark she had. She could barely hear herself over the pounding of her heart. "This is my son, Henry."

"Hi." Henry gave a little wave. "And just so you know—we're single." Meg's mouth dropped open.

"Good to know," Ahmed said with a laugh. He clearly didn't mind Henry's audacity, but Meg sure did. Just *wait* until she got him alone.

"And we don't date," she added. "That's also something you probably should know."

Ahmed tilted his head and studied her and Meg could have sworn she saw the tiniest sadness cross his eyes. He quickly caught himself and made them normal again, but Meg had seen the sadness and it caused her to feel a little melancholy, too. Which she could tell he noticed. Simultaneously, they took big breaths and held them and fell into a serious lock of the eyes, each acknowledging the difficulty of the moment. Starting something was hard. Not starting something was hard, too.

"That's too bad," he said.

"It's stupid. That's what it is," Henry said.

"Henry!" Meg gave him a be-quiet look, which he ignored as he moved his center pawn two spaces ahead.

"It's your turn," he said to Ahmed. "You'd better pay attention to me and what I'm doing if you want to win."

"That sounds like very good advice," Ahmed said, but he didn't break eye contact with Meg.

It was Meg who looked away first.

Sometime in the first year of our marriage, Jonathan and I decided to make Wednesdays I love you *days. Middle of the week. Hump day. Halfway to the weekend. A good day to pause and remember what we were doing it all for: each other.*

We just did nice, little things to show our love. It might be irises from Wild Oats one week. Or ice cream at Austin's. Or we'd put our feet up on the coffee table and watch a movie together. Just something, some little thing to honor our relationship. We did that right up until the end, never missed a Wednesday.

That's one of the problems with starting something with someone. You start out thinking it's just some fun small thing, but then it goes and gets lodged in your psyche and becomes part of you and you can't get rid of it no matter how badly you might want to.

Flowers are never just flowers and ice cream's never just ice cream. Yin and yang. It's all part of the yo-yo aspect of life. Great to have, horrible to lose.

Meg didn't look away from Ahmed for long. Again and again as he played chess with Henry, Meg sipped her coffee and surreptitiously studied him. She noticed the oddest things: how his forehead seemed regal (had she ever noticed a man's forehead before?), how his cheekbones were just perfect, and how his forearms were . . . sinewy . . . and competent . . . and how he wore his watch well. (His forearms! Who cared about forearms? About the way someone's watch fit? Why was she noticing such *stupid* things?)

"Ahmed?" When he finished his move, he looked at her with the beginnings of a smile already in place. "What kind of name is that?"

"It's Persian."

"Does that mean you're from Persia?"

"Yes," he said. "It does."

He smiled at her. She smiled back. He was so full of shit.

"I wasn't aware that Persia's a country any longer," she said.

"It's not," he admitted. "You got me."

"You're from Iran."

"I'm from Iran," he agreed. "And I'm also impressed. Until recently, most Americans haven't even known where Iran is on a map, much less that it used to be called Persia."

"I'm a teacher," Meg said. "I get paid to know these things."

He smiled. "I always thought I'd enjoy being a teacher. What age do you teach?"

"Kindergarten." Meg took a careful sip of her coffee, then set it on the table and looked straight at him. "Why do you try to confuse people about your background?"

Ahmed's eyes lit in surprise. "I'm not exactly trying to confuse anyone."

"You're not exactly trying not to, either," she said. "Why do you say Persia if you know that nobody knows what you're talking about?"

He grinned. "Because nine out of ten people drop it at that point."

"Ah!" Meg laughed. "But I'm not most people. I always find out the truth about a man. Are you ashamed? Of being from Iran, I mean."

"Not at all," Ahmed said. "I'm hardly even from Iran. My mom was American. She met my father in Madison when they were both in college and she went back to Iran with him afterward. It was a much nicer place to live back then. Very Western."

"So you're a halfsie," Meg said.

He laughed. "I haven't heard that phrase before, but I guess I am."

That explained his impossible-to-place look. With his brown eyes, his black hair, his thick brows, and the kind of easy-tan complexion Meg had envied her entire pale-skinned life, Ahmed could have been Mexican, Greek, even French. It was only his name that edged him toward the Middle Eastern side of the world.

"You were born there, then?" she asked.

He nodded. "I was sent to live with my mom's folks—my grandparents—in Wisconsin when I was ten. It was just before the revolution in 'seventy-nine."

"Before the hostages were taken at the U.S. embassy?" Meg asked. "Or after?"

Ahmed bristled, but tried not to show it. "Before. I was here when that happened."

"It must have made you real popular on the playground," Meg said.

"With a few teachers, too," Ahmed said. "I'll never forget

Mr. Paulson in fourth grade. He gave me a zero on a math test even though I got every answer right because I used commas instead of decimals. *You're in America now,* he said. *So act like an American.*"

"What a jerk," Meg said. "I hate mean teachers."

"Me, too." Henry, riveted by Ahmed, watched him as if he was a wondrous creature from far away. "Mean soccer coaches, too."

"He did me a huge favor, actually," Ahmed said. "I never did it the wrong way again."

"But you didn't do it the wrong way," Meg pointed out. "You just didn't do it the American way."

"Good point." He rephrased. "I never did it the Iranian way again."

"Your parents really sent you here all alone?" Henry said. "They made you fly on an airplane all by yourself?"

"Yep." Ahmed's tone was light, but Meg sensed this was a hard memory. "It was just me and my backpack. The stewardesses pinned a little sign on me that said *Unaccompanied Minor.* They were very nice and took very good care of me." He added the last part for Henry's benefit after noticing his wide, incredulous eyes.

"My mom would *never* do that to me," Henry said. "She won't even let me walk to the park by myself and it's only six blocks from our apartment."

A tinge of sadness sweetened Ahmed's tea brown eyes, and Meg wondered what he'd had in his ten-year-old's leaving-home-forever backpack. A teddy bear? A photo album?

"You're lucky to have a mom who looks out for you like that," he said. "My mom died when I was six, so she wasn't alive when I was sent here, and my father couldn't leave Iran for some reason."

"How'd she die?" Henry asked.

"Henry," Meg warned, "don't get so personal."

"It's okay," Ahmed assured her. "She was hit by a car when she was coming to pick me up from school."

Meg hid a wince. "Man, talk about a rough childhood!"

Ahmed shrugged it off. "Plenty of people have had plenty worse childhoods than mine."

"That doesn't mean yours wasn't still hard," she said.

"True." He cleared his throat.

As Henry stared at Ahmed in horrified awe, Meg made big eyes at him in hopes he'd temper his obvious shock. No such luck.

"In any case," Meg added, "don't feel you have to explain yourself to us. We're just some strangers in a coffee shop, after all."

When he searched her eyes, Meg went all soft again. It didn't *feel* like they were strangers. It felt as if their souls went way, way back.

"You're right that I should just tell people I'm Iranian," Ahmed said. "I say I'm Persian out of habit, and as I think about it, maybe I am trying to distance myself a bit. Persia sounds old. Grand. The scent of jasmine in the air. Exotic belly-dancers. Hafez, Rumi, the timeless poets. Saying *Iran* makes you think of . . . well, not any of that."

"I'm sure it makes some people think *Axis of Evil*," Meg said.

"That's right," Ahmed said.

"But you're not evil," Meg said.

"No." His voice was soft, protecting an old wound.

"And I'm not some people."

Ahmed smiled. "You're definitely not just some strange chick in a coffee shop."

Meg burst out laughing. "I didn't say I *was* some strange chick in a coffee shop! I said I was a *stranger* in a coffee shop."

Ahmed's blush was adorable. "You don't seem like that, either. A stranger, I mean. I don't usually share such personal information with people I've just met. I hope . . ." He stumbled as he searched for what he wanted to say.

"You hope what?" Meg asked.

"I hope I'm not saying too much," he said. "I wouldn't want you to think I'm an emotional wreck or anything. Because I'm not."

Meg smiled to put him at ease. "And I wouldn't want you to think I'm just some strange chick."

He laughed. "How about I won't if you won't?"

"Deal." As they beamed at each other, Meg tried to remember what her life had been like an hour ago, before he was in it, but in the frenzy and heat of the moment, she almost couldn't. Which was not good. "You'd better get back to Henry." Meg's voice came out the tiniest bit shaky, which she hoped was noticeable only to her.

"No kidding," Henry agreed. "Because it's all about me. Right, Mom?"

Meg rolled her eyes. Henry could always be counted on to keep her grounded. Ahmed studied the board, then moved a pawn forward to where Henry could capture it, bypassing the capture of one of Henry's pawns that was his for the taking.

Henry eyed him. "You want me to take that pawn."

"Maybe. Maybe not." Ahmed's eyes twinkled. "I never reveal my strategy."

Henry studied the board, made his move, and then looked for Ahmed's reaction.

"I can tell you're a very smart kid," Ahmed said. "But I'm sure you already know that."

Henry basked in the compliment, and when he eventually won fifteen minutes later, Meg couldn't tell if it was a legitimate win or if Ahmed had let Henry win. Ahmed was right: he didn't reveal his strategy. But she was sure he had one. Men always did.

"Want to play again?" Henry asked.

"No, thanks," Ahmed said. "You make me think so hard, my brain hurts."

Henry beamed. "I know! Why don't you play against my mom? She's easy to beat."

The *audacity* of this kid.

"Nice try, Ace," Meg said. "But we've got lots of errands to run."

Henry ignored her. "Do you like soccer?" he asked Ahmed. "Because I do."

"I love it," Ahmed said. "I lived for it when I was a kid."

"Our first game's next Saturday," Henry said. "The team's pretty bad, but I'm not. Do you know where Himmel Park is?"

Ahmed nodded. "I live right near there, on Third Street. Just on the other side of Tucson Boulevard."

"Well, that's where we play," Henry said. "Himmel Park."

"You live on Third Street?" Meg was both jealous and wistful. "That's my very favorite street in the whole city."

Palm trees lined the wide street, which was closed to all but local traffic and used primarily as a bike route for students and professors. The houses were old—some grand, some not so grand. Some had tons of character, others not so much. The street always felt to Meg like the set of a movie. When in college, she'd biked on Third to get to campus and always dreamed of owning a house there one day.

"I have a tiny bungalow," Ahmed said. "Across the street from the school."

"Sam Hughes? That's where Violet goes!" Henry said. "She's my best friend. I want to go there, too, but I have to go where my mom teaches." He made a face, then brightened suddenly. "Hey, you're not married, are you?"

"Henry!" Meg made majorly disapproving eyes at him. "That's crossing the line!"

"What line?"

"The asking-personal-questions-of-men-we-don't-know line." She turned to Ahmed. "Sorry."

"No problem," he said. "I like his spunk."

"We do so know him," Henry said. "What exactly do you call what we've been doing for the last hour?" He rolled his eyes at Ahmed, and while Ahmed laughed, Meg sneaked a glance at his left hand. No ring. He caught her looking, and grinned to let her know.

"You don't date," he confirmed.

"That's right." Feeling her blush spread, Meg stood and moved behind Henry. She pressed her hands into his shoulders. "It was great meeting you," she told Ahmed.

"Thank you." Ahmed stood. "I feel the same."

They fell into another serious lock of the eyes.

"This has been both bizarre and lovely," she said. "But we've got to go."

When she squeezed Henry's shoulders, he clambered up, yet Meg couldn't convince her feet to move.

Ahmed's smile widened. "Maybe you should stay."

"Maybe we should." Meg swallowed hard. "But we're not going to."

"Do you want our phone number?" Henry asked.

Dead meat, this kid was.

"Don't say another word," Meg warned him.

"I was just—"

"Ah, ah, ah!" She stopped him. "Not. Another. Word."

Ahmed looked out the window of the coffee shop for a few moments. Meg watched his chest rise and fall rhythmically as she waited for him to look at her again. To *see* her again, in a way that no one had seen her for a long, long time, if ever. When he did look back at her, it was all Meg could do not to gasp. This guy sparked something in her, something deep and real.

"I could give you *my* number," he said. "In case . . . ?"

"I . . . I . . ."

Meg desperately wanted his number. She wanted to take his hand in both of hers and press it against her chest. She could almost *feel* its impression, so strong was her urge. She wanted to tuck herself into him and feel his arms encircle her waist. To put her head on his shoulder and feel safe, taken care of for a change. She wanted to be six months ahead of now when these urges could be indulged in, when all her single-mom, woman-who'd-been-cheated-on concerns had been appropriately addressed and the need for them declared null and void.

No, Meg, a voice inside her counseled. *Just keep this one moment perfect.*

"I'm going to pass," she finally said. "Reluctantly, I'll pass."

Henry held out his hand. "I'll take your number."

Ahmed laughed. "I think you're part of a package deal."

"Not necessarily," Henry said.

"Hello!" Meg gave him a mental head smack. "We're the packagest of package deals."

Henry leaned back against her and tilted his head to look up at Ahmed. "We come here almost every Saturday," he informed him.

Meg clamped her hand over his mouth. "You thwarter!" she said. "You little thwarter!"

Ahmed winked at Henry, then grinned mischievously at Meg. "Maybe I'll see you guys around sometime, then."

Henry raised his arms in a cheer and then held out a hand for Ahmed to high-five. Meg stood in openmouthed awe, unable to speak, as Ahmed's palm met Henry's in a happy smack.

These boys! These men!

They were incorrigible, every single one of them.

That night, Meg and Henry walked down to campus after having dinner at Rincon Market and bought two general-admission tickets to the University of Arizona men's baseball exhibition game at the Frank Sancet Stadium. Meg knew she'd find her father there, because he went to every home game, regular season or not, and many practices, too. That was him, Phillip Goodman, loyal to the core.

A pang of love and a lifetime of memories hit Meg when she saw him from behind. As always, he wore his navy blue team shirt. As always, he covered his mostly bald head with a UA baseball cap. As always, he sat alone in his season-ticket spot directly behind the home team batter-up box.

Ever hopeful, he bought two seats each season, but one mostly sat empty. Meg and Henry joined him as often as they could. She loved the whiteness of the ball against the greenness of the grass, and the organ music, and the crack of the bat smacking the ball. She loved the very purity and simplicity of the sport. What she loved most, however, was seeing her dad so content.

Henry bounded down the stadium stairs ahead of Meg and threw his arms around his grandfather from behind. "Hi, Grandpa!"

"Hey!" Pleased to see him, Phillip happily patted Henry's forearm and ignored the spilled popcorn his exuberant greeting had caused. "Hi, you two! Nice to see you! What're you two up to? Want some popcorn? It's tasty tonight."

He scooted over a seat. Henry plopped into the chair he'd vacated and dug into the bag of popcorn. Arriving, Meg nudged Henry, who stood to allow her to sit and then plunked his lanky body onto her lap.

"How're you doing, Dad?" Meg asked, accepting a handful of popcorn from the bag he offered.

"Good. I'm doing good." Phillip adjusted his glasses, his most notable nervous habit.

"Mom tells me you have aspirations of being a painter in Paris."

Calmly, her dad shook his head. "I never said I wanted to be a painter. I simply said, more than once, who knows what I might want to do with this next part of my life? I've worked very hard for many, many years. Tax season's hell, pardon my French, and—"

"That wasn't French," Henry pointed out.

"Don't interrupt," Meg scolded.

Phillip shrugged. "I was just making a point, which your mother didn't get, as usual."

"I think I get it, Dad," Meg said. "You're having your well-deserved midlife crisis."

She'd said it teasingly, but his return look was direct and even. "Do I look like I'm in crisis?"

Meg peered at him. His eyes were calm, his skin was smooth, and nothing about him suggested crisis. "No," she said, "you don't."

"That's because I'm not. I'm just thinking through some things."

"In your usual well-reasoned, contemplative way," she said.

"One hopes," her father said.

Henry leapt up from Meg's lap. "Can I get an eegee and then try to catch foul balls with those kids over there?"

Phillip immediately reached for his wallet. He loved to buy treats for Henry. He'd always bought them for Meg when she was little, too. Cotton candy, giant Pixie Stix, those ridiculous plastic-crap rings in gumball machines—anything to give her an easy joy. Her mother, on the other hand, had been the queen of no.

After Henry left, Phillip slid his gaze back to the game. "Nice breeze tonight, isn't there?" he said. "I've always felt best when there's a little bit of a breeze in the air. Keeps the world from feeling too stale, too stagnant."

"Dad?" He raised his eyebrows to acknowledge he'd heard her, but he kept his eyes on the game. "What kind of things are you thinking through?"

His glance to her was quick and a little uncertain, and his swallow came thick and hard. "I'm trying to figure out how to make a few changes in my life without hurting anyone."

"It's okay to put yourself first once in a while, Dad," Meg said. "Do what you need to in order to be happy. If you want to sell your accounting practice or pare it back, go right ahead."

"It's not work so much," he said. "Your mother and I haven't been happy together for a very long time. You know that, right?"

Yes, Dad. Everyone knows that. He was thinking divorce. Or separation, or *something* big. The startling hugeness of whatever it was, even though it wasn't entirely unexpected, thudded through Meg's brain and threatened to waylay the supportive response she wanted to give. She took a moment to center herself before she replied.

"You've got such a big heart," she said. "I hope you make room in it for joy on a scale you've not yet experienced."

Phillip pressed his hands against his heart, touched. "You always see the best in people."

"I get that from you," she said.

He turned back to the game, pressing his lips together to keep his emotions in check. Meg studied him thoughtfully. He'd bottled himself up for years, decades, a lifetime. The idea of making a change—of feeling deeply—had to be scary.

"You've got a safety net, Dad," she said. "I hope you know that. When you're ready to make a leap, I'll be there for you."

Without taking his eyes from the game, he patted her knee. Inexplicably, Meg found herself wanting to cry.

After the game, Phillip declined Meg's invitation to join them at Starbucks, so Meg and Henry settled on the patio after ordering a Mocha Mint Frappuccino for her and an apple juice for him.

For a few minutes, they sat quietly. University Boulevard vibrated with the laughter of college students and the smell of the hookah from Sinbad's and the occasional *ding-ding* as the trolley came by. While taking it in, Meg also ran through the conversation she wanted to have with Henry. Spending time with Ahmed that day certainly had stirred something in her, but it also seemed to have stirred something in him. Several times since then he'd mentioned Ahmed—how nice he was, how brave to fly on an airplane alone, and, more than once, how he wasn't married and wasn't that a pretty neat thing? Henry was smitten with Ahmed in a way Meg found disconcerting.

"Henry?"

He met her eyes. "Mom?"

"On a scale from one to ten, how happy would you say you are?"

Henry, who loved these sorts of questions, got an adorably thoughtful look on his face. "I'd say probably a nine."

Meg laughed, delighted. "What would it take for you to say ten?"

"An iPod," Henry said. "Violet's dad just bought her one, and I want one, too."

"That's it?" Meg said. "Just an iPod?"

Henry nodded. "Will you get me one?"

"I'm fine with you being a nine on the happiness scale," Meg said. "Any happier and you'd be living in la-la land."

"How about for my birthday?"

"I'm not spending a hundred fifty dollars on an iPod, Henry." They didn't even have a computer at home to download music; for e-mail and Web searches, Meg relied on her computer at work. "I can't even remember the last time I spent that much on *myself.* We don't have that kind of money, kiddo."

Henry's lower lip protruded in a pout, and Meg's mind immediately began doing loop-de-loops about the iPod. It wasn't totally about the money. She wanted their world low-tech and high-touch and for Henry's mind to remain unfettered, hence her limits on TV and video games. Stripping away the distracting gadgets resulted in an in-your-face relationship, and while Henry's spirited independence was without question a bit much sometimes, Meg wouldn't trade it for anything. She knew his teenage years would come fast enough and she felt an overpowering urge to

s-l-o-w

l-i-f-e

d-o-w-n.

But life was not cooperating. Henry was catapulting to puberty and Meg knew she'd soon enough lose his affection. Now it was so precious. His class was working on poetry and he'd written "An Ode to My Mother: My mom is like a telephone wire. She connects me to the ones I love." It was taped on the wall outside his classroom. How many more poems like that could she count on? If he had an iPod, he'd walk around with those white ear buds stuck in his ears. She'd become an annoyance to him, an interruption. And then he'd stop writing poetry about her. *You have flowers in your heart,* he'd told her just last week. She'd written it down so she'd never forget.

"Mom?" he said.

"Henry?"

"Maybe I'm not a nine for being happy. Maybe I'm an eight. Or a seven. Or a one."

The flowers in Meg's heart wilted. "Henry, please. You're still very young. Maybe when you're twelve we'll get you an iPod."

"It's not that." He twisted his clear plastic apple juice glass. Meg waited him out, vaguely frightened. "Some kid at Violet's school likes her. I mean, he *like* likes her. Like, he *likes* her."

Meg suppressed a laugh but couldn't help smiling. Fourth

grade. This was the age it all began. "And that bothers you because . . . ?"

"Because *I* like her! Hello!" He looked at Meg like she'd gone AWOL.

"She's your best friend," Meg said. "That's different than like-liking her. Are you saying you have other feelings for her?"

Henry sighed. "I just know that the kid at her school needs to *butt out.*"

Ah, jealousy. Really, a fear of . . . a fear of loss, right? Of something being taken away. His friendship with Violet was priceless to him.

"You want things to stay just as they are," Meg said. The dejection in Henry's nod nearly broke Meg's heart. She, too, wanted things to stay the same. Their life was innocent and simple and so very, very good. *Please don't grow up, Henry. Please don't change. Except—blossom.*

"It's tough when someone comes along and throws everything out of whack and makes you feel things you might not be ready to feel, isn't it?" Henry nodded morosely again. "You've got to stick to who you are," Meg said, "because who you are is really special, and Violet knows that. If you change to try and keep her, you'll end up losing her. Does that make any sense?"

"Sort of," Henry said. "Not really, but sort of."

Meg let out her breath in a disappointed exhalation at how the conversation had gone—maybe a B-minus on the mom report card. An A for effort, but a B-minus for helping Henry make sense of his world, because there just weren't always easy answers where the heart was concerned.

"The same holds true for me, Henry," she said. "You know Ahmed, that guy we met today at LuLu's?"

"Of course I know him!" Henry said. "I was sitting right there at the same table as you—you think I can't remember who I met, like, five hours ago? Um, duh!"

"You and your grandmother are so literal that sometimes it makes me want to scream," Meg said. "What I want to know is what you were up to by telling him we're single and wanting his phone number. What was that about?"

Henry shrugged one shoulder. "I liked him."

"I liked him, too," Meg said. "But I also like our life just as it is. We don't need any complications right now. If we run into him at LuLu's again, great. If not, that's fine, too. But we don't need to exchange phone numbers and you don't need to be telling him where you play soccer. It's not even safe, to tell people we don't know very well things like that. So don't do it anymore. Okay?"

Henry made a maybe/maybe-not face at her, telling her without words that understanding was one thing while agreement was something else entirely.

"I'm serious," she said.

Henry extended his hand. "Nice to meet you, Serious. I'm Henry."

I think Henry might be having father issues," Meg told Amy the next day. They were in Amy's kitchen, with Meg seated at the breakfast bar and Amy standing behind it, chopping vegetables for a salad.

Meg always tried to arrive before Clarabelle and Phillip, because, while Henry played with his cousins, Maggie and Kelly, ages two and four, and while Amy's husband, David, got the grill ready or tinkered with something in the garage, it gave Meg and Amy time to catch each other up on their respective lives before Clarabelle showed up with her intrusive opinions.

Meg looked forward to the time when she could indulge again in long lunch dates with women friends as she had before she'd had Henry, but at the moment, when she was so busy being the single mother of a nine-year-old, it seemed the only friendships that worked were those that came easy and by circumstance. She was friendly with her fellow teachers and the female staff at Foundation, and of course she had the Loop Group and other assorted residents at the apartment complex to socialize with, but otherwise, she pretty much just had Amy.

At Meg's declaration that Henry might be having father issues, Amy looked up from the carrot she was slicing. "Did he ask to see Jonathan?"

"No!" Meg said. "God, no!"

Amy rolled her eyes. "You say that like it would be the worst thing in the world."

"Hell will freeze before Jonathan gets near my son," Meg said.

Amy arched an eyebrow. "Henry's his kid, too."

"Can you say *unwitting sperm donor*?" Meg said. "No, Jonathan had his chance to be a dad and chose not to take it. Thankfully, he has no interest in Henry, so it's a moot point, anyway. But no—we met this guy yesterday, this very sexy guy, and Henry basically threw himself at him. I felt sorry for him, actually."

"For Henry or for the very sexy guy?" Amy asked. "And what made him sexy? Give me some spice. My life is sorely lacking in spice."

"I meant the guy. Ahmed." Meg looked out the kitchen window at Henry, who was playing some sort of fetch game with his cousins. "*Should* I feel sorry for Henry?"

"Of course not," Amy said. "It just wasn't clear from how you said it."

"Let's see," Meg mused, "what made him sexy? Well, his looks, of course. His father's Iranian, so he's got those nice dark features. Thick black eyebrows. He looks like a prince. But that's only part of it. He had this really hard life growing up— his mom died when he was six and he got sent to the U.S. from Iran when he was ten, all alone, and he . . . I don't know. He has this sensitivity to him that's really charming. And he doesn't shy away from opening up, which you don't often see in guys unless it's some sort of get-you-into-bed strategy, or unless the guy's an emotional basket case. He was just, like, *open,* and okay with himself, and, I don't know, *even-keeled* in a way I found very calming."

"Because you're so *not* even-keeled," Amy said, laughing.

"Hey!" But Amy was right. Meg sometimes thought she was just a grown-up version of Henry and that was why she understood him so well and forgave him so fast. They were mother-and-son bobbleheads, springing this way and that as their passions seized them. "I'm working on it," she said.

"This guy's your yin," Amy said. "Or your yang. You know—your complementary thingamajig."

"It felt that way," Meg mused. "It was the oddest thing, but I felt that if I could just tuck myself into him somehow, everything would be okay."

Amy stopped chopping the celery and gave Meg a long look. "Don't freak out, but that's exactly how I felt when I met David. Remember? Didn't I tell you that?"

Meg shrugged. "I was in the midst of crashing and burning while you were falling in love with David." Even now, ten years later, she flinched as she remembered how bad it had been.

"That was so rude of me, wasn't it?" Amy joked.

"Yes," Meg said. "It was."

Amy grinned. "He was wearing this crisp white dress shirt and he'd come into the bank and he was all fresh for the day and I just wanted his arm around me. Literally, that white-shirt-sleeved arm. I swear, I must have missed half of what he said, because all I could think of was how to get it around me. It was weird."

"I was all shaky," Meg said.

"Me, too," Amy said. "Shaky's good."

"Shaky's very bad, actually," Meg said.

"Come on. You're ready," Amy said. "When do you see him again?" She sounded out his name. "Ah-med. Ah. Med. Ahmed."

"I don't," Meg said. "We didn't exchange phone numbers. That was another problem. Henry liked him too much."

"Come on, go out with him," Amy said in a pleading tone. "For my sake. I need some vicarious romance in my life. My love life's the pits."

Meg laughed. According to Amy, since having kids, her sex life had trickled to near-drought status. David had recently suggested they mark on a calendar two days a week to have sex. Amy refused. *You need to woo me,* she'd told him. *Do the laundry once in a while. That's incredible foreplay.* Since then he'd folded the laundry exactly twice. It hadn't helped matters when Amy found a stack of *Playboys* and *Penthouses* shoved in their back closet, asked David why he'd not mentioned them, and he'd mumbled something about how he figured that if Amy knew about them, she'd make him mop the floors before letting him indulge. *If you won't come hither, at least let me have them,* he'd said. *With no housework required.*

His reasoning hadn't gone over well with Amy, to say the least. She felt he should Help Out rather than Jack Off.

"Did you hear about Dad?" Meg asked, changing the subject.

"About how he's having an affair?" Amy rolled her eyes. "Yes, a million times."

"He's not having an affair! Don't even joke about that." Clarabelle tossed out the affair accusation fairly regularly, and it always infuriated Meg. *Jonathan* had affairs, not her father.

"I saw him last night, and I have the feeling he's honestly thinking about moving out. Mom said he's been talking about do-overs and second chances."

"Promise you'll shoot me if my marriage ever turns into theirs," Amy said.

It was already heading in that direction, from what Meg could tell. "Hire a housecleaner," she advised. "And have more sex."

As Amy smirked at her, Clarabelle's ten-year-old Honda Civic pulled into the driveway, and their mother climbed out. She was alone, a most unusual Sunday-morning occurrence.

"Speak of the devil," Amy said.

"Where's Dad?" Meg asked Amy.

"Having his affair."

"Amy," Meg rebuked, "knock it off."

"I will," Amy said, "if you'll take off your rose-colored glasses and grow up."

"Geez," Meg said. "Unnecessary." She did her best flounce off and went to the door to greet Clarabelle. "Hi, Mom," she said. "Where's my dad?"

Clarabelle brushed past Meg and set the bowl of potato salad she'd brought on the counter. "Your father's cleaning out the garage. After thirty years, all of a sudden he's in a rush to clean out the garage."

He's moving out, Meg thought. *He's definitely getting ready to move out.*

"Better late than never, right?" Amy said.

Clarabelle slapped her palm on the counter. "That's exactly what *he* said." Without another word—without even waiting for Meg to pour a glass of wine for her from the bottle of char-donnay she and Amy had tapped into—Clarabelle headed to the backyard, where the kids were playing.

"There's trouble in paradise," Meg said. "Mark my words."

"There's always been trouble," Amy said. "And it's never been paradise."

Meg went through the week as if Ahmed were a fly on the wall watching her every move. She always dressed cute for her kindergartners—kind of bouncy, kind of bopsy—but that week, she took extra time in the morning to make sure her skirts were ironed and to blink on a little mascara. She wore heels to school and reapplied her tinted lip gloss during breaks.

The fantasy she had of Ahmed observing her caused Meg's mood to heighten as well. Colors were brighter. She was funnier. Kinder. Sexier. Quite simply, the very idea of him enriched her life.

Meg realized exactly what she was doing—performing for a guy she'd spent less than an hour with and who, oh, by the way, *wasn't there*. But what was the harm? It didn't hurt anybody.

In fact, it helped everyone. Meg's students got extra attention, in particular sweet Marita, who'd taken to sitting with Meg on the bench outside at recess until Meg joined in the jump-roping and four-squaring and hula-hooping. Only then would Marita participate. When he pestered, Henry got that extra bowl of ice cream and Meg even refrained from commenting more than once a day about the dirty underwear he felt compelled to leave on the bathroom floor.

Meg fantasized about looking to her classroom door and

finding Ahmed there, leaning against the doorframe, maybe holding a sprig of daisies. He'd admire the passion with which she taught. She fantasized, too, of Ahmed passing by the pool while she was there with her Loop Group friends, perhaps visiting a friend of his own. Their boisterousness would catch his attention. He'd see Meg midlaugh, her head thrown back, pure living-in-the-moment emanating from her being. And he'd think, *I want that. I want her.*

And then he'd come to her.

It was the pursuit Meg fantasized about—only the pursuit. Him wanting her and finding her worthy.

But in reality, Ahmed had no idea where she lived and no idea where she taught. The only link that could possibly bring them together was the coffee shop. Frequently throughout the week, Meg wondered whether she should go to LuLu's the following Saturday.

Ultimately, she decided not to. Daydreaming about him was enough. In her fantasies, she could keep him perfect in a way the real world would never allow.

Henry's soccer practice was the only black mark against the week. At his first practice, he'd thrown an embarrassing temper tantrum at Bradley, a boy who continually blocked the ball with his hands. Henry had spent most of practice on the sidelines, not an auspicious start to the season.

So this week, Meg made brownies to take as a snack, sort of as an apology and sort of to earn them a do-over. When they arrived, Henry took off at a sprint, dropped the juice boxes near the parents, and ran to join the other kids, who were climbing the fence behind the baseball diamond. Meg's heart lightened when she saw that the kids didn't seem to be holding a grudge.

"Afternoon, everyone!" Meg called to the parents, who were almost uniformly seeking refuge in a strip of shade generated by the lone palm tree near the practice field. "Hot enough for ya?"

Anytime the temperature was over ninety-five degrees, as it was that day, that was what people said. *Hot enough for ya?* It was the standard Tucson greeting.

"It's ridiculous," said one mom. She was a stressed-out yoga-mom type, seated on the ground with her legs in a strange contortion. Her eyes remained focused on the text message she was punching out with her thumbs.

"I left my purse in the car today for ten minutes and my lipstick melted," said another. "It was my new Clinique, too!"

"I hate when that happens," said the only dad there. Everyone laughed—dads were always popular among the moms—and Meg was hopeful she'd been forgiven for Henry's outburst the previous week.

"Is Coach Debbie not coming today?" she said. "Should we maybe run a few drills with the kids?"

"She's just late," said the yoga mom. "She's always late. Drops her kids off late to school every day."

"She'll *be* here. She's *got* four kids, you know." This from the team parent. Meg couldn't recall the woman's name but knew the type: on a power trip, with a fake smile. *Wound up.* Maybe she needed a chocolate fix. Meg gave her a big smile and extended the prettily arranged tray. "Would you like a brownie?"

"We don't *do* brownies on this team," the woman said. "Did you not read the e-mail?"

What was this chick's name? Cindy? Connie? Something with a C. Whoever she was, she was rude, and uncalled-for rudeness was Meg's ultimate pet peeve.

"I'm sorry," she said in a tone that perhaps indicated otherwise. "I didn't catch your name."

"It's Catherine," the woman said.

"Well, Catherine, I suppose I did miss the e-mail. Was it the same one that contained the snack sign-up sheet? Because I haven't seen that, either."

"I think it was very nice of you to bring something," said a mom.

"Thank you," Meg said to her new ally. "Would *you* like a brownie?"

"No, thank you." The woman smiled apologetically. "I'm sort of macrobiotic in my eating." She gave Catherine a pointed look. "Where *is* the snack sheet? I like to plan for these things."

"I left it on my printer last week, but I have it right here." Catherine pulled it out of her team-parent binder, handed it to the macrobiotic woman, and then turned to Meg. "I have to ask you not to offer anyone else a brownie. Please."

Meg met Catherine's firm gaze. Oh, the things she would not say! They were delightful to think of, anyway.

"Catherine, I get the sense that you're personally offended by my brownies."

As the other parents laughed, Catherine sneered. "We don't *do* sugar on this team," she said. "We do organic fruit.

Otherwise the kids go crazy. We witnessed some of that last week, remember?"

Meg's mouth dropped open. The nerve of this woman! "You mean Henry? My son?"

Catherine nodded smugly.

Unbelievable! Did her kid never misbehave?

"Oh!" Meg chastised herself for taking so long to figure it out. "Let me guess. Your son's Bradley, isn't he? The one Henry yelled at?"

"That's right," Catherine said. "And he was very upset afterward."

She stepped closer and bulked up her shoulders, and all of a sudden, it turned into the full-fledged mom's equivalent of a pissing contest. One version of Meg's imagination had her throwing down the plate of brownies and tackling Catherine.

It was not the response she chose, of course.

"How about we get the boys together for a playdate soon?" she said. "Maybe Bradley can come over and swim."

"We'll see," Catherine said. "I don't know that he'd feel comfortable."

"Have you looked at him recently?" Meg said. "He seems pretty happy to me."

While the other kids ran around and sprayed one another with their water bottles, Henry and Bradley kicked a soccer ball back and forth. Bradley was positively beaming. To Meg, it looked like the start of a beautiful friendship.

"Look." Meg pointed them out. "They've let bygones be bygones. Forgiveness comes so much easier to kids than it does to us grownups, doesn't it, Catherine?"

Catherine ignored the saccharine smile on Meg's face and

didn't answer, but when the lone dad on the team winked and grinned at Meg, it took absolutely every single ounce of self-control she had not to offer him a brownie.

"Organic fruit," Meg complained to her Loop Group friends as she chomped on a rejected brownie that night down by the pool. "I can't even afford organic fruit for myself, much less for fifteen kids. What planet are these people from?"

"They're from the land of plenty." This from Kat—Crazy Kat, Crazy Sexy Kat—who had a penchant for short skirts, high heels, low-cut tops, and men who were into that sort of thing, as were most men, from what Meg could tell. Kat was a parole officer, tough and strong, African-American, and with the most solid thighs Meg had ever seen on a woman. Meg wondered about her motives in choosing to wear such provocative clothes to work, as it very much seemed to be asking for trouble, but parole officers were a breed unto themselves. Besides, Kat was a girl with a gun. She packed heat and her aim was fearless. No one messed with Kat.

Also at the table was Harley, resident manager of the complex. He'd gone by Jeff until a few years ago when he got a divorce and bought a motorcycle and grew his hair ponytail-long and stuck pirate-hoop earrings in both ears and let someone ink a string of tattoos down his arms. Now he brought home women who wore superblack eyeliner.

Absent from the table was Opera Bob, a man whose age Meg couldn't quite figure out and for whatever reason felt she shouldn't ask. He had a pregnant-man paunch and worked by day as a phone technical-support representative, a faceless voice to those crying out from the nanotech wilderness. At night, he watched the national news—Meg often saw him alone in his apartment, leaning forward on his beige couch, letting his senses be bombarded for thirty minutes with everything that had gone wrong in the world that day. When it ended, he turned off the TV, stepped outside, and for the next twenty minutes wandered the paths of the apartment complex singing the most beautiful arias Meg expected she'd ever hear in her life. That was what he was doing at the moment, serenading them all as he strolled through the complex grounds.

Henry was on the opposite end of the pool playing cards with Violet. They'd had two brownies each—and look! No craziness! The land of plenty, indeed.

"So that makes me from where?" Meg said. "The land of not enough?"

"You're from the land of single motherhood," Kat said. "And from the land of underpaid teacher-hood."

Meg laughed. That pretty well summed her up, all right. "There's a very exciting rumor going around that we might get a one percent pay raise this year. I think that would put me officially above minimum wage."

"Woo-hoo! Organic fruit for everyone!" Harley held up his bottle of Corona in a toast. Meg clinked her plastic margarita glass against it and happily took a sip.

Life was good, with or without a one percent pay raise. She had a job she loved and was good at. She got summers off, and she did make more than minimum wage—she just felt poor in comparison with her friends who'd majored in marketing and business and in comparison with Jonathan, whom she imag-ined was by now a high-end defense lawyer in New York. It didn't help that early on he'd reneged on paying child support and she'd been such a wimp that she'd let him.

But money meant little to Meg in the overall scheme of things. She had a boy she was crazy about, and a boy who was crazy about her. She got the gift of lingering watercolor sunsets each night with her Loop Group friends.

She had opera. She had the warm desert breeze and the comforting smell of fabric softener, which wafted over from the nearby laundry room. Meg felt pretty sure she'd already attained her little slice of heaven. Sure, it wasn't how she'd expected her life would go, but it was a good life nonetheless. She and Henry were not only surviving—they were thriving, and that was even without the benefit of eating organic fruit.

On the morning of Henry's first soccer game, Meg stepped on her patio and was thrilled to see the sky bursting with clouds. And while there wasn't a chill in the air, there was a noticeable lack of hotness. This was it! The official end of Tucson's six-month summer. She and Henry could walk the six blocks to Rincon Market at high noon without frying like eggs on the sidewalk. The animals would emerge from their shaded corners and move around their habitats at the zoo, making going there fun again. Tucson came alive at summer's end, and it always felt like a well-earned reward for having endured the summer.

Henry was so nervous about the game that he couldn't stop eating. He ate four hard-boiled eggs before Meg noticed.

"Hey, stop," she said. "You'll throw up if you eat any more."

"Do you think I'll start?"

"That depends," Meg said. "If Coach Debbie goes with who's the best, you'll definitely start."

Henry slumped. "She won't start me. She hates me."

When they arrived at the park, Coach Debbie was changing her toddler's diaper while the kids on Henry's team played keep-away. Meg set up their blanket as far away from Catherine as possible. Henry stayed nearby and hopped up and down until the referee blew his whistle for the players to line up and have their cleats checked.

When Meg saw a huge smile erupt on Henry's face during the team huddle, she knew he'd start, which was a good thing, because within minutes it was clear that if they had any hope of winning, Henry would have to carry the team. The others ran around like headless chickens, bunched up around the ball, kicking it for the sake of kicking it. Not a bit of strategy or discipline was evident. Meg understood perfectly well why Henry got so frustrated.

"Well, hey," a voice behind Meg said. "Funny running into you here. I can hardly believe the coincidence."

Meg, recognizing Ahmed's voice, smiled even before she turned and saw him. He was in runner mode, wearing a T-shirt and running shorts, which showed off rock-hard thighs that would be nice to bump up against. Heart pounding, she scrambled to her feet and put out her hand for a handshake, and *yowsa*, the chemistry was still there.

"A coincidence, indeed," she said with a tease in her voice. "Exactly how many times have you run through the park this morning looking for just such a coincidence?"

"Every hour on the hour starting at seven." There was pride in his voice.

In-*corrigible*, Meg thought, laughing. It was ten o'clock now. "How did you know we'd be here?"

"Henry told me, remember?"

"Ah, yes," Meg said. "My son. The boy who needs to learn discretion. That was shortly before he asked if you were married, right?"

"Right," Ahmed said. "Which I'm not."

"Right," Meg said. "Hence the lack of a ring."

They exchanged the dopiest of smiles. Meg's embarrassment

was huge. She'd spent perhaps an hour with him the previous week at LuLu's but days and nights dreaming about him, having imaginary discussions in which she revealed her innermost secrets, and she now had the feeling that he knew her too well. She had to remind herself that he didn't. He hardly knew her at all.

"What if we'd gone to the coffee shop?" Meg said. "What if we skipped the game and went there in hopes of running into you?"

"Ah! I thought of that." Ahmed held up his pointing finger. "I gave LuLu my cell phone number and made her promise to call if the two of you showed up."

"That was very good thinking," Meg said.

"How's the game going?" Ahmed scanned the field until he found Henry, scrawny number nine in his black uniform shirt that hung to the middle of his thighs. "There he is! Playing his guts out. He's sure fast on his feet. Fearless, too. That's great. The less fear you have of getting knocked around, the better off you'll be."

"Their team pretty much sucks," Meg said. "Plus, the coach and the team parent think Henry's the devil incarnate."

"No," Ahmed murmured more to himself than to her. "How could anyone think that?"

Man, oh, man. He knew exactly how to turn her heart to mush.

They watched the game, pileup after pileup on the ball. When after a few minutes Ahmed asked to borrow her phone, Meg got it from her blanket and handed it to him. She considered asking him to join her on the blanket, but the thought of sitting so close to him made her shaky, which was *not good*, no matter what Amy said.

Ahmed flipped open her phone, dialed a number, and hit SEND. Instantly, a buzz sounded from his shorts pocket. He clicked off her phone and handed it back and the buzzing from his shorts stopped. "There. I've got your number. That solves that problem." His smile was broad. "I can't tell you how many times I wanted to call you this week."

Be still, be still, be still my heart.

"And I can't tell you how many times I wished I'd given you my number this week, as much as it pains me to admit that," Meg said. "I'm really not in the market to date right now."

"There's a part of me that doesn't believe you," Ahmed said.

They looked at each other for a long, conflicted moment. It was that starting/not-starting something feeling again, and all Meg knew for sure right then was that the way he looked at her made her feel as if they were alone. As if she was tucked into him, dancing in the moonlight, and they were looking into each other's souls and finding a kindred spirit.

It was disconcerting, the feeling. Disconcerting in the loveliest of ways.

"There's a part of me that doesn't believe me, either," she admitted.

Even though the rest of Henry's team played like a soccer version of the Bad News Bears, he performed great. Several times, he emerged from a pileup of kids with the ball and twice he scored. The quarter ended with the other team up, 5–2. Red-faced and sweaty-haired, Henry ran over to gulp from his water bottle.

"Excellent job, Henry," Meg said. "You're playing very well."

"Did you see my goals?"

"Absolutely, I did. Didn't you hear me cheering?" Meg waited for Henry to acknowledge Ahmed's presence, but he gulped and gulped from his water bottle and completely ignored him.

"*Pssst,* Mr. Self-Absorbed," she said. "Can you say hello to Ahmed, please? He just *happened* to be jogging by." She gave Ahmed a friendly smirk.

"I knew you'd come," Henry said to him. "Did you see my goals?"

"Hi," Ahmed said.

Finally chagrined, Henry smiled. "Hi."

"I did see your goals," Ahmed said. "I was very impressed. I was telling your mom that your fearlessness is going to take you far in life. And you know what? If you played halfback, you could probably stop numbers five and eight from the other team. Those are the real tough guys."

"Coach Debbie told me to play forward," Henry said.

"No one else is playing his position," Ahmed pointed out. "They're running around all bunched up wherever the ball goes."

"Thank you!" Henry said. "That's what I keep telling them: *stay in your stupid positions.* I don't know why it's so hard for them to get it right. It's not that hard."

"Henry's on a bit of a tight leash with the coach," Meg said.

"I wouldn't exactly call her a coach," Henry said.

Ahmed laughed. Meg did, too, for while disrespectful, his sense of comic timing was impeccable. Besides, it was true. Coach Debbie wasn't much of a coach.

When the whistle blew, Henry ran back to his teammates. Meg finally felt composed enough to invite Ahmed to join her on the blanket.

"Henry, you're still in," they overheard Coach Debbie say. "But I expect you to pass more this quarter."

Ahmed, who'd been casually leaning back on his arms and stretching his legs in front of him, now tilted toward Meg. "Who's he supposed to pass to?" His lips grazed her hair as he spoke confidentially in her ear.

Electric.

"Be nice." Meg leaned against him ever so slightly as she murmured back, "They're doing the best they can."

"They need a better coach." He said it seductively, so seductively in fact that what Meg heard was, *I want to make love to you right here, right now.*

"Oh my God," Meg said, blushing. "What did you just say?"

Ahmed tilted his head at her in curiosity. "I said they need a better coach."

She burst out laughing. "I thought you said something else."

"What'd you think I said?" It was an invitation, the way he asked.

"I'm not telling." But she did tell him, with her eyes. And she could tell he understood what she was intimating, or something close enough, because he chuckled, pleased.

"Pass it! *Pass it!*" Coach Debbie's screeching voice interrupted them. Her scream was directed at Henry.

Ahmed frowned. "He's got an open path to the goal."

"They really do need a better coach," Meg said.

"Pass it!" Coach Debbie's face was blistering red.

"Pass to me! I'm open! To me! To me!" It was Bradley, who indeed was open, but Meg knew what Henry was thinking. If he passed to Bradley, it would be intercepted because Bradley waited for the ball to come to him, and there were plenty of kids from the other team who could easily get in the ball's path before it did.

Meg could see Henry's hesitation as he went against his better instincts and passed the ball to Bradley. Sure enough, it was intercepted.

"Bad pass," Catherine said loudly to the other parents.

"This is ridiculous," Ahmed said.

The other team scored. Henry kicked the ground. Almost immediately after the kickoff, he again got possession of the ball from midfield and Meg winced in worry. She had a feeling things would not end well.

"All the way, Henry!" Ahmed shouted. "Take it all the way!"

"Pass it!" yelled Coach Debbie. "Pass to Bradley!"

Meg could see Henry's confusion.

"Pass to Bradley."

Henry passed to Bradley. Meg flinched as Bradley blocked the ball with his arms. Would this kid never learn?

"What's he *doing?*" Ahmed said. "What's he touching the ball for?" He shook his head. "This is crazy. He's old enough to know better."

Henry's face had turned cold white. He ducked his head as

he tried and failed to shake off his anger. And then the moment turned slow motion in the most horrible of ways as he
charged across the field.

Toward Bradley.

While Meg froze in absolute horror, Ahmed jumped up and
waved wildly to get Henry's attention. "Henry, no! Stop!
Henry!"

There was a horrible thud when Henry knocked Bradley to
the ground.

Catherine reached the boys first, grabbed Henry's arm, and
hauled him off her son. "What's *wrong* with you? Don't you
have *any* self-control?"

The referee raced to intervene, as did Coach Debbie and
Meg and Ahmed. Ahmed arrived first.

"Your kid's out of control!" Catherine hissed and shoved
Henry to him.

Meanwhile, Meg arrived and pulled Henry close. The poor
kid was shaking. Ahmed let Catherine's incorrect assumption
about his relationship to Henry stand and instead of answering
her turned to Bradley, who remained sitting on the ground,
flanked by a half-circle of players. Bradley was watching his
mother in frightened awe.

Ahmed offered a hand to help Bradley to his feet. "Are you
okay?"

"Yeah." Bradley brushed himself off. "He shouldn't've done
that, though." He walked over to Henry and abruptly punched
him in the arm. That set Henry off again.

"Why do you keep messing up?" Henry yelled. "You're not
supposed to catch the ball!"

"I didn't mean to!" Bradley said. "I can't help it!"

"Yes, you can!" Henry yelled. "You need to get it right!"

"Enough, boys! Henry, enough." Meg turned to the referee. "What happens now?"

"He should be kicked out of the league!" Catherine said.

"That's enough from you, too," Meg snapped at her. "Try being decent for a change." She sensed Ahmed's discomfort, but he remained silent beside her.

The referee ejected Henry from the game and asked that they leave the park. The three of them left the field together, with Henry in the middle and Meg hugely embarrassed. They paused to collect their things and then continued on their conspicuous walk of shame. After they were a good distance from the rest of the team, Ahmed stopped and turned Henry by the shoulders so they faced each other. "Are you okay?" he asked.

Henry's eyes glistened as he nodded.

"There's this Persian saying I want to tell you," Ahmed said. "'If you want a rose, you've got to respect the thorns.' Do you know what that means?"

Henry sniffed and shook his head.

"It means that if you want Bradley to be a good player and someone you can pass to, you should respect the fact that he needs help to get better," Ahmed said. "I was on the sidelines getting really upset with him myself, but then when I was over by him, I felt bad for him, because it sounds like he really wants to get better but doesn't have anyone to help him. Did you have that same sense?"

As Henry nodded, Meg was delighted to see actual sympathy in his eyes.

"Maybe you can be the one who helps Bradley," Ahmed suggested.

"Could you help him, too?" Henry's voice came out raspy, as if he were afraid Ahmed would say no.

Ahmed glanced at Meg before answering. "How about I give you some tips and tricks that you can then use to help him? Would that work?"

Henry nodded and latched on gratefully to the decency in Ahmed's eyes. Ahmed's return look was fatherly, and seeing it, Meg was struck with a longing she thought she'd left far behind.

On the way to Meg's car, Ahmed caught her eye over Henry's head and mouthed, *Ice cream?* Meg processed it as *I scream* and gave him a puzzled look. *Ice cream,* he mouthed again. As he did, Henry caught the exchange. "What'd you say?"

"I was asking your mother if we should take you for ice cream," Ahmed said. "I know that mint chocolate chip ice cream always makes me feel better when I've had a rough day."

"Ice cream?" Meg laughed. In retrospect, it was obvious what he'd been saying. "I don't know—that's really a harsh punishment. I mean, it's not like Bradley lost an eye or anything." The beginnings of a smile crossed Henry's eyes.

"What were *you* thinking?" Ahmed said. "Hanging him upside down by his ankles?"

Meg loved being on the same humor wavelength with a person, and she and Ahmed definitely were. "Something like that," she joked back.

Even as Meg was still embarrassed by and mad about what Henry had done, her heart melted when he laughed. As a mom, she constantly worried that some big trauma was going to come along and break his spirit. His laughter told her that *this*—getting kicked out of the soccer game—wasn't it. His little psyche would survive.

They reached the parking lot and stopped in front of Meg's car. "Can you imagine what Catherine would think if she saw us having ice cream after Henry just pounded on her kid?"

"Come on—please!" Henry said. "We'll be done by the time the game's over!"

"That's not the point," Meg said.

"I learned my lesson," Henry said.

"Yeah, right." Who did he think he was kidding? "Don't think you're getting off that easy."

"Sorry," Ahmed said. "I didn't mean for him to hear."

"I thought you were saying *I scream*," she said. "I just couldn't figure it out."

"I scream." Ahmed laughed. "That's cute."

Meg blushed. It was as good as if he'd called *her* cute.

"I know!" Henry said. "We've got Popsicles at home. Can Ahmed come over and have one?"

Whish. The idea of Ahmed in their apartment felt dangerous. Delicious, yes. But dangerous, too.

"That still doesn't seem like a punishment," she said.

"Please?" Henry said. "I won't have any fun. I promise!"

"I won't, either." Ahmed's smile was sexier than hell. "I promise."

Hoo-rah.

Meg considered. It would be letting Ahmed in, which was one thing in and of itself, but even worse were these wild impulses she kept having where he was concerned. The entire past week, she'd seen her storage closet at school or the laundry room at the apartments or even her kitchen counter, and she'd gotten lusty little thrills and thought, *There's a nice place I could shove him up against.* She wasn't sure she trusted herself where he was concerned.

She shook her head. "That won't work."

"Come on! Why not?" Henry said.

"Because first of all, you misbehaved," she said. "And boys who misbehave don't get treats."

"Ahmed's not a treat." Henry stuck out his lower lip in a pout.

Oh, yes, he is. Meg carefully avoided looking at Ahmed because he'd know exactly what she was thinking. And he'd be very, very amused.

"My mind's made up," she said.

"What's the second reason?" Henry asked.

"I beg your pardon?"

"You said *first of all.* That means there's a second of all."

"Oh, right." Meg glanced at Ahmed before answering. "We don't know Ahmed well enough to have him over."

"We do so," Henry insisted.

Meg shrugged an apology to Ahmed. "Sorry, but I'm protective when it comes to my son."

"As well you should be," Ahmed said. "How about I'll take my leave here. But can I call you sometime this week?"

"You *have* to," Henry said. "You have to show me your tips and tricks, remember?"

"Oh, right. So you can help Bradley." Ahmed's eyes twinkled. He turned his twinkle on Meg. "What do you say?"

I say I find you irresistible.

"You can call us," she agreed. "And I'm very glad you happened to so innocently jog by today."

Ahmed's smile broadened. "I don't recall saying there was anything innocent about it."

Henry denies it, but when he was a little kid he was crazy about Barney, enough that I was willing to put up with Baby Bop's incredibly annoying voice. He'd go all sweetly trancelike at the end of each show when they sang the closing song: I love you. You love me. We're a happy family.

So precious, the purity of their love: You exist. Therefore, I love you. Kids have no history to fall back on, to trip them up. They don't sit around and wonder, What is love, anyway? What does it really mean, to love a person? And why bother? For them, love just is. They couldn't get it wrong if they tried.

Of course, I'm not talking about all kids.

Only little ones.

Say, kids under the age of nine.

After that, their hearts start getting complicated. Their love, just as deep, is not nearly as easy.

For better or worse, they become more like us.

"I think maybe I'll quit soccer," Henry said on Monday morning as they drove to school. Meg knew as they passed the junk-filled yards and the angry graffiti and the bullet-ridden windows of the tough South Tucson neighborhood where Foundation

Elementary was located that in the overall scheme of things, Henry's desire to quit soccer was minuscule.

She knew this.

But still. Henry loved soccer and he was good at it. Meg eyed him in the rearview mirror. "I think maybe you won't," she said.

Henry kicked the back of Meg's seat.

"Knock it off," Meg said. "You know I can't stand that."

"And *you* know I can't stand the coach." Henry kicked the back of Meg's seat once more for good measure, as he always did upon being told to knock it off. "It's just going to happen again, the same stupid thing. Bradley's going to keep catching the ball and I'm going to keep getting mad, and his mom is one mean person all right, and I don't think I like soccer very much anymore, anyway."

"You sure looked like you loved it after you made those two goals on Saturday," Meg said. "Remember how good that felt?"

In the mirror, she watched him cross his arms and reject the memory.

"The world's full of people who are all too eager to make your life difficult," she said. "You just can't let them. Whatever happened to you wanting to help Bradley get better? I thought you were excited about that."

"Ahmed didn't call," Henry said. "He was supposed to call, and he didn't."

The sharpness in his tone set off alarm bells in Meg's gut. "He said he'll call sometime this week," she reminded him. "That means anytime up until next Saturday."

"But I have practice tomorrow!" Henry said. "How am I supposed to help Bradley if I don't know how?"

"You know how perfectly well," Meg said. "You just kick the ball around with Bradley and help him learn how not to be afraid. Just show him how to stop the ball with his chest, or how to turn his body so the ball hits his back. Just show him what *you* do."

Henry was obstinate. "But Ahmed has tips and tricks, and I need to learn them."

Once she and Henry parted ways at school, Meg delved into her day. During morning circle, she and her students sang songs and then Meg read them that week's story, "The Three Billy Goats Gruff." On Mondays, she simply read the story. On Tuesdays, which she nicknamed Tie It Together Tuesdays, she read the same story again and they tried to connect the theme or plot to their own little lives. On Wednesdays, half the kids acted out the story while she narrated it. On Thursdays, the other half acted it out. By Friday, they owned the story. They owned it, told it, loved it, knew it, became it.

From story time they moved on to art, otherwise known as Messy Mondays. Once they were properly smocked and poised in front of their poster paper, Meg called out a word and they chose a color to associate with it, then painted as much or as little on their posters as they wanted. When Meg said *happy*, most chose yellows and reds. When she said *outdoors*, they chose greens and blues. When she said *sad*, Lucas refused to participate.

"Sad is black and I don't want black on my painting." He looked at her in spirited defiance.

Meg smiled, delighted by the way his mind worked. "How about just a tiny dot?"

"No."

"How about brown? Is brown ever a sad color?"

"Yes!" Antonio said. "I put brown *and* black on my painting for sad. And purple, too!"

Except for Marita, Meg's sweet and silent wallflower, everyone else shouted out what colors they'd used to show *sad*.

"Look at hers," Lucas said, pointing to Marita's painting. "That's crazy sad."

"Marita's painting is Marita's business. You just worry about your own self." Meg said it even as she herself was alarmed by the blackness of her quietest student's work. "So, Lucas, no sadness in your painting, that's your final answer?"

"That's my final answer," he said.

"Good for you," Meg said. "Why don't you pick the next word for the class?"

Lucas scrunched up his eyes and thought real hard. "I know! *Dancing.*" Then he took a paintbrush in each hand and, after dipping one in the orange paint and the other in the red, made jazzy swirls on his poster. Dancing, indeed. Meg watched as he leaned over to Marita's painting and began to paint an orange smiley face on hers.

"Lucas!" Meg scurried over. "Hands to yourself."

"It's okay, Miss Meg." Marita's voice was so soft it was almost nonexistent.

"Yeah." Lucas threw his arm around Marita's shoulders. "She likes for me to do stuff like this." He turned to Marita.

"Doncha? Doncha? Huh, huh, huh?" He poked her with the nonbrush end of his paintbrush until she giggled.

Meg, who would have paid a million dollars to hear that giggle, bent to Lucas and tapped him on the nose. "You are a beautiful goof."

Alone in the teacher's lounge on her lunch hour, Meg noted a message on her cell phone. Hi, Meg. It's Ahmed. Can you call me, please? Thanks.

Her heart raced as she dialed him back. He picked up on the second ring. "Meg! I'm glad you called back."

Meg felt her smile grow stupidly wide. Thank goodness she was alone. "And I'm glad *you* called," she said. "I've got a boy on my hands who very much wants to learn your tips and tricks."

"Those would be my soccer tips and tricks?"

"You have other kinds?" Meg asked, teasing.

"Oh, yes," he said. "Many, many others."

Was it possible to smell a person over the phone? Had the subtle-cologne scent of him crossed through the phone lines, or was it just Meg's memory of him? Or was it a trick of his?

"I can meet with Henry any night this week after work except for tonight because I've got golf plans," he said. "You just tell me when and where. And then I was hoping you could stop by my office one day this week because I have something I'd like to give you. You're welcome to bring Henry, of course."

His office. Meg realized she didn't even know what he did for a living. It seemed she absolutely should know this by now, but she'd only seen him twice, after all, and both times, Henry had sucked up much of the spotlight. Was Ahmed a college professor? Owner of an art gallery? "What do you do, anyway?" she asked.

"I'm the assistant city manager," he said.

"The assistant city manager of what?"

"Of Tucson."

Of Tucson! "You're a bigwig!"

Ahmed laughed. "I'm just a cog in the wheel."

"Can you do anything about the sidewalks in my neighborhood?" she asked. "Because I think it's crazy that I live in one of the nicest neighborhoods in town and I can't even walk from my place to Rincon Market on a sidewalk. Sixth Street needs sidewalks all the way through! Tucson's so schizophrenic with its sidewalks that it drives me nuts. We need sidewalks and we need handicap curbs."

Ahmed chuckled. "The RTA's supposed to help with that."

"You sound like a politician." Meg tried to remember what RTA stood for, but couldn't. She only knew that it and something called Rio Nuevo were supposed to be the answer to everyone's transportation and downtown redevelopment prayers, although no one in Tucson seemed to expect much from either.

"Nope," Ahmed said cheerfully. "I'm just a cog in the wheel. I live in the same neighborhood as you. If I had any clout, we'd have better sidewalks. I agree with you that they leave something to be desired."

"You're probably just all ethical and honest and don't want to put your own neighborhood ahead of others," Meg said. "Am I right?"

"Lack of clout." He laughed after saying it.

"Is this why you didn't tell me what you do for a living?" Meg asked. "Does everyone always come up to you and ask you to fix things for them?"

"Pretty much." Ahmed's chuckle was low and sexy. *Man,* he gave good phone. Meg suspected he was probably a pretty good fixer of things, too.

"So, do I need to make an appointment to see the assistant city manager?" she asked.

"You? Never," he said. "I keep the last hour of my day open, so just stop on down to city hall at your convenience. I'm on the tenth floor."

Ahmed met them at the park the next night and showed Henry some drills he could do with Bradley, and then a few days later, Meg left Henry to tag along with Harley on a plumbing project in 108-D while she went to see Ahmed.

Tucson's downtown was small but complicated, with its myriad one-way streets and its resistance to a grid structure, which left the V-shaped streets sending people in the wrong direction from their desired destinations. It all felt deliberately hostile, and sensible people avoided downtown if they possibly could.

But Meg wasn't sensible.

She was a fool in lust.

She parked in the library parking lot and then walked the few blocks to city hall. In her infinite wisdom, she'd worn heels, the sexiest she owned, which admittedly weren't very sexy, but they made her feel Like a Woman, as did the autumnal orange nail polish she'd painted on her toes the previous night. She wore a simple sleeveless dark blue linen dress that her father always complimented, going for a deliberately care-less but man-she-cleans-up-good look.

Once at city hall, she rode the elevator to the tenth floor and stopped at the reception desk. The woman behind it was cool and professional and her entire presentation was exactly of a certain type—perfectly highlighted hair, whitened teeth, long French nails that must have made typing a challenge, and a plethora of bling. Meg always wondered how people in normal-paying jobs could pull off looks like this. It seemed she must spend her entire paycheck keeping up her appearance. Meg also always wondered: if she'd remained married to Jonathan, was this how she'd look—nice, certainly, but some-what . . . interchangeable?

"I'm here to see Ahmed. . . ." *Shit.* She couldn't remember his last name! The things she didn't know about him could fill a book. "Ahmed . . . Bour-something? I'm Meg Clark. He's sort of expecting me."

"Bourhani." The receptionist smiled. "His name's a mouth-ful. I'll let him know you're here."

"Do you happen to know if he has any pull when it comes to putting in sidewalks?" Meg asked.

The receptionist's smile was practiced. "The RTA's sup-posed to help with that."

"Right," Meg said. "So I keep hearing."

She scoped out the lobby while she waited. It was pretty typical, nothing special, but *right there* was the mayor's office. No matter how he tried to downplay it, Ahmed was a big fish in Tucson's small pond.

When a burst of cool air tickled Meg's neck, she knew even

before turning that he was on his way down the corridor toward her. Sure enough, she turned and there he was, in linen pants, a crisp white shirt, and a rich-but-casual blazer. He carried himself with a self-possession that seemed earned rather than inherited. Along with kindness, Meg found confidence about the sexiest trait a man could possess. There was no denying it: Ahmed was hot. Meltably hot.

Perhaps best, he was clearly happy to see her. He walked toward her with intention, his eyes focused on hers with a captive intensity. Even the receptionist noticed and turned to study Meg with a new appreciation.

When Ahmed was a few feet from her, he stopped. He was close enough that Meg could have kissed him if she wanted to. And yes, she wanted to—she could hardly stop herself, actually. This was *crazy,* this whatever-it-was between them.

With a roguish grin, Ahmed extended his hand, and after he had his hand in hers, he was disinclined to let hers go. "Thanks for coming," he said. "I haven't seen you without Henry before."

"He's more or less an appendage," Meg said, glad Henry wasn't there. He'd steal all of Ahmed's attention, and Meg was quite enjoying it. The way he looked at her made her feel beautiful.

"Come on back." They walked side by side down the corridor, which was narrow enough that it was harder for them not to touch than it would have been for her to take his elbow or for him to put a hand on the small of her back, *sizzle sizzle.* Meg simply wasn't brave enough, and she supposed Ahmed was being gentlemanly, damn him.

Ahmed's office was of a generous size but otherwise unrevealing. He had only stock framed Tucson prints, a few standard plaques, and fake plants.

"No pictures of family," Meg said.

His eyes were pleased she'd noticed. "My father's a bit of a disapproving sort of fellow, and I don't exactly want his face staring at me all day. Glaring at me, I should say. And my grandparents—well, I have a picture of them at home."

"Are they still alive?"

"No."

"Ah," Meg said. "I'm sorry."

"Thank you."

Meg walked to his large picture window. He had a perfect view of A Mountain, which was marred only by the unavoidable view of I-10 that went along with it. "Do you watch the fireworks from here on the Fourth?"

"I have." He stood a few feet from her, studying her. "I like that dress."

I'd like you out of that dress, was what Meg heard. She swallowed hard and her heart pound-pound-*pounded.* "You said you have something for me?"

"I do." When he leaned past her to get to his desk, Meg honestly and ridiculously worried she might pass out. From lust! Was such a thing possible? His neck, his jawbone, his *cheekbones,* for God's sake, taunted her, dared her to engage. She sighed helplessly. Regardless of what happened with Ahmed, it was time to rethink her vow of celibacy.

Ahmed picked up a sealed envelope from his desk and handed it to her. Stapled to the envelope was the business card of Samuel McFarland, private investigator. "It's not very romantic," he said, "but I'm really hoping you'll reconsider your policy about not dating. I know you're a single mom and you've got Henry to worry about and I tried to put myself in your shoes to see what . . . well . . ." He swallowed and cleared his throat. "I imagine you've got a lot to consider before you'd say yes to even a simple dinner date, so I thought maybe you might find this helpful as you think about it. Because I'm officially throwing it out there. Consider the request-for-a-date gauntlet thrown down, Meg Clark. You can let me know your answer at your convenience. On your own timetable. Say, by Friday."

Meg laughed and felt the flush of delight in her face. "That was quite the . . . quite the *something*." She waved the envelope. "What is it? Should I open it now?"

"I had a private investigator do a background check on me." Meg tilted her head at him, curious, and he shrugged sheepishly. "Kind of weird, I know, but this buddy of mine, this guy I run with in the mornings, his daughter got massively taken to the cleaners by her boyfriend, and when my buddy got hold of his credit report and his criminal record, there were red flags all over it. So I just . . . I don't know. A background check might not tell you who I am, but at least it should give you a good indication of who I'm not." He cleared his throat. "I'm not a bad guy, Meg. At least, I don't think I am—I haven't actually read the report! If I'm a bad guy, I don't know it. But you can call him and talk to him if you want. His card's right there."

Trying to steady her breathing, Meg stared at Ahmed, dumbfounded. He *got* her—even though he barely knew her, he understood her essence. He recognized the scared yet hopeful heart inside her that wanted love and yet wanted even worse not to mess up.

Ahmed might think it unromantic to hand her an envelope that laid bare the official facts and figures of which he was composed, but he was beyond wrong.

Hands down, it was the most romantic thing anyone had ever done for her.

When I look back on myself as a young wife, I see a girl so slight she could have been blown over by a strong wind.

I vividly remember the final hours of that last, horrible weekend. I was on my knees on the bed, begging Jonathan for probably the hundredth time to tell me exactly what I'd done that was so wrong as to make him want to hurt me so badly by cheating on me. By leaving me. By preferring her.

He never did tell me why.

After he left, my body stopped working. My heart stopped beating, and this baby we'd planted needed to grow. I was terrified by the depth of my rage and grief, and one day several weeks after he left, as I lay furled under the bathroom vanity unable to move, I realized that I needed help.

For a while, I saw my therapist twice a week. I'd sit next to her at this small, round conference table, and as she got to know me, it became such a comfort because when she'd look into my eyes, I knew I was still there. That I was safe, because she'd let me fall only so far.

She said: you can choose to be bitter, or you can choose to be better. It was only then that I realized I had a choice as far as who I'd become, as a woman and a mother and a person in my own right.

I decided I wouldn't be bitter. I'd be better.

❖

"I think it's kind of creepy," Amy said when Meg called to tell her about the background check. "It's like he's trying too hard."

Meg had just left city hall. She'd made her way to the grass behind the library, found a shady spot, sat down and opened the envelope. The report was blessedly innocuous, with nothing to cause alarm. Beyond a reasonable mortgage balance, Ahmed had no debt. No arrests. Two speeding tickets. No lawsuits of any kind filed against him. But the fickle happiness she'd allowed herself crumbled at Amy's words. It seemed to Meg that he'd been trying exactly the right amount. But then again, she wasn't the best judge of men, as history had proven.

Glumly, she stared at the short Guatemalan-looking man who carried an armful of rose bouquets and was systematically approaching everyone. No one was buying. Meg hated being solicited, especially when Henry was with her, which was nearly always, and she dreaded the man's needy sales pitch. Besides, roses made her sneeze.

"Creepy?" she said. "Trying too hard? You really think so?"

"Background checks are meaningless," Amy said. "Most child molesters are never caught."

"But the vast majority of people aren't child molesters," Meg said, even as she knew Amy was right. "And I just don't think he is one."

"What makes you say that?" Amy said. "To an outside observer, he seems to be doing everything possible to get into Henry's world. Running into you at the coffee shop—"

"We ran into him," Meg said. "He was there first. I already told you that."

The Guatemalan rose seller was working his way toward Meg. She pressed her hand against her purse and shifted her direction away from him.

"Playing chess with Henry," Amy continued. "Drawing out personal information from him like where he plays soccer and that you're single . . ."

"Henry's the one to blame for all that," Meg said. "In fact, Ahmed seemed uncomfortable with how much Henry was telling him. He sort of pulled back and didn't engage with him until I said it was okay."

"And yet then he showed up at Henry's soccer game, using that same information." Amy was making everything sound so nefarious that Meg felt compelled to play devil's advocate, even while her insides felt hacked up by the possibility that Amy might be right.

"You sound like Mom," Meg said. "Like a nicer version of Mom. Does there have to be something wrong with him?"

"If you want me to sit here and say he sounds like the greatest guy in the world, fine," Amy snapped. "Just tell me that's what you want. I was under the impression you wanted my honest opinion."

"And I was under the impression you thought I should date him," Meg said. "In fact, I clearly remember you telling me that in your kitchen a few days back. You wanted me to date him for you, because your own love life was so . . ."

"Pathetic," Amy said miserably. "I know. Don't listen to me. I swear I'm not myself these days. I walk around feeling *mad* all the time, and then I feel bad for feeling mad."

"I'm telling you, hire a housecleaner," Meg said. "I know I would if I could afford it, even though we've got only eight hundred square feet." Amy's poking had rekindled the fear Meg had been trying to smother. Now she wondered about Ahmed's agenda. Maybe he *was* a master manipulator. But why? To what end?

"I should," Amy said. "But it feels wrong. I'm a stay-at-home mom! It's my job to keep the house clean! I already get the impression that David thinks I sit around eating bonbons all day. Although, what is a bonbon, anyway? Have you ever actually eaten one?"

"It's your job to raise your daughters," Meg said. "To read them stories and lie on the floor and play games with them, right? To linger with them. To live on their little-kid time. That's what you don't want to hire out for. The house? Let it go. Let someone else worry about it. Your house should be your refuge, your sanctuary. Not something you resent. I think bonbons are those fluffy things."

"Chocolates?"

"I really don't know," Meg said. "I don't even know if people make them anymore, actually. Maybe they were just a fifties thing."

"I'm doing it," Amy said resolutely. "I'm going to find a housecleaner before the week's out. Someone who does laundry, too. I can at least have someone come in every other week—*that* I can justify. I'm *sure* that someone still makes bonbons."

"You don't have to justify anything," Meg said.

"Neither do you," Amy said. "If your gut's telling you that Ahmed's a good guy, then he is."

Meg stared at the background report. Ahmed wouldn't have given it to her if he hadn't known it would be clean.

And sealing the envelope had been overkill. He *was* trying too hard. She folded up the report and shoved it back in its envelope.

Meg sneezed. Without turning to see whether the rose-wielding man was near, she leaned forward, elbows on her knees, and put her head down. Hopefully, the guy could take a hint. Although probably not. Men seldom did.

"Men are idiots," she said. "They're either criminals or idiots."

Amy groaned. "No, no! Don't regress because of me! Just because I'm always mad at David these days doesn't mean Ahmed's not a great guy. You've been on such a nice upswing lately. I'm sure Ahmed's on the up-and-up, and I'm sure the two of you will fall madly in love and go on to have oodles and oodles of happy babies like you always wanted. Oops, hey. I've got to run. Kelly just woke up from her nap and she's calling. I don't want Maggie to wake up if at all possible."

Startled, Meg straightened, cotton-brained all of a sudden. "Did I really?"

"Really what?"

"Want more kids."

"Oh my God, you don't remember?" Amy said. "You had their names all picked out when you were, like, ten years old, and all the girls had flower names. Iris and Heather and Rose and that sort of thing. You couldn't decide if you wanted four kids or six, but you for sure wanted an even number."

"So everyone would have someone and no one would be left out." Meg remembered now. "How on earth did I forget that?"

"I don't know, babe," Amy said. "Maybe reality set in when

you had Henry and saw how much work one kid was. Plus, you know . . . no husband, no babies, unless you're turning all Angelina Jolie on me."

Meg laughed. As much as she wished she could be a fearless collector of kids à la Angelina Jolie, the truth was she was a conservative girl at heart—a single, unmarried mom by circumstance, not by choice.

As soon as Meg clicked off her cell phone, the Guatemalan man was in front of her.

"Flowers, pretty lady?" His teeth were remarkably crooked, but very white. And his smile was so hopeful that it almost broke Meg's heart.

"No, thank you." She sneezed.

"Bless you." The man was just a few inches taller than Henry and had one of those thick-skinned, ageless faces. "Do you know why people say *bless you* when somebody sneezes?"

Cringing at having to engage, Meg forced a smile and shook her head. She had no idea.

"It's because your heart stops when you sneeze," the man said.

"Oh right," Meg said. "I did hear that somewhere."

"I've always thought people should say *welcome back* instead. So welcome back, pretty lady." He bowed at her and moved on, and Meg chastised herself for being so negative.

People were good and decent and more often than not they had innocent hearts. And if she couldn't accept that there was an opportunity cost to her fear, then the plain fact was she might very well miss out on something beautiful with Ahmed.

After Meg got home, she settled on the patio with a hot apple cider. As she watched Henry and Violet play two-square on the sidewalk, she phoned her father for advice.

"Hey, Dad! You busy?" She'd called him at his office so Clarabelle wouldn't nose her way into the conversation.

"I'm never too busy for you," he said.

"So I've got a question for you—how do I know if a man's intentions are sincere?"

"Have I met the man in question?" Phillip said.

"No," Meg said. "This is a new man, one I'm thinking of potentially dating."

"Good for you, Magpie!" Phillip said. "I'd say you're definitely ready to start dating. And Henry's at a good age."

"I don't know about that," Meg said. "He's at an age when I think pretty soon he's going to acutely sense the absence of a father figure. He's already all tangled up liking this guy, which, of course, will only make things that much more difficult when it ends."

"Maybe it won't end," her father said. "Does this guy have a name?"

"His name's Ahmed," she said.

"Ack-med?"

"No, Dad. *Ahmed*. Ah. Med. The emphasis is on the -Med."

"Ag-med," her father said. "Where's he from?"

Meg sighed. She could only imagine how tiring it must be for Ahmed all the time—already she was sick of explaining his background and she had yet to go on a date with him! "His father's Iranian," she said. "He's been in the U.S. since he was Henry's age."

"So he's Iranian, too."

"Well, he's a halfsie," Meg said. "Half American, half Iranian. His mother was American."

"You mean he's fractured," Phillip said. "One foot in both countries, both cultures. Never really feels that he belongs to either one. I have several clients like that. African, Latino. It's the immigrant experience, after all."

"Then shouldn't we all feel that way?" Meg asked. "Since we're a nation of immigrants?"

"People like us just feel vaguely unsettled all the time," Phillip said. "I'm sure our ancestors felt it more acutely."

"Well, I don't get the sense that Ahmed's fractured," Meg said. "He seems very well adjusted and definitely more American than Iranian. Not that there's anything wrong with being Iranian."

"Of course not," Phillip said. "And I have friends who are black, so I can't possibly be racist."

"I beg your pardon?" Meg said. "Are you trying to make me get mad at you?"

"You never get mad at me," he said evenly. "What would it look like if you did?"

"I feel like you're trying to pick a fight with me, Dad," she said. "You want to just come on over and duke it out?"

"I just find it curious you felt the need to say there's nothing wrong with being Iranian," he said. "The old me thinks you doth protest too much. Tell me more about this Ack-med guy."

"Ahmed, Dad." Meg laughed. "I'm going to have to insist you practice that."

"You asked how to know if a man's intentions are sincere, and my advice is—if you want to know how a man feels about you, don't listen to a word he says. Instead, watch what he does. What does Ahmed do for you?"

"You got his name right!" Meg said.

"I was teasing you a little bit," he said, chuckling. "His name's not all that hard to pronounce."

"Do you mean, does he open doors and that sort of thing?"

"Not just that. Not that at all, actually," Phillip said. "Although he'd better open doors for you."

"I don't think we've actually walked through a door together yet," Meg said. "He asked me on a date earlier today, and I'm trying to decide if I should go. You know how for the longest time I haven't wanted to date, right?"

"You've pretty much screamed that from the rooftops, yes," Phillip said.

Henry and Violet had abandoned their two-square game and were now playing hangman with sidewalk chalk. *L-O-V-E*, Meg thought.

"He fits in with me and Henry," she said. "We make a good threesome. He was so sweet to Henry the other day after he'd gotten kicked out of the soccer game." She briefly updated her dad on what had happened. "I swear, Dad, there was a moment when I was watching them that I saw the future, and he was in it. I'm freaking out a bit, because I didn't want to feel this way about anyone. Not at this point in my life, anyway."

"You're not getting any younger," Phillip pointed out.

Meg's mouth dropped open. "You *are* trying to pick a fight with me!"

"Just think how nice it would be to have someone looking out for you," he said. "Someone to come home to at night who actually gives a shit how your day went."

Ouch. That was a crack against Clarabelle.

"It would be nice," Meg admitted. "I bet you'd like that, too."

"Someone you could enjoy the gran—enjoy Henry with," he said. "You're still young enough to have another baby or two. How nice would it be to have a partner in that process?"

A baby, my God.

Or two! Two babies! A boy and a girl, Meg decided.

"You're putting dangerous thoughts in my head, Dad," she warned. "I don't even know if Ahmed wants kids." She shook the notion out of her head. "I'm just talking about a date. One date."

"I don't think you are, Magpie. I know you pretty well. If you didn't see a potential future with this guy, you wouldn't bother."

He *thought* he knew her pretty well.

"Maybe I just want to jump his bones," she said mischievously. "Have some great sex."

Phillip cleared his throat. "That has its place, too, I suppose."

Meg imagined him alone in his office, blushing. "I'm just

kidding, Dad. You do know me, better than anyone. So you think I should just plunge on in, huh?"

"Has he been married before?"

"I didn't ask, and he didn't mention it," Meg said. "Do I need to know that before I go on a date with him?"

"I suppose that's what a date's for," her father said. "To find out things like that."

"I think I'm going to do this," Meg said. "I mean, not all men completely suck. There are a few good ones left, right? Besides you, I mean."

Her father sighed. "The world's not black-and-white," he said. "There's a complexity to things. There's a complexity to you, too, Meg, that I'm not sure you always honor."

Meg sat back in her patio chair, warmed by the idea that he recognized her as more than just a simple, happy-go-lucky kindergarten teacher doing the single-mom thing with aplomb, which was truly all she ever showed the outside world. But her heart sure had its disturbing secrets. For instance, there was the fact that she still sometimes missed Jonathan so much, she could hardly stand it. And that she sometimes pretended he was doing this all with her, this raising Henry, and that he was going to walk through the door and say, *Hi, honey. I'm home,* and it would be *normal.* It would be the *Hi, honey* of her dreams, with no layer of lies beneath it. She'd have nothing to forgive, because he wouldn't have betrayed her in the first place.

To Meg, this was the fantasy of someone who was weak. "There's a stupid side to me, too," she said. "And I don't want to give it any encouragement."

"There's no part of you that's stupid," Phillip said. "There are just parts of yourself you don't understand, and maybe you're not meant to. But you still have to honor them, even as you don't understand them."

"When did you sneak off and get all philosophical on me?" Meg asked.

There was ruefulness in his chuckle. "I've been reading a lot of self-help books lately. Thomas Moore's got some good ones."

My daddy, Meg thought. *He sounds sad.*

Now it was Meg who cleared her throat. Some questions were so hard to ask. "Are you okay?" she questioned him. "It's fairly obvious something's going on with you, and I want you to know I'm here if you ever need to talk. Okay?"

"I appreciate that," he said. "Although I hate the idea of you seeing chinks in the old armor—weakness in me. I like that you still have that little-girl belief that I can do no wrong. I'm not sure I'm ready to lose that."

Touched, Meg watched Henry being chased across the grass by Violet. He ran past the patio, beaming a smile at her. She knew exactly what her father meant. It *was* nice to be idolized, and there sure weren't that many people in the world willing to do it.

"You're my hero," she said. "Now and forever."

"Everything ends," Phillip said. "The only unknowns are how and when."

"And sometimes why," Meg said, thinking of her marriage. "I hate the unknown. I'm terrified of it, actually."

"There are no guarantees in life," he said. "The best you can hope for is to have someone by your side who loves you for you and who can provide the kind of solace you need as you struggle through your hard times. To not be alone in your hour of need."

Meg exhaled heavily. "I don't want any hard times. I've already had my share."

"No one wants hard times," Phillip said. "And yet the hits, they keep on coming."

That Sunday when Meg and Henry arrived at Amy's house, Henry immediately slipped past Amy and went in search of his uncle and cousins.

"Hello to you, too, Henry," Amy called after him.

"Hi, Aunt Amy!" He didn't look back.

Meg stepped inside somewhat warily. Amy wore a baggy T-shirt, her hair was stuck in a careless ponytail and the scowl on her face looked like it had been there awhile. Meg held up the plate of chocolate-chip cookies she'd baked. "Want a cookie?"

"Hell, no," Amy said. "They'll go straight to my ass."

"You're chipper today," Meg said, thinking, *Damn.* Now she couldn't eat a cookie, either, without Amy resenting her. She should have left a few at home for later. "Bad morning?"

As Meg walked behind Amy to the kitchen, she grimaced at the back of her sister's head. Amy simply *had* to stop letting her hair go so long between highlights. Meg took her usual place at the counter as Amy yanked open the refrigerator door, aggressively pulled out ingredients for a fruit salad and plunked them on the counter.

"My life sucks," she said.

Meg withheld a sigh. It had been such a pleasant few days, as she meandered through life in a fog of idle wonder about Ahmed. There was so much she didn't know, so much to imagine. His hobbies. Friends. Reading habits. Movie choices. Boxers . . . or briefs? She'd fallen asleep considering that last question, ultimately deciding that since Jonathan had been a boxers guy, Ahmed would be a briefs guy. Picturing this was not a bad way to fall asleep, if one had to fall asleep alone.

Then this morning, Henry's Tootsie Roll breath was in her face, asking if they could bike to University Boulevard for breakfast, so they'd had a lovely ride through campus, their world painted in an autumnal hue, as a few campus trees managed to change colors this time of year, and then shared an egg burrito on the patio of Café Paraiso. Around them, bicyclists whizzed by on their Sunday-morning group rides. People parked their dogs at patio tables at the Starbucks across the plaza, and the fountain from which Henry often stole quarters burbled a pleasing background melody. After such a mellow morning, Amy's mood was fingernails against a chalkboard—screechy and unwarranted.

"Please don't say your life sucks, Amy," Meg said. "You're living the dream."

"Not everybody has the same dream as you, you know!" Amy snapped. "Maybe your dream is other people's hell!"

"I just aspire to have a congenial brunch at my favorite sister's house, and she's not being very congenial at the moment," Meg said. "Let me help you. Why don't you go take a bath, relax yourself out of this mood, and let me make the fruit salad?"

Amy was territorial in regard to her kitchen, often waving a knife in the direction of anyone who dared to encroach, so Meg was not surprised when she refused. "The only person I want help from around here is David." She said his name like it was a swear word.

"What'd he do now?" Meg said it dispiritedly, hoping Amy would realize that she didn't really want to hear about it.

She didn't. "It's more like what he doesn't do." Amy positioned a cantaloupe on the cutting board and hacked into it. "I was up all night with Maggie—she's got this horrible cough—and I'm sick of it. He *never* gets up. I'm *punished* for being a light sleeper. And then *he* slept in this morning! I swear, sometimes I think being a single mom's the way to go."

"I don't know what to tell you, Amy," Meg said, "except that I feel for you. And that they grow up so fast that soon you'll be wishing you could get these days back."

"They're ingrates," Amy said. "All of them. Ingrates."

When Meg laughed, Amy glared at her. "It's not funny. Sometimes it seems all I am is their maid."

"Let me take the girls back home with me after brunch," Meg said. "You and David can go catch a movie. Or stay home and have s-e-x in an empty house."

"Oh, yeah, right," Amy said. "Having sex with David is exactly how I'd spend my precious free time—not! That would be rewarding him for his bad behavior."

Meg shook her head in disapproval. The longer Amy withheld sex because David didn't help around the house, the crankier he became, and the crankier he became, the less Amy was willing to have sex, and so on and so on.

Amy looked at her accusingly. "You think I should just sleep with the guy, don't you?"

"With *your husband*?" Meg said. "Yes, I do."

Amy slammed her hand on the counter. *"He needs to woo me!"*

"Fine!" Meg said. "Geez. Just so you know—I wouldn't

woo you, either, when you're acting like this. He's probably afraid you're going to bite his head off if he tries to say anything nice to you."

"Maybe I will," Amy said.

Just then, David came around the corner from the great room into the kitchen. From the imitation cheer on his face, Meg knew he was well aware of his wife's mood, whether or not he'd overheard their conversation.

"Hi, David." Meg didn't want him to think she held Amy's frame of mind against him.

"Hi, Meg." There was no hint in his voice that anything was amiss. "How's your school year going?"

As Meg was in the middle of assuring David she was fine, the doorbell rang and the muscles in his face involuntarily tensed. In addition to his cranky wife, the poor guy now had to deal with Clarabelle, too.

"I'll get it." Meg slid off her stool. "David, I know Henry was hoping you'd teach him to play cribbage today."

"Love to." David smiled at her, thankful for this escape hatch. He followed behind her to greet her parents and stood back as she opened the front door wide enough to allow them both entry. Her father stood behind her mother, as usual.

"Your father tells me you have a new suitor," Clarabelle said to Meg by way of greeting, as Phillip smiled apologetically at her.

"Hello to you, too," Meg said. "Is that my favorite green Jell-O with maraschino cherries in it?"

"No," Clarabelle snapped. "It's red, with mandarin oranges."

When Meg was small, she'd thrown up oodles of red Jell-O with mandarin oranges and had since been unable to eat it.

Clarabelle's making it was payback for Meg confiding in her father and not in her, plain and simple.

"I'll help with that." David took the dish from Clarabelle and escaped to the kitchen.

"What kind of name is Ahmed, anyway?" Clarabelle asked as she brushed aggressively past Meg.

"It's a first name," Meg said. "And I don't want to talk about him with you."

Clarabelle harrumphed. "Does he speak English?"

"Oh, for God's sake," Meg said. "He's the assistant city manager. Of course he speaks English!"

Clarabelle narrowed her eyes. "Does he have an accent, I mean."

He didn't have an accent, but Meg wasn't about to tell her mother that. She crossed her arms and responded with a defiant look.

"He's been here since he was a kid, right, Meg?" her father said. "Came from Iran when he was ten, didn't you say? His mother was American?"

"Don't bother, Dad," Meg said. "I'm not looking for her approval or permission."

"Of course you aren't," Clarabelle said. "When have you ever?" She stomped off to the kitchen, now about the last place Meg wanted to be. She looked at her father.

"What is it with the women in this family?" she asked. "Why are they so grumpy all the time? I'm not grumpy."

"You're never grumpy," Phillip said.

"That's because life is good," Meg said.

She suggested they go out back and join the kids in the backyard, where they were playing some sort of running-around-and-squealing game that seemed to have no rules, and together they spent a pleasant thirty minutes with the kids, until they were called in for brunch.

Soon enough, Clarabelle was at it again. "How old is he?" La, la, la.

"Please pass the fruit salad," Meg said. David passed it over.

"Has he been married? Is he divorced?" Clarabelle said. "I hear a man can have four wives in Iran."

"Leave her alone," Amy growled.

"Mother, get a life of your own and stop butting into mine." Meg made big eyes at Henry in response to his look of disapproval.

"He's really nice," Henry offered. "He helps me with soccer."

"Those Middle Easterners do like their soccer. Is he Muslim, I suppose? Does he eat pork?" Clarabelle machine-gunned her questions. "Does he pray five times a day and face Mecca like they do? I wonder how that goes over down at city hall. Does he go to a mosque?"

Meg felt her left eye twitch.

"So what if he goes to a mosque?" Amy snapped.

"He doesn't." Meg had asked. When he'd said no, she'd been both relieved and ashamed of her relief. "Not that it matters."

There was nothing wrong with being Iranian!

"Oh, it matters," Clarabelle said. "In this day and age, it most certainly does matter."

"He's really nice," Henry said again.

"Leave her alone," Phillip told Clarabelle. Meg looked at him in surprise. Most often, he let whatever Clarabelle said roll off him as if she were a fly whose pestering he'd gotten so used to that he didn't bother to swat it away anymore.

"Excuse me, Phillip." Clarabelle glared at him. "Am I not allowed to ask my daughter a question?"

"This is what I mean." Phillip said it matter-of-factly. "Exactly what we were talking about before. You aren't just asking questions. You're judging. Criticizing. Acting like she's not an intelligent woman who can come to good decisions on her own."

Ha. Yes! Thank you, Dad.

"She's not making decisions on her own, Phillip." Clarabelle said his name with venom. "You're making them for her."

"No, he's not!" Meg said. "He gives me advice. And he doesn't judge me."

"He doesn't judge you because he doesn't want *you* to judge *him*!" Clarabelle practically yelled.

Meg glared at Clarabelle, who swirled the ice in her glass with a screw-you snippiness and then took a swallow of her gin and tonic.

"Enough." Phillip stood and tossed down his napkin. "I've had enough."

I've heard it said that when a husband cheats on his wife, it's never really about the sex. I've never quite fully believed that— even as I know that in my case, it was probably true.

Jonathan and I were always good together, always sexually compatible. Whatever he suggested, I was willing to try. I initiated sometimes; other times, I followed. He was playful in bed. Thoughtful. Funny. Sex relaxed him, released him from himself. Sex wasn't what we got wrong.

When I hear the word affair, this is what I think: Ugly. Torrid. Selfish. Sneaky. Hurtful. Jonathan's affair, at least the one I know about, was all that and more. There aren't words to describe how horrible it was. The damage it wreaked lingers in me until this day.

But my father . . .

Well, I know my father pretty well. I know my mother, too.

What my father wants is someone who gives a shit how his day went. He wants someone to listen with an open and nonjudgmental heart when he talks. He wants to be heard, and understood, and loved. He doesn't want someone who nags him to change. He wants someone who accepts him as he is.

An affair, it's true, is never just about the sex.

❖

A date!

Meg, who didn't date, was going on a date!

With Ahmed!

A date was just a date, she kept reminding herself. Nothing more and nothing less. In the hokey-pokey scheme of things, it was putting her right foot in, just to test the waters.

What she obsessed over was: would they kiss? There was an etiquette to it, she knew. Perhaps the first date was only supposed to be a kiss on the cheek—but since this was really the fifth time they'd seen each other, even if only their first official date, did that rule still have to apply?

Meg worried he'd be all gentlemanly about it. She, herself, was not feeling particularly ladylike. Kissing Ahmed, she thought, would be like having an extremely interesting conversation.

Meg had decided to have Ahmed meet her by the pool rather than at her apartment. Since Harley was watching Henry, it would make her leave-taking that much smoother. Plus, she wanted her Loop Group friends to meet him so they could discuss him at length later.

Kat spotted him first. "Ooh-la-la," she said. "Is that him?"

When Meg saw Ahmed heading down the path to the pool in his jeans and white shirt and Calvin Klein–ish sports coat, she gave herself official permission to disregard first-date etiquette, because *ooh-la-la* was right.

"That's him." Meg started down the path to greet him. She'd decided to go simple-sexy and wore a sleeveless black knee-length dress and open-toed heels. For makeup, she wore mascara, lipstick and just a hint of eye shadow. The clincher was the diamond necklace she wore. It had been a gift from

Jonathan on their first wedding anniversary, and while she'd thrown their photo albums in a garbage Dumpster and simply walked away from their household items, she couldn't bring herself to abandon the diamond necklace, because while the marriage ended up being far from perfect, the diamond itself was flawless.

The chain on which it hung was so translucent as to be almost invisible, and it had the effect of causing one to lean close to examine what held the diamond in place at the base of her throat . . . which then caused one to inhale the delicate Estée Lauder perfume she wore. So many women wore low-cut tops and high-cut skirts and two-inch fake nails to pass themselves off as sexy (Kat, for instance), but Meg's belief was that a woman should have one signature item that made *her* feel sexy, and the rest would follow naturally. For Meg, it was the diamond.

As they closed the distance between them, Meg kept her eyes on Ahmed's. His radiated unabashed lust—he didn't even try to hide it. She grinned when she recognized it for what it was and then fell into intense seriousness as they moved, yet again, to that deeper level they couldn't seem to avoid. Maybe it was the luck of her diamond or maybe it was the look in his eyes, but Meg's approach was perfect. Her hips swayed gracefully; her heels clicked confidently. Her chin was raised and her posture, ballet-strong.

Sultry, that was how she felt.

She stepped into Ahmed's space and stopped mere inches from him. Silently, she apprised him of her intentions: sultry women don't say hello. They *take* a man.

Thankful for the oleander bushes that blocked Henry's view

of them, Meg pulled Ahmed to her. Though it was their first kiss, there was nothing awkward about it. It was deep, and leisurely, and lingering. It was a fine first kiss.

"There," Meg said when she let him go. "Now I don't have to wonder all night whether or not you're going to kiss me."

Ahmed grinned. "I was definitely going to kiss you."

When they kissed again, the world beyond Meg disappeared. It was just the two of them, softening toward each other, connecting, revealing themselves. It was a kiss to get lost in, until from the pool area Henry called out.

"Hi, Ahmed! Over here!" He pressed himself up against the bars of the pool enclosure and waved wildly. Inelegantly, Ahmed stepped back from her.

"Hi, Henry!" Ahmed grinned at Meg. "Oops."

"It's okay," Henry said. "You can kiss my mom."

Together, Ahmed and Meg entered the pool area and went to him.

"Hey, Henry," Meg said, "guess what."

"I know," Henry said. "He doesn't need my permission."

Ahmed burst out laughing. Meg led him over to the Loop Group and introduced him to everyone, and then they went back over to Henry to say goodbye. He and Violet had created a tent using two tables and a bunch of pool towels.

"*Psst*, Henry!" Meg said. "Come here for a minute."

She guided him to a lounge chair and sat with him. "Are you sure you're okay with me going out with Ahmed like this?"

Henry shrugged. "I think I should get to come, too."

"Another time." Henry's face fell into sadness and Meg felt horrible. This was what she'd wanted to avoid. This was part of the reason she didn't want to date, so Henry would never get confused about her priorities. *He* was her priority. "Do you want me to stay home?" she asked.

"No!" Henry was earnest all of a sudden. "I want you to go! It's just that I wanted to go, too."

"Well . . ."

"But, no, it's okay," Henry said. "Harley's taking me for ice cream and I want to keep playing with Violet. But maybe Ahmed can take *me* somewhere sometime."

Meg laughed. "And here I thought you were sad because I was leaving, but really, it's got nothing to do with me, does it?"

Henry threw his arms around her neck and pulled her down heavily in a way he knew she hated. "You're my favorite mom in the whole world!"

Meg disentangled herself from his smothering happy-cobra grip. "And you're my favorite boy. You know that, right?"

"Um—yeah! You tell me all the time."

"Say it." Henry rolled his eyes. Meg poked his belly and made him laugh. "Say it. Who's my favorite boy in the whole world?"

Henry acquiesced. "I am."

"And when you're being exceptionally naughty and driving me nuts, *then* who's my favorite boy in the whole world?"

"That would still be me."

"That's right," Meg said. "And is there *anything* you could *ever* say or do to make that not be true?"

"Mom!" But this was how it went—one, two, three times he had to acknowledge the absolute nature of her love.

"Answer me," Meg said. "And then I'll let you go back to playing."

"I will always be your favorite boy."

"Yes, you will." Meg kissed the top of his head.

As he dashed off and crawled back into his tent, Meg stood and brushed down her dress. When she looked at Ahmed, his eyes were twinkling.

"Fairy dust," he said. "When I see the two of you together, that's what I always think. It's like you've been sprinkled with fairy dust."

Hoo-rah.

Not every man could get away with saying such corny things. Ahmed could, because there was nothing the least bit corny about him.

As they drove down Broadway Boulevard toward Euclid, Meg studied Ahmed in profile. He was still such an unknown. All she knew with certainty was that being with him gave her a steady burn deep inside, a rumble of rightness she hadn't felt since . . . well, since things had been good with Jonathan.

At Meg's suggestion, they went to the Frog & Firkin on University Boulevard. Music, beer, pizza. What more did a girl need in life?

"The Frog's good," Ahmed agreed when she suggested it. "That's my neighborhood hangout, you know."

"Ah, right," she teased. "I forget you're a Sam Hughsie."

"You are, too."

"Yes, but you're a home-owning Sam Hughsie. I'm just a renter, crashing your neighborhood, bringing down the property values."

He laughed. "I wouldn't say that."

"What would you say?"

"That you're cute." He glanced at her, then back to the road. "And that there's something different about you tonight."

"You're just saying that because I kissed you."

Ahmed smiled. "Maybe."

"Well, also I'm trying to get over myself," Meg said. "That could be what's different. I'm putting my right foot in."

"Meaning?"

"I haven't told you my Hokey-Pokey Theory of Life yet, have I?" Ahmed shook his head. "Well, that's what I'm doing tonight. Living it."

"You'll have to explain it to me over a beer," he said.

The Frog was crowded, but a large group was leaving just as Meg and Ahmed arrived and so the waitresses separated a few tables and they barely had to wait. After they ordered their pizza and after their beers were delivered and dutifully sipped upon, Ahmed prompted her to explain her theory.

"The Hokey-Pokey Theory of Life is that you've got to put your whole self in," she said. "To life, to whatever moment you're in, no matter what it is. If it's wonderful, go with the wonder. If it's painful, go with the pain. You know? You just . . . you shouldn't hold back. I forget it sometimes, but that's what I believe. Or it's what I *want* to believe, anyway."

He studied her. "Tonight's the first time I feel as if you're not holding back with me."

Meg fingered her necklace. "I used to wear my heart on my sleeve," she said. "I used to be much more sure of my place in the world. And then one day, I wasn't anymore."

"Got beat up by life a bit, did you?" Ahmed had about the most beautiful, accepting eyes she'd ever seen. A girl could get lost in those eyes for days.

"I used to come here with my ex-husband, Jonathan." Meg's heart pounded just remembering it. "I used to meet him here on Fridays after I got off work. He'd be here with all his law school buddies and they'd all be yapping back and forth, using these multisyllable million-dollar words, and I'd just sit there like this stupid trophy wife in training. And the worst part was,

I liked it. I was happy being his arm candy, being the cute little wife with the smart guy for the husband. I was just— *God*—I was so shallow back then."

You were young.

You were as deep as you knew how to be.

Meg sipped her beer. Suddenly scared, she looked away from Ahmed to the band of four middle-aged men in Hawaiian shirts performing Beatles songs. *Yesterday, love was such an easy game to play. Now I need a place to hide away.*

A place to hide, indeed.

She looked back at Ahmed. "What's your story, Ahmed? Have you ever been married?"

He glanced away from her and watched the band. *I said something wrong—now I long for yesterday-ay-ay-ay.* Meg waited him out. After a long moment, he turned back to her. "I was married once," he said. "To an Iranian girl. It didn't last."

"What happened?" Meg wanted to get right up in his face and peer into his eyes, his heart, his soul. She needed not so much to hear what he told her, but to feel the truth of what he left out. But she made herself stay reclined and casual.

"We were young, and we didn't know each other very well when we got married," he said. "That caught up with us pretty quick. I was still in college—way too young to be married."

"I was twenty-three when I got married," Meg said.

"That's also young," Ahmed said.

"Please don't tell me you cheated on her," she said.

Ahmed shook his head. "It wasn't like that. We really had no business being married in the first place. Looking back, it was so obvious I was trying to please my father."

"By marrying an Iranian girl?"

"By marrying Avesha in particular," he said. "But it's impossible to please my father. It's not even worth the attempt."

"Are you still in touch with him?"

Ahmed took a sip of his beer and set the glass back on the table, twisting it idly with one hand. "I call him the first Friday of every month. Like clockwork. He is my father. I feel a responsibility."

"He never calls you, I take it."

"Oh, no," he said. "That would be too much trouble, to actually pick up the phone and dial it."

"When's the last time you saw him?"

"Three years ago in France," Ahmed said. "I met him there when he was on business. He gave me three hours of his time."

Meg took his hand. "See, this is why I think it's best that Henry's father hasn't ever been in his life. I think it'd be harder to have his affection be half-assed than for him not to be around at all."

"Henry doesn't mind that he's not around?"

Meg bit her lip as she considered his question. Henry almost never asked her anything about Jonathan. Plus, he had David and his grandfather. And Harley. And now maybe even . . . Ahmed?

"He somehow always manages to get what he needs," Meg said.

"I think Henry's about the coolest kid I've ever met," Ahmed said. "I think he's great."

Meg looked at him for a long moment. "He thinks you're great, too."

Ahmed looked back squarely at her. "Your husband cheated on you—am I right?"

"It's that obvious?"

Ahmed smiled. "When you asked if I'd cheated on my wife, that pretty much gave it away."

"Jonathan told me about his affair the same day I told him I was pregnant with Henry." Meg took a quick sip of beer, feeling very self-conscious all of a sudden. "I had no idea. Never saw it coming. I thought we were perfectly happy. I swear, sometimes I *still* think he was happy right up until he left."

"It's hard to end a relationship," Ahmed said, "especially when the person you're with is a great person. He probably did love you even as he left. Just not in the way he needed to in order to make it work."

"That sounds very wise," Meg said. "Are you speaking from personal experience?"

Ahmed smiled. "Sure, maybe."

Meg tapped her fingernails on the table. "Come on. Do tell. This is what a first date's for—you tell me yours, I'll tell you mine."

"Fair enough," Ahmed said. "I'm thinking of my last girl-friend, Caroline. We dated for probably two years when she got a transfer to the Bay Area—this was last fall; she was in marketing—and it just made no sense for me to go, professionally."

"Don't you think if she was the one, you would have taken the hit professionally to be with her personally?"

"I do," Ahmed said. "Absolutely. And she wasn't the one. But if that transfer opportunity hadn't come up, I'm sure we'd still be together. We got along really well and we had momentum in our favor. Nothing was wrong with the relationship."

"That sounds horrible," Meg said.

Ahmed laughed. "It wasn't horrible. It was just . . ."

"Cordial," Meg said.

Ahmed laughed again. "It was very cordial. But it wasn't . . ." He gestured back and forth in the space between them. "It wasn't like this."

Meg felt herself redden. "What *is* this? If you have any idea, I'd sure like to hear it, because I'll admit I'm confused."

"I'm not sure what this is, either." Ahmed took a long moment to find his words. "I know that you somehow draw me out," he said. "I consistently find myself wanting to . . . I don't know . . . let you see who I really am. You always say what's on your mind and you don't hide your feelings, good or bad, and you're just . . . healthy. I don't know. I almost never share personal information about myself. Part of that's being Persian, I think. Culturally, we're guarded. But I find myself wanting to let you get to know me. You're . . . you give people what they need to feel safe."

Meg was flattered by his words, impressed by his openness and scared by the depth of his feelings. Her heart beat insanely fast. "So it's more than cordial?"

"It's more than cordial." Ahmed's smile was serious. "And, Meg, I don't cheat in any aspect of my life. I'd never cheat on you."

Meg leaned forward to study his eyes. They had the calm confidence of a lake at sunrise, and Meg *loved* lakes at sunrise.

She loved diving into them and causing ripples, but she especially loved it once the ripples faded and the lake turned placid again and she, having dived in, became part of the calmness, part of the confidence, part of the whole. She realized as she looked in his eyes that she wanted to be part of the whole. That she was ready, finally.

"Kiss me," she said. "Kiss me cordially and with passion, too."

He leaned forward and obliged, and as they kissed, Meg thought how she'd been right. Kissing him *was* like having an interesting conversation—a gentle, searching, questioning-and-answering kind of conversation.

It was the kind of conversation she wished could go on forever.

In the afterglow of their first date, they went on several more. There was a miniature golf outing with Henry, a sunset hike in the Rincon Mountains without him. Horseback riding with, intimate dinners without. They often met at Rincon Market for iced tea and something from the bakery. He met her father. She met his friends. Meg and Henry made room for Ahmed on their Saturday coffee-shop dates at LuLu's, although Meg adamantly maintained Friday Night Movie Night as a mom-and-son-only ritual. Ahmed didn't mind, as he had his own Friday-night ritual to close out the workweek and usher in the weekend—hitting balls on the driving range, either alone or with the guys.

Over time, Ahmed filled in the puzzle pieces of his past. He'd stumbled socially through middle school in small-town Wisconsin until he'd stripped himself of his accent and foreign mannerisms, and by high school, he hung around with the popular crowd. It helped that his high school was so small that any kid could play on any sports team. He played soccer and football and ran track. His grandparents hated his father at a time when Ahmed still idolized and missed him, so his relationship with his grandparents was strained. He'd married while in college at the University of Wisconsin–Madison and moved to Tucson for a fresh start after the relationship fell apart (she'd moved back to Iran), working full-time while attending graduate school at the U of A, eventually earning a master's in public administration.

Meg, too, shared her past with Ahmed piece by piece. Her story felt less interesting in comparison. They hugged spontaneously, and often. They stole and gifted kisses. Holding hands became habitual, and if Henry was around, he always managed to end up in the middle. Now that Ahmed was part of their life, Meg couldn't imagine being without him.

"Mom?" Henry said one Sunday morning. "Who would I live with if you died?"

He asked this when it was just the two of them, eating their early bowls of apples-and-cinnamon oatmeal, which would hold them over until brunch at Amy's.

Meg hated moments like these. The idea of her not being there for him was such an ugly one that she'd never been able to think about it. She'd never made a will, never had any difficult would-you-take-my-kid conversations with friends or relatives. Even though she knew it was ridiculous, she sort of believed that if she planned for her death, then it would happen. As a result, she had no idea what actually *would* happen to Henry if she died.

"I take very good care of my health," she said. "I'm not going to die."

"But if you did," Henry said. "Like, if you got ran over by a car."

She knew the important thing was to be decisive in her response. The actual person who'd care for him wasn't as important as was conveying with confidence that everything would be under control. "You'd live with Amy and David," she said.

"What if they died, too?" He wasn't angsty, just matter-of-factly curious.

"Then you'd live with your grandparents," Meg said.

"What if they don't stay married?" Henry said. "Or what would happen if you and Ahmed got married and *then* you died? Would I keep living with Ahmed?"

Meg set her spoon back in her oatmeal bowl, folded her hands in front of her on the table (even though what she really wanted to do was pull her hair out) and looked evenly at Henry. "We've only known him for a month," she said.

"Six weeks," Henry said. "Six and a half, actually."

Meg took a deep breath. "You like him, don't you?"

With his burning blue eyes, Henry looked straight at her. "I think we should marry him."

"Henry . . ." Meg felt helpless, waylaid and vastly unprepared for this discussion. "Buddy, my dear. Love of my life. Please be happy with how things are. Please don't get your hopes up. The fact is, I don't do marriage very well. I'm not very good at it."

"Why not?" He looked at her pointedly. "It can't be that hard. Whatever you did wrong before, just don't do it anymore."

"It's not that easy," Meg said. "I don't know what I did wrong."

"Then you need to find out, because this is important," he said. "What we have with Ahmed's important."

Meg sighed. "You know what they say—yesterday's history and tomorrow's a mystery but today is a gift and that's why it's called *the present*. We need to be happy with things just like they are now. Six weeks isn't long enough to know whether we have a future with Ahmed."

"Six-and-a-half weeks, Mom." Henry glared at her. "And yes, it is long enough."

Henry pushed back from his chair and left the table without waiting to be excused. Meg thought about calling him back and making him take his bowl and juice glass to the kitchen sink but decided against it. Instead, she stirred her oatmeal in hopes of smoothing it out, but it had turned hopelessly clumpy.

It didn't matter, though, because Meg had completely lost her appetite.

The following day, when Meg was called to Mrs. Anderson's office, she left her three-afternoons-a-week aide with her kindergartners and arrived to find Henry pouting in the naughty-kid chair with his arms crossed. Mrs. Anderson sat behind her desk, calmly reading her *Journal of Educational Administration* while she waited for Meg.

"Sorry to pull you out of class," she said when Meg arrived, "but your son's earned himself a two-day suspension."

Meg's stomach plunged as Henry gave her a defiant look and straightened from his slumped position. "What for?" she asked.

"He got into a shouting match on the playground with Enrique and grabbed him by his jacket collar and pulled him to the ground," Mrs. Anderson said. "The playground monitor witnessed the whole incident."

"What part of *zero tolerance* do you not understand?" Meg asked Henry.

"He called me a bastard."

"I work for a living, Henry. You know this, right?" Meg said. "I need to be here every day, because it provides me with the money to put a roof over our heads and food on the table. I can't take two days off from work because some kid called you a name and you didn't like it. You know better than to fight. I'm very disappointed in you."

"I hate this school," Henry said. "I want to go to Sam Hughes."

"This has nothing to do with that," Meg said.

"The kids here are rude," Henry said.

"Kids at Sam Hughes do plenty of name-calling, too," Meg said.

"I don't care," he said. "That's where I want to go."

Meg exchanged a look with Mrs. Anderson.

"Did you fight with Enrique on purpose because you thought you'd get to change schools?" Meg said.

Henry slumped again. "No."

Meg felt her left eye twitch. Something about his denial was insincere.

Because the school day was almost over, Mrs. Anderson permitted Meg to bring Henry to her class until the dismissal bell rang. Meg made him spray the tables clean and cut out the twenty-five capital letter Gs she needed for tomorrow's lesson. He refused to join the kindergartners for closing-circle time, refused to put any or all of his pouting self in.

On the way home, Meg called her mother to see if she could watch Henry. Clarabelle agreed to watch him the next day but informed Meg she was unavailable the following one because she was scheduled to work.

"But you don't have a job," Meg said.

"I do now," Clarabelle said. "As of this afternoon, I'm a seasonal associate at Ann Taylor at the Tucson Mall."

"Hey, hey! That's great!" Meg said. "Discounts all around! Good for you—what made you decide to do this?"

"My daughter told me I needed to get a life," Clarabelle said.

"Since when have you ever taken your daughter's advice?" Meg asked and then quickly added, "Just kidding. I think it's a perfect job for you."

Clarabelle would be forced to be friendly, which might spill over into her private life. It would get her out of the house. Maybe she'd even venture beyond her standard black, brown, and gray clothing choices.

"Why does he need someone to watch him?" Clarabelle said. "Don't you have off from school, too?"

"It's not a free day," she said. "He got suspended for shoving a kid down on the playground." Meg cringed, waiting for her mother to pronounce Henry a deviant and herself a bad mother and was pleasantly surprised when Clarabelle didn't.

"Do you remember when I had to come get you from school?" Clarabelle asked. "You took on both the Thompson girls."

"Oh my God—those horrible girls!" Meg remembered them. Their whole family was big, loud and the very definition of uncouth. "But no, I don't remember."

Clarabelle tsked. "They took your sister's little poetry journal or some such thing and ripped all the pages out."

Poor Amy. She'd been such a dreamy girl. Utterly defenseless. Which meant . . . she—Meg—had been the strong one? How did she not remember this about herself?

"Were you mad at me when I got sent home?" Meg asked.

"I wasn't, actually," Clarabelle said. "I was usually pretty good about big things like that. It was the day-to-day things that drove me crazy."

Meg laughed. "Well, I'm glad you're doing this job at the mall. It sounds fun. And don't worry. I'll figure out a solution to my Henry problem."

"Try Amy," Clarabelle suggested. "She's always home."

Meg wrapped up the call and looked at Henry in the rear-view mirror. She was the opposite of her mother—good with the small things and maybe not so good with the big things. She wanted to be good with everything. "Okay, guy," she said. "One day down, one to go. I'll call Amy when we get home."

"Can I see your phone for a minute?" Henry said.

Against her better judgment, Meg handed it to him in the backseat. Ten seconds later, she heard, "Hi, Ahmed? It's Henry. Can I go to work with you the day after tomorrow?"

Dead meat this kid was.

"Henry!" Meg said. "Give me the phone!"

"Cool," Henry said. "Hang on. My mom wants to talk to you."

"Sorry about that," she said to Ahmed when Henry gave back her phone. "Ignore his question."

"No school?" Ahmed said. "And hi, by the way."

Meg smiled. "Hi, yourself. He got suspended. For fighting."

"What's that all about?" Ahmed asked. "I thought he was calming down."

"I thought so, too," she said. "But apparently not."

"He's impetuous." The tease in Ahmed's voice came through loud and clear. "Like someone else I know."

"Hey," Meg said, grinning.

"He can come to work with me," Ahmed said. "I think it'd be fun."

"He's not supposed to have fun," Meg said. "It's a punishment. Make him shred paper all day or something."

"I like shredding paper," Henry said.

Meg ignored him as she and Ahmed said their goodbyes,

and then she narrowed her eyes at Henry in the rearview mirror. "Are you even sorry for what you did?"

"Enrique called me a bastard."

Broken record. "So what, Henry?"

Henry kicked the back of her seat twice, hard. "So I don't want to be one anymore!"

In that moment, Meg finally got it. They drove the rest of the way home in silence. Once inside, she pulled out the dictionary and had him look up the word *bastard*. *A person born of unmarried parents. An illegitimate child.*

"See?" she said. "You don't even qualify. I was still married when you were born."

"Enrique said it means I don't have a dad."

"He's wrong," Meg said. "The dictionary doesn't lie. And besides, if memory serves, Enrique's dad's in prison."

"At least he *has* a dad."

Meg made Henry sit at the dining room table and look her in the eye. "What's this about?"

Henry shrugged and wouldn't meet her eyes.

"Can you tell me, Henry? Since when is the two of us not enough?"

Henry didn't answer, but he didn't need to. Meg knew the answer. Life had been good before Ahmed came along, but as they got to know him, Henry, like Meg, wanted more, more, more.

They both wanted a never-ending supply of more.

When I was married to Jonathan, I honestly thought nothing bad would ever happen to me.

Because I'd led a charmed life, I had no idea how much I was defined by my naive belief that tragedy wouldn't touch me. But in an instant, I went from being that—a la-la land girl who lived in a little fake snow globe bubble of happiness—to being the sort of person bad things happened to.

After Jonathan cheated on me, I didn't know what to believe about myself anymore. Take the husband, you know? Take the husband and the house and the car and the money and all the things I thought my future would hold. I could live without any of that. But did he have to take away everything I thought I knew about myself as well?

My father once shared with me an expression: only a broken heart can be whole. He said we find ourselves in the broken pieces, and we build ourselves back up.

After Jonathan cheated on me, I cracked. Humpty Dumpty all the way, only the king's horses and the king's men were nowhere to be found. I alone had to put myself back together again, to make myself whole, and my dad was right: I did find myself in the broken pieces.

❖

On the day Henry went to work with Ahmed, he emerged from his bedroom dressed not in his usual T-shirt and shorts but in khaki pants (the pair that did not have a hole in the knee), a button-down shirt and a clip-on tie. He was hand-over-heart adorable.

"You look precious," she said. "You *are* precious."

"He's making us pancakes," Henry said. "We need to be there in, like, ten minutes. He can't be late to work because of us."

Precious.

The smell of pancakes and the sound of blues music greeted them from the sidewalk after they'd parked the car in front of Ahmed's house. Blues music? At seven in the morning? Meg felt a lusty thrill tickle her skin. It was so unexpected. She would never have suspected that Ahmed was a fan of the blues. She would have thought he'd be more of a Kenny G kind of guy. Not that there was anything *wrong* with soothing light jazz, but there was no denying the fact that when you imagined how someone might be in bed, the difference between a light-jazz guy and a blues guy was huge. Blues was plaintive. Insistent. Focused on the heart of the act. Jazz seemed so much more . . . obsessed with the foreplay. And not that foreplay was bad, but too much of it was . . . well, Meg listened to jazz sometimes and thought, *Will that saxophone never shut up?*

Henry ran up the steps ahead of her and rang the doorbell three times right in a row. Through the screen door, Meg saw that Ahmed, in khaki pants like Henry and with his shirt collar open, holding off on his tie for as long as possible, was beaming in a way she'd not seen before.

"Good morning, you two!" he said. "I've got pancakes all ready."

Someone was cooking for them—for her—how amazing was that? And then there was his porch, with two Adirondack chairs just waiting for a couple to grow old in together.

His view across the street was of Sam Hughes Elementary, one of the best schools in the district and the one Violet went to and the one Henry could go to if only it wasn't so inconvenient. If they lived here, she and Ahmed could sit on the front porch together and watch Henry cross the street to school. And then they could go inside, turn on some blues music and have themselves a blues-inspired quickie before they went their separate ways for the day.

"Hey, you." As Meg stepped across the threshold, she patted Ahmed playfully on the cheek. Henry was already in the kitchen, checking on the pancakes. "I didn't know you were a fan of the blues. It seems so uniquely American."

"I am uniquely American," Ahmed said.

"Indeed, you are," Meg said. "Who is this?"

"Marcia Ball," Ahmed said. "From her *Blue House* CD."

It was a soulful, mournful ballad. *In a lonely heart there's a tiny spark that keeps the love alive. And if it's just a dream no one else believes, why do I? Why do I?*

"Nice music to slow dance to." She stopped mere inches from him, unabashedly undressing him with her eyes.

"Mmmm." The look he gave her was lustful. Nakedly so.

"It's got a nice saxophone," she said.

"It does." Ahmed said it as if he knew what she meant by that.

She stepped farther inside. His house was a small shotgun bungalow with wood floors and built-in bookshelves. His furniture was mission-style, and he had an old upright mahogany

Baldwin piano against an inside wall, which Meg had yet to hear him play, although he'd mentioned he'd been taking lessons for the past year. A few pieces of original artwork by local artists adorned the walls.

As they ate, she felt as if they were in a scene from some movie—a romance, of course, the part where some telling detail sparks the single mom's realization about the rightness of her new relationship. The flourish with which Ahmed served the chocolate-chip pancakes, for instance. Or the cute way Ahmed and Henry clinked juice glasses. Or how sweetly Ahmed cleared their plates and how clearly happy he was to have them there. But she realized there wasn't just one thing about him that made them such a good match. It was everything.

As Meg drove to school, her heart was light and she cranked her radio when Melissa Etheridge's "Message to Myself" came on and she sang at the top of her lungs. She didn't even mind the empty backseat, because she knew Henry was with Ahmed and that, therefore, he was in a very good place.

At that afternoon's snack time, her students went a little crazy in the most beautiful of ways. Everything in her kindergarten classroom was part of a well thought-out routine, and the afternoon-snack routine consisted of all the students pushing their desks into groups of four. Chairs were to be silently slid and tucked under the new arrangement.

The children sat two boys and two girls to a table, and Meg sat with the leftovers, one of whom always happened to be Marita. Three kids got to be the cracker kids, and they counted out five baskets of twenty lightly salted whole-wheat saltine crackers and distributed them to the tables. Three other kids got to be the carrot kids, and they counted out five paper plates of twenty baby carrots, along with a small bowl of ranch dressing for dipping, and distributed them to the tables.

Usually, it was all very orderly and quiet, but in a kindergarten classroom, it takes only one kid to throw everything into utter chaos. And that kid, that day, was Lucas, lovely little Lucas.

While Meg's back was turned, he made race-car noises while sliding his chair across the floor. Still lost in a dreamy fog that involved Ahmed and blues music, Meg ignored his transgression. The other boys took it as permission to make their own race-car noises, and soon the whole classroom was buzzing with boys.

"All right, everyone. This isn't the Indy Five Hundred," she said. "Take your chairs, and I'll put the music on."

When Henry was a baby, Meg had played classical music to him each night as he'd fallen asleep, which had an unintended and unfortunate consequence: classical music now put Henry in a droopy, Pavlovian stupor. Meg sometimes pictured him as an adult, snoring through symphonies his wife dragged him to. But Meg felt classical music was important, and she wanted her kindergartners to appreciate it (without the resultant sleepiness), so another ritual of afternoon-snack time was the playing of classical music.

When Lucas began to sway and bop his head to Mozart's Serenade No. 13, Meg ignored him, which his tablemates took as permission to join him. Not only did they sway and bop their heads, too, but when the music swelled in the middle of the serenade and when Lucas waved his arms like a zealous-but-perhaps-drunk conductor, the others followed right along, sheer joy on their misbehaving faces.

Soon, with the exception of Marita, who sat quietly next to Meg and watched with her big brown eyes as she nibbled her square cracker into a circle, the entire class joined in with sweet abandon and ineptness. Meg watched, tears in her eyes from the beauty of the moment. She felt Marita's hand on her knee.

"Please don't cry, Miss Meg," Marita said. "They don't mean to make you feel bad."

"I'm not sad," Meg whispered. "I'm crying because I'm happy."

Less happy was her father, whom Meg visited at his office after school, since she had some extra time before she was supposed to pick up Henry from Ahmed's house. She'd called Phillip on a break at school and asked if he could squeeze her in that afternoon.

Her father's tax practice specialized in accounting for the medical profession. With an office located on Grant Road near Tucson Medical Center in a small complex, he was a sole practitioner, although in recent years, since he was nearing sixty, he'd talked about finding someone to buy into the business and eventually succeed him. For now, it was just him and Sandi, his longtime secretary and bookkeeper, whom Meg had never quite figured out.

Or maybe she had—maybe there just wasn't much *to* figure out. Meg had known Sandi, who was about her father's age, for more than a decade and yet she knew little about her beyond that she was remarkably large-breasted, had a black beehive hairstyle and read romance novels at her desk during slow times. Her husband was a man named Bud, who liked to go fly-fishing.

When Meg arrived, Sandi gave her a cheery greeting and announced she was heading out for the day. *Must be nice,* Meg thought, and then felt guilty for thinking so. From the first of January, both Sandi and her father burrowed into their tax work and emerged on April sixteenth blurry-eyed and pale-faced, having crammed a year's worth of work into ten weeks. Sandi was well within her rights to leave early this time of year.

Meg settled with her father in his office—his inner sanctum, as he called it—on his steel-and-black-leather Copenhagen couch. A few years back, he'd donated his old no-style furniture to charity and gone modern.

It had been a surprising choice, because in every other way, he was, to put it kindly, somewhat . . . bland. His glasses were a decade out-of-date, and nearly without exception, he wore khaki pants that sagged in the behind and muted oxford shirts. Even his ideas about secretaries were old-fashioned—he honestly expected Sandi to make and bring him coffee each morning (which she gladly did).

Today, he looked at Meg uneasily. "I think I know why you're here."

"It's your turn, Dad," she said. "I want to know what's going on in your life."

He looked at her for a long moment and then pushed against the bridge of his glasses with his middle finger. At the same time, he searched her eyes, looking, it seemed to Meg, for a way to ground himself, or maybe to find common ground.

"I've been married for nearly thirty-five years," he said.

"That's something," Meg said. "Not many people can say that."

"It's something, but it's not enough," Phillip said. "Just being married isn't enough for me anymore. If I'm married, I want to be *happily* married. And I'm not."

*   *   *

On the way to Ahmed's house to pick up Henry, Meg pulled into a parking lot to call Amy and fill her in on the conversation she'd just had with their father.

"I totally get what he's talking about," Amy said. "I'm on his side completely."

"It's not about sides," Meg said.

"When does the shit hit the fan?"

"My sense is pretty soon." Meg got an ugly feeling in her gut, because while a divorce between her parents might be for the best, it wasn't going to be easy.

After the call, Meg tried to figure out how she felt about her parents' impending separation. It was like a heart attack waiting to happen, surprising only in that it hadn't occurred sooner. Still, it left her feeling numb. Where would her father live? It would be so strange visiting him in a new place! And was she supposed to warn her mother?

Her mother had to know or at least sense it was coming. Getting a job—a reason to get up in the mornings—was probably at least partly in preparation for Life After—a social network, a little extra spending cash, new clothes. Maybe she'd surprise them all and blossom.

When Meg arrived at Ahmed's house and approached the front door, she saw through the screen that Henry and Ahmed were leaning over his dining room table from opposite sides, engrossed in a game of chess. Dark and light, big and small. She stopped still and watched them.

Since that first day at the coffee shop when she'd gotten all shaky after seeing the two of them huddled together over the chessboard, she'd given some thought as to what had so startled her about the moment, and what came to her was this: when she closed her eyes and let an image of her and Henry float forward, mother and son, the image was most often of them side by side, him knocking into her and her arm loosely around his shoulders, pulling him to her in a bumpy, hanging-out-together sort of way. But when she imagined Henry with a father figure in his life, the image was that of two guys, one big, one small, heads focused downward, working on airplane models or electronic thingamajigs—some guy thing, important only to the two of them. She always pictured herself watching from a distance, swelled with love for the guys in her life, the man and the man-to-be.

And here was that image, working its way to the surface, from dream to reality. Nearly breathless, Meg watched for a long moment before interrupting them.

"Knock, knock," she finally said through the screen door.

Both Henry and Ahmed looked up and smiled at her.

"Who's there?" Henry said.

Meg grinned. "Carly."

"Carly who?"

"Car leaves in five minutes, so hurry up and finish your game."

"Very funny, Mom. *Not.*"

Ahmed approached to unlock the door. "How was your day, dear?"

"Lovely, thank you." She kissed him on the cheek, deciding she didn't need to tell Ahmed about her parents right away. The door on her parents' relationship might be closing, but the one on theirs was just opening. The newness in the pleasure of coming home to someone at the end of the workday should be relished and protected. "And yours?"

"We had a great day, didn't we, Henry?"

"Yep, except that meeting with the mayor got really boring."

"You met the mayor?" Eyebrows raised, Meg walked over and gave Henry a kiss. His clip-on tie was gone, but he still looked adorably preppy. "How cool are you?"

"Very cool," Henry said. "Ahmed, it's your turn."

Ahmed's amused gaze was on Meg as he answered Henry. "Let's take a break and catch up with your mother."

"Chopped liver," Meg said. "That's all I am to him."

When Ahmed asked if she wanted a glass of wine, she said yes and followed him into the kitchen. He first filled a wine-glass with grape juice for Henry, then uncorked a bottle of merlot and poured them each a glass. She stepped close to accept hers. "Did you take good care of my boy?"

"As if my life depended on it." Ahmed's eyes danced with hers and they fell into a dopey-smiling moment again. She was going to bed him soon—she knew it. How could she not, when he had eyes like that? How could she not, when she found him appealing in virtually every way?

"I have a question for you," she said.

"Ask away."

"You said this morning that you're uniquely American, which you are. But there's so little in the house to suggest your Iranian background and I wonder why that is. I mean, you don't even have a Persian rug."

"I'd say I'm only sort of just now tiptoeing my way back into my culture," Ahmed said. "I spent a lot of time in my youth rejecting it."

"Did nine-eleven have anything to do with your change of heart?" Meg asked. "Awaken some new sort of pride or something?"

"Sure." He shrugged. "Overnight, all of us had to measure every word, gesture, e-mail, phone call, trip abroad."

"The land of the free suddenly became a lot less free," Meg said.

"That's right," he agreed.

"Well, I'm sorry." Meg quickly hugged him. "I'm sorry for every bad thing you've ever experienced."

Ahmed's hold on her was tight. "You're so sweet. You make me feel good about who I am."

"You *should* feel good about who you are," Meg said. "You take care of people."

Ahmed pulled back. "But I don't," he said. "Not like I want to. Until you and Henry, I haven't had anyone—I mean, I've wanted to in the abstract, but—"

"You do on a community level," Meg said. "You're part of a group down there at city hall that works to make this town a good place to live. With the glaring exception of providing good sidewalks."

Ahmed laughed, but quickly turned serious again. "I want to take care of you two," he said. "Not that you can't take of yourselves perfectly well, because you can, obviously. You've been doing it for a long time, but—"

"How about we'll take care of each other?" Meg swallowed hard, barely believing this conversation was actually happening.

Ahmed nodded. "I like that. And the RTA will take care of the sidewalks."

Meg slugged him playfully in the arm.

"People," Henry said from the dining room. He'd used the interruption to line up all the chess pieces he'd acquired from Ahmed, but apparently he'd then run out of things to do. "We're in the middle of a game here."

Meg pulled back from the embrace to reprimand Henry. "Can't you see we're having a moment here?"

"Have it some other time," Henry said. "Can't *you* see that I'm waiting to make my move?"

Ahmed raised his eyebrows at Henry and then at Meg. "I do, as a matter of fact, have a Persian rug," he said in a suggestive undertone. "It's in my bedroom."

"You're such a tease!" she said.

He laughed. "I really do have one in my bedroom."

"Do you have a Persian cat?"

"In my bedroom." He made his voice low and husky.

"Now *that* was a line," Meg said.

"You got me."

"Excuse me, peoples," Henry said. "It's my turn."

No, Meg thought. *It's my turn.*

She took the wineglass of juice to her son and ruffled his hair. "Give us a minute, Henry. I want to see the rug in Ahmed's bedroom."

As Ahmed grinned at her, Henry crossed his arms in a pout.

"Hey, Henry, if you want, you can check in my freezer and see if I have any ice cream. You can get yourself a bowl if I do." Ahmed turned to Meg. "If that's okay with you."

"Sounds like a very healthy dinner to me," she said as she took Ahmed's hand and began to pull him down the hall.

Cheered, Henry bolted from the table and disappeared into Ahmed's kitchen. "Mint chocolate chip! My favorite!"

"He's such a sucker," Meg whispered. "Now show me that rug."

Once in his room, Ahmed gestured toward the floor. "My token Persian rug."

Meg looked oh so meaningfully into Ahmed's eyes. "I don't care about the rug."

"What is it you care about?" He said it in that low, sexy way he had as he put his hands around her waist, making her feel all skinny.

"You," Meg said. "Us. Me getting it right this time around."

"Kiss me cordially," he said. "And with passion, too."

"I don't think so," Meg teased, backing him toward the bed. Ahmed's house was at most a thousand square feet, so Henry was definitely not far out of earshot, but this was Ahmed's *bedroom* and on the stereo Etta James was wailing out "Cry Like a Rainy Day" and how sexy was *that*?

Gamely, Ahmed half fell onto his mattress, leaving his legs dangling over the edge. "You lured me to the bedroom under false pretenses," he protested happily.

Meg stepped into the space between his legs. She leaned over him and put her hands on either side of his shoulders so he was fake trapped. Also, so he had a decent view of her cleavage. "Do you mind?"

"Can't say that I do." He ran his fingertips up the back of her thighs, giving her the chills.

She traced a finger over each of his eyebrows in turn, then kissed his cheek. She kissed his forehead, then several points along his jawbone, and when she finally kissed his lips, he tasted of the merlot and of a spice she couldn't place.

"What did you have for lunch today?" she asked.

"I took Henry to Ali Baba for Persian food," he said.

Meg couldn't recall Henry ever having eaten Middle East-ern food before. "Did he like it?"

"He loved it."

"Will you cook Persian food for me sometime?" she asked.

"I don't know how," he said. "But for you, I'd be willing to learn."

"Let's learn together." Meg kissed him again, a deep and persistent and satisfying kiss.

"I have a question for you," he said when they came up for air. "Henry spent a good chunk of time today complaining about his soccer coach, and she really doesn't sound competent."

"She's not," Meg said. "And she never wanted to coach in the first place. It was just that no one else volunteered. And she's been horrible to Henry. I almost feel I should let him quit and start fresh next year with another team."

"What if I volunteered to coach?" Ahmed said. "I'd love to do it, and I think it would be good for Henry, too."

Meg pulled back, awed and stunned. She stared at Ahmed in a daze as her father's words came back to her. *If you want to know how a man feels about you, don't listen to a word he says. Instead, watch what he does.*

This counted, Ahmed's offering to coach Henry's team.

It counted for a lot.

Later that week, Meg was in the school office before the beginning bell, making copies of a permission slip for a field trip to Centennial Hall, when she overheard the school secretary say to someone on the phone, "Oh, Ms. Clark's right here. Hold one moment, please."

Meg turned from the copy machine. "Is it a parent?"

Alicia Diaz held out the receiver. She was fiftyish, short and fleshy—Meg thought of her as squishy. As long as Meg had known her, Alicia had always worn the same soft Dior J'adore perfume. "He says he's an old friend."

Meg's gut kicked a warning. "Take a message, will you?"

Alicia tried, but then held the handset out again. "He says it's important."

Meg shook her head. "Find out who it is."

"Just take it." Alicia shook the handset at Meg. "I've got work to do."

Meg's chest pounded in terror as she reached for the phone. "Hello?"

"They still call you Ms. Clark, I see," the man said.

Eeek, eeek, eeek.

It was like the shower scene from Hitchcock's *Psycho,* all the way. Jonathan's amused tone stabbed her, quick and sure. *They still call you Ms. Clark.*

He'd taken every other goddamned thing from her. The least she could do was keep his name.

"Meg?" he said when she didn't reply. "How've you been?"

As if he cared.

"What are you calling me for?" she demanded. "What do you want?"

"I'm coming to Tucson in a few weeks," he said. "I'd like to see you. There are some things I need to say."

The nerve.

The *nerve* of this guy.

"I'm all booked up." Meg clenched the handset. "No room for cheating ex-husbands on my schedule."

Alicia stared at Meg with her mouth open, not even pretending not to listen. She'd been there when Meg was a glowing newlywed. She'd been there during the three years Meg had put Jonathan through law school on her teacher's salary. She'd been there when Meg learned she'd been duped, and she'd been there when Meg was dumped, and when she'd grown round with Henry and had to face person after person who congratulated her on *their* happy news when there was no *them* anymore. *It looks like it's going to be just me raising this precious baby,* she'd say with a shaky voice and wavering smile. Alicia had been there through it all.

"Meg—"

"Don't *Meg* me," she snapped at Jonathan. "How dare you call me now, after all these years? How dare you? Ten years you didn't call me, and you call now? What? Did you sense I was finally completely happy and you just couldn't stand it? Huh?

Is that why you're calling? You're trying to ruin me again? Well, I won't let you."

"But, Meg, I—"

"Don't *Meg* me!" With that, she firmly laid the handset back on the receiver and stared at Alicia, dumbfounded. After he'd first left her, she'd expected his call on a minute-by-minute basis, the pathetic wreck that she was. Then hourly. Then daily, then weekly. And then Henry was born, and then a year had passed and then ten and Jonathan never, ever called.

Why now?

Alicia moved to comfort her, but Meg waved her off. If anyone showed her kindness, she'd fall to the floor and wail and be no better than she'd been back then. She needed to get a grip. She needed for this not to be happening. She needed . . . she needed . . .

Oh God.

Meg rushed from the office. All around, a blur of early-arriving bright-shirted kids called greetings to her, but she didn't reply, couldn't reply. What she needed was to make it to the bathroom, to find a toilet, because the very thought of Jonathan reappearing in their lives made her sick.

Marita came to school that day sporting a big bandage on her left arm. She approached Meg on the playground from behind and tucked herself into Meg's skirt.

Still in shock from Jonathan's call, Meg didn't notice the bandage at first. "Hey, Marita. How are you?"

Clutching Meg's skirt, the little girl didn't answer. Meg draped her arm around Marita's bony shoulder and drew her out where she could get a good look at her. "You got an owie," Meg said, finally noticing. "What happened?"

"I got hot water spilled on me," she said and then added, much too quickly, "But it was an accident."

Meg clenched her teeth and cursed the red flags that waved desperately at her. She *hated* this. There was always one, it seemed. Every goddamned year, there was one. And not that she'd wish harm on any of her kids—she wouldn't—but she'd give anything for Marita not to be this year's one.

From her years of teaching, Meg knew all too well that no one ever knew what went on behind closed doors, and that it was actually a blessing when things spilled out so the child could be helped. But that didn't make it easier. What a crappy, crappy day this was turning into. She led Marita to the nearby bench, sat her down and took her hand.

"I'd like you to tell me what happened," she said. "And I'd like you to tell me the exact truth. Can you do that?"

"I got hot water spilled on me," Marita repeated, her eyes big and dutiful. "But it was an accident."

Meg's sigh was deep. These kids' duty was always to the parent, no matter how much pain the parent caused. She lifted Marita's chin to ensure eye contact. "If anyone ever hurts you or scares you, I will help," Meg said. "I'll help you and I'll never be mad at you, no matter what. Okay? Do you understand what I'm saying?"

Marita nodded.

"Was it scary, when the hot water got spilled on you?" Meg asked gently.

Marita nodded again.

"Was it hot water, or was it more like a teakettle or a hot pan that got pressed against your arm by accident?"

Hesitation crossed Marita's eyes, and she didn't answer. Meg knew it was because no one had helped her rehearse a response to that particular question.

"Did somebody put some lotion on your arm to help it get better?"

Marita nodded.

"Was it the same person who helped you with your bandage?"

Marita perked up. "It was Anna. Anna helped me."

"Is Anna your sister?"

Marita shook her head. "She's my . . . I share a room with her. She's *like* my sister, but she's not my sister. Her mom's Rosa."

"And who's Rosa?"

"My mom's friend. They pay rent together."

"How old's Anna?"

"Fourteen."

Meg ran her fingers down Marita's braids. Thank God for Anna. "Is she the one who braids your hair so pretty?"

Marita nodded and smiled.

"Anna must love you very much," Meg said.

Marita's beautiful smile broke through. "I love *her*. And I love you, too, Miss Meg."

"I love you right back, sweetie." Meg stroked Marita's smooth braids again and prayed that Marita wouldn't hate her for what she had to do next, which was everything in her power to get her out of the only home and away from the only family she'd ever known.

As she and Henry approached the soccer field after school that day, Meg saw kids running drills through cones and remembered that today was the day Ahmed had planned to surprise Henry. Because of everything that had happened in the last hours with Jonathan and then with Marita, she was not in the mood to play along, but she did, seeing it as her motherly duty.

They were far enough away that Meg knew Henry hadn't yet recognized Ahmed. She squinted, then raised her hand to shield her eyes from the sun, ostensibly to see better, but really just for effect.

"Your team never starts on time," she said. "So that can't be your team . . . can it?"

"There's Bradley," Henry said. "See? Right there." Meg followed Henry's finger. Yes, indeed it was Bradley, tripping his way through the drill.

"But where's your coach?"

They scanned the field. Henry found her first. "Over there! On the sidelines!"

Sure enough, Coach Debbie was sitting on a blanket and looked to be reading a book. "Well, then, who's that?"

"Mom! That's Ahmed! Ahmed's coaching!" Henry jumped with glee. "Oh my God! This is the best week ever!"

Best week ever. Right.

Meg tried valiantly to make her expression match her son's. Ahmed turned at the sound of Henry's voice, winked at Meg, grinned, tooted his whistle and told Henry to join the drill.

He worked the kids hard, and they loved it. There were no grumbling, no fooling around, and—best of all—no outbursts from Henry. The other parents encouraged Meg to stand with them—she was suddenly cool by association.

Even Catherine was in good spirits. She approached Meg after practice ended. "Bradley's had his father in the backyard every night practicing his passing," she told Meg. "Did you see? He didn't touch the ball with his hands today. All his hard work is really paying off."

"Hard work usually does." Meg didn't feel she needed to be particularly kind to Catherine. Not after the day she'd had. Catherine was a power abuser when she had it and a suck-up when she didn't, and since Ahmed was a few yards away packing up the team equipment, Meg figured Catherine's friendliness was intended more for him than for her.

"The boys seem to be getting along," Catherine persisted. They'd raced ahead to the playground.

"They always get along," Meg said. "Except when they don't."

Catherine stepped closer and extended her hand. "No hard feelings?" Out of the corner of her eye, she looked to make sure Ahmed had heard her. Meg looked, too, and when Ahmed winked at her, she decided to go along.

"No hard feelings," she agreed. But when Meg returned the handshake, Catherine's grip nearly crushed the bones in her hand.

"Geez, Catherine!" Meg yanked back her hand. "Were you trying to break my fingers?"

"Meg?" Ahmed rose from his squatting position and stepped forward. "Would you help me carry some equipment to my car?"

"With my one good hand, I will," she said.

"I'll help!" Catherine said. "We're parked right next to you in the lot."

"Thanks, anyway," Ahmed said. "But Meg's the only one I need."

Meg reached for a box of extra jerseys and shin guards. Ahmed asked if she was all right as they hauled their load to his car. "You seem out of sorts," he said.

"I've had a shitty day." Meg hadn't yet decided how or if to tell him about Jonathan's phone call.

Ahmed stopped and faced her. "Anything I can do?"

Meg stopped, too. Ahmed was a beautiful soul. "When Henry saw that you were the coach, he said this has been the best week of his life."

Ahmed beamed.

Meg tried to smile, too, but failed. "He also more or less told me that if I happen to get run over by a car and die, he'd like to live with you for the rest of his childhood. And he said he doesn't want to be fatherless anymore."

Ahmed's smile widened.

"No," she said. "This is *bad*. We moved too fast and Henry's confused and what's going to happen when you decide you don't want to be with me anymore? It's going to break his heart."

"Henry doesn't seem confused to me," Ahmed said. "It

seems he knows exactly what he wants. And so do I. I think you're the one who might be confused."

"I'm scared of losing you." Meg's fear wasn't only because of Jonathan's call. It also had to do with her parents' marriage breaking up, and with Amy, who was married but miserable. "The problem with letting someone in is that they eventually want out."

"Hey." Ahmed dropped the duffel bag of gear he was carrying and took her hands in his. "I'm not going anywhere."

"You say that now." Meg couldn't keep the tears out of her voice. "But doesn't everybody think that early on? Right now, I think you're perfect. But you're not. You can't be. I don't even know your bad habits."

"My closets are very disorganized." His eyes twinkled and Meg could tell that his playful manner was deliberate, meant to soothe her. "And I always forget my cell phone in my gym locker. And I eat too fast and I don't drink my eight glasses of water every day."

Meg set down the box of shin guards and jerseys and threw her arms around him, squeezing him, so thankful he was who he was, which was a good guy—the best of all good guys.

"I dream about you sometimes," she confessed. "And when I do, I always wake up smiling. I just can't stand the thought of losing you."

He pulled back to look in her eyes. "Seriously, Meg. You know my weaknesses," he said. "I'm more guarded than I probably should be. I'm new to dating the mother of a young kid, and I didn't exactly have a father I'd want to model myself after."

"You don't need to model yourself after anyone," Meg said. "People should model themselves after you."

He was visibly moved by her words. "I think everything we've experienced up until now in our lives has been practice for this," he said. "Can't we choose to look at things that way?"

Meg looked over at Henry on the playground. He was standing on the seat of a swing, pumping with the force of his entire body, so high he'd take off and fly in a moment. She looked back to Ahmed. "So every stupid mistake I've made is okay because it means I'll be smarter with you?"

"Right." Ahmed grinned. "And vice versa."

Meg looked back at Henry with a fluttering heart. He swung himself so high, he was almost parallel to the ground, not at all afraid of falling. She looked back at Ahmed, desperate.

"What matters is that we try," she said. "Right?"

He shook his head no. "What matters is that we keep on trying."

Every weekday at dinner I ask Henry to tell me the most inter-esting thing he learned in school that day. Once he told me how in 1954 a lady in Alabama was taking a nap on her living room sofa when an eight-pound meteor crashed through her roof, landed on her—and she lived. With his typical good sense of tim-ing, he said, It must have hurt like h-e-double-hockey-sticks in the morning.

Another time, he was doing a research report on great white sharks and he said the most interesting thing he'd discovered is that baby sharks stay with their mothers for twelve to fifteen months after they're born and before they go off on their own—but if they're attacked, they have to fend for themselves. Their mothers won't fight for them.

After he told me this, he said, I don't know why they're called great white sharks. If that's how they treat their kids, I don't think there's anything great about them.

It was a funny thing about a voice—the memories it could evoke, the time it could erase.

Meg lay awake in bed for hours that night and thought about Jonathan. She hadn't heard his voice in years, but the way it had softened when he greeted her—*They still call you Ms. Clark, I see*—now, hours later, brought her back to the bedroom of her youth, to all the late-night phone conversations they'd had in high school, in the days when Ronald Reagan was president and *nothing* came between a girl and her Calvin Klein jeans.

They'd begun dating early their sophomore year. New to Tucson from New York City, Jonathan seemed older than his almost-sixteen years—certainly more self-possessed than most sophomores. A bit aloof, he nonetheless went out for varsity cross-country and joined the debate team and quickly created his own place in the world of Catalina High. Besides sharing an introduction to geometry class, they passed each other twice a day in the stairwell. There could be a rush of fifty people and yet Jonathan's blue eyes always locked on hers, instantly causing her to blush. He'd unsettled her from day one, and within weeks, they were inseparable.

Late at night, with Meg's top-40 radio station playing hits like Howard Jones' "No One Is to Blame," she'd lie in bed freshly showered and shampooed, relishing the absence of the nose-curdling Aqua Net from her hair. She'd wrap the phone cord around her index finger until the tip turned white, and talk to Jonathan for hours. Sometimes she'd just listen to his breathing and think, *That is mine, that breath. His heart beats for me.*

It had been enrapturing, the wonderment and possession she'd felt back then to have the power—of teenage angst, the awakening of lust—to keep him on the phone for hours at a time, to feel physical pain at the thought of having to disconnect.

Often they'd fallen asleep on the phone, each in their respective teenage beds—she in the same bed in which she'd later lie, pregnant and in tears, trying and failing to pinpoint the exact moment when things had gone wrong between them.

It was so intimate, a voice.

It contained a history that was impossible to deny.

The next morning, Mrs. Anderson stopped in Meg's class-room to talk with her before school started. "You were right about Marita," she said. "And it's worse than you suspected."

Meg's heart fell. She'd already thought it must be pretty bad. "Please don't tell me there's a father or an uncle involved," she said. "Please tell me it's just the mother and it hasn't gone beyond physical abuse. Let's let this girl have *something* resembling a second chance here."

"Before Child Protective Services could do a home visit, Marita's mom was arrested for selling crack to an undercover officer," Mrs. Anderson said. "It's a felony offense and she's looking at a long prison term. Marita's going to stay with her aunt for the duration."

Meg pressed her open palm against her chest, willing her lungs to expand, to function properly so she could go on with the business of breathing. "Does her aunt use, too?"

Mrs. Anderson shook her head. "I can't imagine she does."

"Will Marita be in school today?" Meg's voice came out fearful, tentative, pleading. "She'll stay at Foundation, won't she?"

"She'll stay at Foundation," Mrs. Anderson confirmed. "But they're keeping her in her new home for a few days to get settled."

After Mrs. Anderson left, Meg crossed the room to the CD

player and put on Mozart's Symphony No. 40. She kept it low and sat in a small-person chair next to the table it rested on. Tears welled behind her closed eyelids as she listened to the music, its beauty so incongruous with what she expected Marita's home life must have been like, incongruous as well with what she imagined her life was like at this exact moment—a little girl in a new place. Who knew what this aunt was like? Maybe she was great, but why hadn't she stepped forward earlier? Why was it Meg who'd reported her suspicions and not this aunt?

Meg knew now why Marita always put herself on the sidelines. To be the child of a drug addict meant your world didn't rotate in the same imperceptible trajectory as everyone else's. It lurched, and you were always in danger of falling off without notice. It made perfect sense now why Marita had always tucked herself into Meg. She was holding on for dear life.

As a teacher, Meg heard plenty of sad stories. To be a teacher was to have your heart ripped out regularly—it was part of the job description. Always, there was a child who suffered. This year, it was her very special Marita, the girl who'd sat and watched while her classmates danced to Mozart.

Despite the addition of Ahmed to their lives, Meg still reserved Friday nights for Henry. It was their time to reconnect and cuddle in bed, watching their movie and eating their ice cream.

Meg began that particular Friday night by having a margarita with Harley and Kat. Opera Bob, in his apartment watching the news, had yet to serenade the complex. In answer to Meg's questions, Kat informed them about the Pima County Jail, where Marita's mother was awaiting her next hearing. She told several gruesome stories of people whose lives were ruined by crack. Meg would have thought her mood couldn't get any worse, but Kat's stories achieved that.

And then Clarabelle arrived. It took Meg a moment to process the sight of her, because for the first time in years, she wore a decidedly undrab outfit—a kelly green shirt worn with winter cream pants. From a distance, she looked like a whole other version of herself.

"Mom—hi!" Meg called. "I love your outfit!"

"Hello!" Clarabelle called back. She visited first with Henry and Violet, who were reading books in lounge chairs across the pool from the grown-ups. A few days earlier, Harley had offered to give them a dollar for each age-appropriate book they read, which was keeping them both industrious and out of his hair.

Meg met her mother halfway. Ever since her conversation with her father, she'd felt horribly guilty about what she knew that perhaps her mother did not—namely, that Phillip was, in fact, serious about leaving her. Meg wasn't sure how she was supposed to handle it, if she was, which she sort of doubted. It was their marriage and it looked as if it couldn't be saved. Her job was to be there for her parents, in whatever way they needed her.

"How are you enjoying your new job?" she asked.

"It's fun!" Clarabelle said. "The girls I work with are quite pleasurable. Some of the customers, though—how hard is it to hang up the clothes you don't want? I'm not saying you need to hang them back on the rack. Just don't leave them on the floor! You never do that, do you? I mean, who does?" She held out a little Ann Taylor bag, one of two she carried. "Here. I bought you some earrings."

"Thank you! That was very thoughtful." Meg peeked at them. They were big hoops and cute, in a cheap-metal sort of way.

"I bought the same pair for your sister," Clarabelle said. "Remember how the two of you used to dress alike all the time? Whatever I bought for you, I had to buy one size smaller for her."

Clarabelle smiled brightly and then sniffed. Meg, who didn't remember ever dressing like her sister, tilted her head and studied her mother. Because Clarabelle had on dark sunglasses, Meg couldn't see her eyes. "Mom?"

"I'm fine, Meg!"

"I didn't ask if you were fine," Meg said. "Do you need to talk? Should we go to my apartment?"

"No, no. You're busy with your friends." Clarabelle looked wistfully over at the Loop Group table. The hint was clear.

"You want to join us for a drink?" Meg said.

"Oh! Well, why not?" Clarabelle said. "It is Friday night, after all."

Meg hid a snort. On Sunday mornings, Clarabelle would say why not to a Bloody Mary, and on Wednesdays at noon she'd say why not to wine with lunch. And, indeed, why not? That wasn't Meg's point. Her point was it seemed disingenuous of her mother to suggest there actually might be a time when she *wouldn't* have a drink.

Meg led Clarabelle to the table. Harley stood and pulled out a chair for her. "Hello, Meg's mom," he said. "What's your poison, beer or a margarita?"

"One of each, please." She gave him a big smile. "Just kidding. A margarita would be lovely."

While he poured her drink from the pitcher of margaritas, Clarabelle put her other bag on the table and pulled out a foil-wrapped bundle. "I brought tamales."

A giving mood, her mother was in. Meg had the distinct impression that her mother was attempting to turn over a new leaf.

"Tamales! I'd kill for a good tamale," Kat said. "It's hard to get really good ones in this town."

"These are gourmet, and they're delicious," Clarabelle said. "I had a sample when I picked them up. Spinach and wild mushroom. It was so good I can't stop thinking about it!"

"Where'd you get them?" Kat said.

"From the new place near here. The Tucson Tamale Company. It just opened," Clarabelle said. "And the owner's got these incredible blue eyes and thick, thick eyelashes that are simply wasted on a man."

"I hate blue eyes," Meg said, thinking of Jonathan.

"You have blue eyes," Harley reminded her. "And so does Henry."

"I mean on men," Meg said. "They get me all weirded out."

"Meg's right." Clarabelle unwrapped the foil and set the dozen tamales in the center of the table. Kat grabbed two. "You can never trust a man with blue eyes."

Meg's father had blue eyes.

While they gorged themselves, Opera Bob stepped out of his apartment, turned, locked his door and gave a nod to the Loop Group. Three steps into his stroll, his rich baritone permeated the crisp desert air, beguiling them all. Well, all except Clarabelle. She wrinkled her nose and pointed at Opera Bob with her white plastic fork. "Is that *him*?"

"Yes, it is." Meg said it with an edge. Ever the optimist, she hoped her mother would recognize her tone and back off.

"He really does this every day?" Clarabelle said. "What on earth is he thinking?"

Meg's mood was souring fast. Her mom had started off admirably nonjudgmental, but she simply couldn't sustain it. "It's not noise pollution, Mom. We all appreciate it."

"I can't completely unwind from work until I get my opera fix," Kat said. "His singing reminds me there's always been tragedy in the world. Wars, murders, lost loves. And there always will be."

"As long as there are men in the world, there will be tragedy," Clarabelle said, then smiled sweetly at Harley. "No offense."

When he was finished singing, Opera Bob silently un-latched the gate and slipped into the sole empty seat at the table, which happened to be next to Clarabelle.

"Bob?" Meg said. "Margarita?"

He nodded, and she poured him one. "Here you go."

"This must be the opera singer," Clarabelle said. "I'm curi-ous, Bob. Why do you sing like that every day? Your voice is *lovely*, don't get me wrong. It's just a little *unusual*."

"Leave him alone, Mom," Meg said.

"I'm just making small talk. Is this the fulfillment of some sort of dream of yours?" Beet red, Bob said nothing. "Bob?"

"Bob doesn't like to talk about his singing, Mom." Bob didn't like to talk about anything. He was the king of one-word answers. *Yes. No. Maybe. Sure. Mmmm. Hmmm. Well.* Clara-belle wasn't going to get much more out of him.

"Oh, but I'm not really talking about the singing. I'm talking about dreams. Men and their dreams." She turned to Harley. "Do you have middle-aged man dreams? Like, I don't know, becoming a painter in Paris, or hiking the Himalayas?"

Ah. So that was what this was about. "Mom," Meg cau-tioned, "don't get carried away."

"I'm just curious," Clarabelle said. "What do men dream about, besides sex? And is it really true that men think about sex an average of once every seven seconds? Bob? Is that true?"

Bob froze in place like a startled iguana.

"MOTHER! *Jesus.* Leave him alone." Henry's head popped

up over the back of his lounge chair to see what Meg was yelling about.

"I'm just making an effort to get to know your friends." Clarabelle enunciated her words. "That's what the girls at work suggested I do. Get to know your friends. Learn to treat you like one. But I can see I'm not welcome here."

With that, she burst into tears.

Jaw dropped, Meg scanned her circle of friends. They looked back with varying degrees of shock and concern.

Meg put her hand on her mother's arm. "Mom?"

"I don't want to talk about it!" Clarabelle said.

Meg scanned her friends again. "Should we go up to my apartment?"

"Your father said some things to me today that were very hurtful," Clarabelle said. "He blew up at me, said I was the biggest nag he'd ever met and he was quote 'sick and tired of me crushing his spirit.' "

Crushing his spirit? Her father should have known better than to use words like that with Clarabelle. They were too . . . froufrou. Meg laughed. She couldn't help it.

"It's not funny," Clarabelle said. "He took a suitcase with him when he left."

Ah, Meg thought. That answered the question as to when he planned to leave. "Do you know where he went?"

"Probably to his horrible girlfriend's house!" Clarabelle burst into fresh tears. "And don't tell me he's not having an affair, because he is! I know it! Talking all the time about quote 'second acts' and 'pursuing one's passions.' Those aren't your father's words. He doesn't have passions! Someone's brain-washing him."

Meg sighed. Her mother as a woman scorned was going to be ugly. "Mom, I'm sure he's—"

Henry stuck his head around his lounge chair. "Yo! Mama! Can we watch our movie now?"

"Not the best timing, bud," Meg called.

Henry came over and tugged on her arm. "Movie time."

"Go ahead. Don't mind me." Clarabelle waved them off, but more tears spilled from behind her sunglasses.

"Grandma?" Henry took a worried step toward her.

Clarabelle covered her mouth to hold back her emotions. Meg took a big breath and asked a question she very much did not want to ask. "Do you want to stay and watch Harry Potter Five with me and Henry?"

"Oh, no. I couldn't." Clarabelle knew what a ritual their movie night was, and she'd never been invited before. But then she took off her sunglasses and looked at Meg with her raw red eyes. "Could I?"

"Yes," Meg said. "Tonight, you can."

"Awesome!" Henry said. "Three spoons for the ice cream!"

It happened just as Meg had imagined in the past, with all three of them crawling into her bed, Henry in the middle. They dimmed the lights, dug into the ice cream, and it wasn't so bad.

Halfway through the movie, Clarabelle fell asleep.

When Meg woke the next morning, she was gone. Meg couldn't help but wonder what it would be like for Clarabelle to arrive at an empty house and couldn't help but think her mother wouldn't like it much at all.

There was a cloudy sky and a November chill in the Old Pueblo that Saturday morning and Meg was glad she'd gotten a cup of coffee from LuLu's to warm her insides during Henry's soccer game. It was Ahmed's first game as coach and Henry was sure they were going to win. Meg was less so. They'd practiced twice that week and certainly had improved, but an actual win would be remarkable.

When they arrived, Meg waved to Ahmed and took a spot on the sidelines, stomping her feet to keep warm. Henry, his cheeks wholesomely flushed, trotted over to Ahmed, who put his hand on Henry's shoulder and drew him into the team warm-up. Ahmed was undeniably sexy in his cuddle-with-me blue flannel shirt, and Meg imagined the three of them cozied up around a fire later that day, sipping hot chocolate at Ahmed's house. Henry would *not* get the middle spot.

After setting the boys up with a drill, Ahmed called the parents to gather around him. "We need some ground rules for today's game," he said. "We've worked very hard this week at practice to get the boys to stay in their positions. We can't have them running around all bunched up like they have been, and part of the reason they do this is they're hopelessly confused."

He scanned the circle of parents, his expression serious. "You can clap," he continued. "And you can cheer if they score, but I don't want you to yell anything while they're playing. Not *good job* or *get it* or *throw to so-and-so.* They need to listen to me, to do what I tell them. Beyond that, they need to figure out how to play on their own. If they'd just stay in their positions, we might actually win once in a while. Can everyone agree to this?"

All the parents nodded. "Good idea, Coach," Catherine said.

Meg upped her one. "*Great* idea, Coach."

Ten minutes into the game, the boys were playing their positions admirably. They hadn't scored yet, but neither had the other team. It had been a hell of a week for Meg and she actually found it pleasant to be relieved of the burden of cheering. She sipped her coffee and spaced out a bit until someone spoke into her ear, startling her.

"Who's winning?" It was Clarabelle.

"Hey—hi!" Meg said.

"Henry invited me," Clarabelle said.

"Good," Meg said. "I'm glad." She wasn't, of course. She'd been delaying the moment her mother and Ahmed met, since Clarabelle so rarely had kind words to say about anyone. "How are you today? Heard from Dad?"

"*Pfff,*" Clarabelle said. "If I never hear from him again, it'll be too soon." She eyed Ahmed. "Is that *him*? Your man friend? You never said he was so handsome."

Meg looked at her mother in surprise. "Thank you. He's exactly my type."

"Exactly your new type," Clarabelle clarified.

"Right," Meg said.

"He looks almost Mexican."

"Well, he's not." Meg sipped her coffee and shifted her attention back to the game in hopes of preserving the fragile peace between them.

"Oh! Did you see that?" Clarabelle said. "Henry almost got it in! GO, HENRY!"

"Shhh," Meg said. "We aren't supposed to cheer."

"Not cheer? That's ridiculous!" Clarabelle raised her voice to a yell. "Over there, Henry! To that big kid over there— number twelve!"

Ahmed's head snapped around. He looked from Meg to Clarabelle, who smiled broadly. "I don't think he'll reprimand me, do you?" Clarabelle said this out of the corner of her mouth as she waved to him. Meg shrugged at Ahmed apologetically. He gave her a wink and turned his attention back to the game.

When her cell phone rang, Meg was glad for the interruption. She fished her phone out of her pocket and flipped it open. "Hello?"

"Meg, it's Jonathan."

Meg gasped. Had she really just been glad for the interruption? *I take it back,* she thought desperately. *I take it back and then some.* Helpless, she watched as Henry made a great shot, scored a goal and ran straight to Ahmed for a high-five slap. For the first time that season, their team was in the lead.

"Meg?"

Stop saying my name. Meg walked away from her mother

and tossed her coffee cup at the garbage can, missing it. "How did you get this number?" If a voice could be icy and shaky at the same time, hers was.

"I have my ways." Jonathan's tone was supposed to be teasing. "How are you today?"

She'd been a hell of a lot better a minute ago. How was she supposed to answer that—*instantly soul-withered by the sound of your voice?*

"What do you keep calling me for?" she asked. "And why now?"

"We have some unfinished business," he said.

"We had unfinished business ten years ago," Meg said. "Now there's nothing between us."

"Except our son."

Meg gasped. "How dare you even refer to him as your son?"

"We need to meet."

Meg's blood ran cold as her eyes seized upon Henry, whose hair curled at the ends just like Jonathan's, whose long fingers and blue eyes were his, his, his. That was what Jonathan was after: the boy whose name he dared not speak. All of a sudden, Meg was sure of it.

"No," she said.

"Come on, Meg," he said. "Please."

"Funny, your use of the word *please*," she said. "It never worked when I used it on you." She'd begged him that last weekend. *Please, just tell me what I did wrong. Please, let's try to work this out. Please, don't make me raise this baby by myself.*

"I'll never let you near my son," she said.

"Who do you think gave me this number, Meg?" Jonathan asked.

"I have no goddamned clue." Her heart pounded in terror. There'd been an implication in his question that she didn't like one bit.

"Henry called me last weekend," Jonathan said. "He's the one who asked me to get in touch with you."

"He wouldn't." Meg felt light-headed. Dizzy. In danger of floating away. "He doesn't care a thing about you and he knows you're not worth our time."

"He called me," Jonathan repeated.

"You're lying," Meg said. "That's all you are—a liar."

"I'm coming to Tucson over Thanksgiving, and we need to meet," he said. "There are some things I need to say to you in person."

"Are you in some sort of twelve-step program and you're at that stage where you've got to apologize for your past transgressions? Because if that's the case, consider yourself forgiven and leave me the hell alone."

"*Am* I forgiven?" he asked.

"Are you in a twelve-step program?"

"No."

"Then hell no." Meg flipped her phone closed, turned off the ringer and stood dazed, looking toward the Catalina Mountains. The innocent cotton-candy clouds crushed the mountaintops where she'd once hiked, camped, made love with Jonathan. Three military planes from David-Monthan Air Force Base, so clean and competent, cut through the sky overhead that belonged to the park. Had Jonathan *really* just said that her son, the flesh of her womb, had placed a phone call to her mortal enemy?

The next time there was a break in the game, Henry grinned at her and made a peace sign. She stared at him as if he were a stranger. If he'd really called Jonathan, there'd be no peace in their household that day.

They won, 1–0.

Because of Henry's goal, his team won. Henry was the hero, and Meg could barely stand to look at him. She led her mother over for introductions. "Mom, this is Ahmed," she said. "Ahmed, this is my mom."

Ahmed warmly shook Clarabelle's hand. "It's so nice to finally meet you."

"You, too." Clarabelle seemed mesmerized by his eyes. "I don't know why my daughter has insisted on hiding you away from us." Henry tugged on Clarabelle's sleeve and whispered something to her. "Would you like to join us for Thanksgiving dinner?" she asked when she straightened. "We're having it at my other daughter's house."

"Ho, ho. Hold up," Meg said. "Mom? Can you take Henry to the car and I'll meet you there in a few minutes?"

Clarabelle, sensing Meg's mood, led Henry off without protest. As Meg watched them walk away, she felt light-headed again. Loose. Worthless. As if she could blow away in a slight breeze and no one would even notice.

But Ahmed noticed and took her gently by the arm. "What's wrong?"

She looked at him desperately, drowning. "Pretty much everything." How could she tell him that Jonathan had called, and not only that, but it had been Henry who'd asked him to? Henry hadn't betrayed just her. He'd betrayed Ahmed, too. Ahmed, who'd been more of a father to Henry in the past couple months than Jonathan had been in ten years.

The ingrate.

Ahmed would remember the moment she delivered this news for the rest of his life. *You know how crazy you are about my kid? Well, it doesn't matter how great you are with him. It seems he's more fascinated with his father, who's ignored him for the past ten years.* Meg owed it to Ahmed to tell him right. Without anger. Without sarcasm. With compassion. And so she decided to hold off.

"My parents separated last night and it's hitting me like a ton of bricks," she told him. "I don't think Thanksgiving is going to be especially thankful this year. I think it's going to be hell, actually, and I'd rather it not be your first official introduction to my family."

"Poor Meg." Ahmed pulled her close. "Tell me what I can do for you."

"I just . . . Damn it." She stopped as tears sprang to her eyes. In a world that didn't seem to reward it, Ahmed was so very kind. "I just wanted us all to be happy. I didn't want anything to get ruined."

And now it is. Jonathan's going to ruin everything. That's what he does. That's who he is. A ruiner. A destroyer. A breaker of hearts, mine in particular.

Ahmed pulled back and took her hands. "No pity parties, Meg. There's a happy ending ready and waiting for us, like an apple on a low-hanging branch and all we've got to do is stretch the tiniest bit and it's ours. Maybe a happy ending's waiting for your parents, too."

He honestly believed it. Meg could see it in his eyes. She didn't feel nearly as hopeful.

"But that's what ruined Adam and Eve," she said. "Reaching for the low-hanging fruit. Wanting more than they were entitled to."

When Meg arrived at the car, Henry was up in a nearby tree, while Clarabelle watched him from below.

"Okay, Henry," Meg said. "Let's go."

"Hold on." Henry reached for the next branch. "I want to climb higher."

"We're leaving now." Meg turned to her mother. "I told Ahmed I'd prefer that he not come for Thanksgiving. Henry doesn't run the show, and I really need you to talk with me before you issue invitations. We're not welcoming Ahmed into the family quite yet."

"Yes, we are," Henry called down.

"Get in the car, Henry."

"I *said*, in a minute."

"The car won't be here in a minute." It took Meg about fifteen seconds to get to her car, and as she unlocked it, she saw out of the corner of her eye that Henry *still* wasn't coming. They were a mere six blocks from home, and Clarabelle was there and wouldn't let Henry walk alone, and damn it, he was being such a brat. She was going to leave him. Teach him a lesson for a change. Make him take her seriously. Meg got in, buckled up and started the ignition before he even looked over. He held up two fingers, for two minutes. She put the car in reverse. So sure she'd wait for him, he sat leisurely on the branch dangling his legs.

When Meg backed out of her spot, Henry finally jumped

down and started over. Meg inched forward a few feet. When she saw that Henry had begun to run, she considered whether she should keep going and really teach him a lesson or if she should give him a break. Not that he'd cut her any breaks lately. Far from it. But still. She stopped for him and stared straight ahead, shunning him at the same time she was chauffeuring him.

Henry got in, buckled up and waved goodbye to Clarabelle. "Hey, Mom? Mom, Mom, Mom? Can we go for ice cream?"

"Are you kidding?" Was it even conceivable that he didn't know she was mad at him? Or was he just so sure her forgiveness was a given?

"Can we?" he asked.

"No! When I say it's time to go, we go. *I'm* in charge. *I* make the decisions."

"I thought we both made the decisions," Henry said.

"We aren't a democracy," Meg said.

"But I thought we were a team."

"If we're a team, then I'm the coach and you're the player," Meg said. "You don't tell Ahmed how to run the practice, do you?"

"That's different." Henry kicked the back of the seat. "Why didn't you say anything about my goal? You saw it, right?"

"Of course I saw it," Meg said. "That's how I spent my Saturday morning. Out of all the things I could have been doing, I chose to stand in the cold and stomp my feet and watch you and cheer for you and *be there* for you. And, yes, congratulations. It was a very nice goal."

"Thank you," Henry said. "When we get home, can I play pool in the clubhouse with Violet?"

"No, you may not." Meg felt like knocking her head against

the steering wheel. How thick in the head was this kid? *Who* was this kid?

"Why not?" Henry said.

"Because I said so."

"I hate when you say that."

"And I hate saying it," she snapped. "So when I say no, that's it. End of discussion."

"Can I later?"

Meg gripped the steering wheel to keep from screaming at him. "I'm not talking to you right now."

She jerked to a stop at the sign on Third and Treat streets and started up again with a whiplash-worthy acceleration. A woman coming in the opposite direction on Treat in a green Mercedes station wagon made a slow-down gesture at her and Meg's first impulse was to flip her off, even though she knew perfectly well the woman was right.

"Mom," Henry said.

"Not now, Henry."

"But why—"

Meg yanked the steering wheel to the right and came to a fast stop on the side of the road. She twisted to look Henry dead in the eye. "Enough with the questions. Let me ask *you* one. What in God's name possessed you to call your father, and where did you get his number?"

Henry shrank back in his seat. "That's actually two questions."

Meg glared at him. "I *actually* have never been so mad at you in my entire life as I am right now."

"I won't talk anymore." Henry's voice was a squeak. "I won't say another word all the way home."

"Thank you," Meg said. "We will drive in silence, and when we get home, we will talk."

"Okay," Henry said and then added, "Oops."

Meg faced forward, closed her eyes and tried to summon her place of central calm. But Jonathan's face popped into her mind and then Ahmed's appeared right next to it, and when *Henry's* face popped in between them, Meg knew the pursuit of calm was useless. She inched Coop back onto the road and drove five miles below the speed limit for the final few blocks.

Once home, they walked in silence from the parking lot to their apartment, Henry behind Meg, head down. Her little soccer star was drooping, and sympathy tugged at Meg's heart-strings. It was so easy to get mad at him, yet so hard to stay that way. He clearly had no idea about the can of worms he'd opened—of the unintended consequences, of which Meg was sure there'd be many. After she unlocked the door, she turned and gruffly kissed his sweaty scalp.

Henry went directly to the living room couch, sank down onto it and began unlacing his soccer cleats. Meg poured him a glass of lemonade and set it on the end table nearest him and went to her favorite armchair. Sitting down, she felt dissatis-fied. They were supposed to be cuddled together on Ahmed's couch, drinking hot chocolate, and Meg was supposed to be getting off on the softness of Ahmed's flannel shirt. Instead, here she and Henry were, about to embark on their most dif-ficult discussion to date.

"Okay, Henry, I love you. Let's start there," she began. "It's obvious I'm angry. I don't know what's going on with you that you felt you needed to call Jonathan. I simply don't under-stand. Tell me what was going through your mind."

And how the hell did you get his number?

Henry pulled off his shoes and stripped off his shin guards and long socks as if he hadn't heard her. Meg watched him, expressionless, until he met her eyes.

"What did he tell you?" he said.

"All we're going to talk about right now is why you felt the need to call him." Meg's voice was even-tempered, but her anger bubbled beneath the surface because once again, unsurprisingly, Henry was pulling a Henry. He just sat and looked at her, rock-dumb.

"Speak," she said, "or I will begin to yell."

"Why should I?" he said. "You're just going to get mad at me."

"I'm already mad at you," Meg said. "Trust me, you've got nowhere to go but up."

"Did he tell you that I called him? Is that how you know?"

"How else would I know, Henry?"

"Did he tell you *when* I called him?"

"Henry," she warned.

"Did he tell you *why* I called him?"

"Henry, you've got less than one second to start explaining."

Henry stood, defiant. "If you want to know, call him back and ask him." As if frightened by his own audacity, he sprint-walked to his bedroom and slipped inside. Meg heard the soft click of the lock and decided not to go after him.

Eventually, Meg's maternal instinct kicked in and she grew worried about the silence in Henry's room. She knew he was in there—he'd promised her once that he'd never run away, and so far, he'd never broken a promise to her. But he was an antsy kid, not one to sit still, not one to take naps, not one to read a book for this long.

She went to his room and tapped on the door. "Henry?" She made her voice soft, loving, and then tried the knob, which was still locked. "Open up, please."

She heard the covers on his bed rustle, and seconds later, he unlocked the door and opened it. Meg's heart broke a little when she saw his pale, drained face, complete with raccoon circles under his eyes, which he only got when he had a headache. Or, possibly, when he'd cried his guts out. Meg followed him back to his unmade bed, and when he lay down, she sat next to him and put her cool palm against his warm forehead. He relaxed instantly.

"Let's talk," she said. "And let's remember we're on the same side. Okay?"

Henry sighed and gave the slightest of nods.

"I thought you liked Ahmed," she said softly.

Henry abruptly sat up. "I do!"

"Don't you see how calling Jonathan and asking him to get involved in our lives can threaten what we've got with Ahmed?" Meg asked. "Calling him just wasn't very smart."

"You said you wouldn't marry Ahmed!"

"Shh. Shh." She brushed his bangs off his forehead. "First off, it's not like Ahmed has even asked me to marry him. He hasn't. But no matter what, I'm not going to get back with Jonathan. That's *never* going to happen."

"I know that!" Henry said. "That's not why I called him."

"Well, then, why did you? Do you want a relationship with him? Is that what this is about?" Meg shuddered, unable to help it.

"Can we not talk about this anymore?" Henry begged. *"Please."*

"You can't make life difficult for me and then expect me to go easy on you. You see how that's not fair, right?" Meg asked. "Your calling Jonathan has raised a whole host of problems. How do you think Ahmed's going to feel? He coaches your soccer team. Plays chess with you. Helps you feel better when you're sad. Takes you to work with him. Your calling Jonathan—when you've never before expressed even the slightest interest to get to know him—sends the message that none of what Ahmed has done for or with you means anything to you."

Henry's eyes brimmed with fresh tears. "But it does," he whispered. Meg brushed his bangs off his forehead to soothe him.

"I don't mean to make you feel bad," she said. "And I don't want you to think I'll keep you away from your father if you have some intense need to meet him or something. But you come to me. Okay? You don't go behind my back, ever. You come to me for everything."

"But, Mom." Henry put his hand on her knee. "Mom, Mom, Mommy. Sometimes you're not enough."

*S*ometimes *you're not enough.*

That trumped all the hurtful things Jonathan had ever said to her. It trumped *everything.*

Meg lay in bed that night and mentally catalogued the times and ways she'd been there for Henry. Year by year, from the croup he'd had as a toddler to the ear infections too numerous to mention, to helping him face his fear of the dark, to teaching him to swim, to watching Harry Potter ten thousand times. They laughed all the time! Took great summer vacations together!

How could he say she wasn't enough?

It was only after she'd gotten up at about two in the morning and warmed a glass of milk and honey—something her father had done for her at bedtime when she was young—and lit a candle and curled up on the couch with a blanket and sipped the drink, thinking of pretty much nothing, that the answer came to her. *You've been enough, Magpie, but he's getting older and his needs are changing.*

It was her father's voice coming to her in her hour of need. And his words made perfect sense.

After she finished her glass of honeyed milk, Meg took her blanket and crawled into Henry's bed to sleep next to him. "I'll get you what you need," she whispered. "Whether it's me or Ahmed or Jonathan or all three of us, I'll make sure you get what you need."

Remembering the peace sign he'd flashed at her during the soccer game earlier in the day, Meg made the sign back at him, and when she closed her eyes this time, sleep came easily.

The next morning, Meg sat at Amy's breakfast bar and drank a mimosa while Amy prepared a salad. Henry, Kelly and Maggie were in the backyard playing some sort of Wiffle Ball game. David had been sent to the grocery store for half-and-half to prevent Clarabelle from throwing a small fit. Their father would not be coming. Meg had spoken with him the previous day and he'd sublet a condo a few miles east of his office. He'd seemed to be in good spirits.

"Have you talked to Mom yet today?" Meg asked Amy.

"She called to say she's bringing brownies for dessert," Amy said. "She didn't mention a word about Dad."

"I suppose that's good," Meg said. "I'd rather she not talk about him than complain about him."

"Whose side are we on?" Amy peered at her. "And why do you look so tired? Are you okay?"

"We're not taking sides." Meg ignored Amy's other questions, not wanting to talk about anything involving Jonathan quite yet, if ever. "We're just helping them both move forward in the best way possible."

"You can't not take a side with Mom," Amy said. "You're either for her or against her."

"Who knows?" Meg said. "Maybe she'll surprise us for a change."

She did. It began with a toot of the horn as Clarabelle

pulled into Amy's driveway. Henry ran inside. "Mom! Mom, come quick! Come see Grandma's new car!"

"Oh, shit," said Amy.

Together, they went out front and found Clarabelle sitting proudly behind the wheel of a shiny blue Ford Mustang convertible, wearing a Jackie O scarf and sunglasses.

"Nice car, Mom," Meg said. Amy walked around the vehicle, inspecting it from all sides.

"I've never had a new car before," Clarabelle said. "Your father always talked me out of it. 'A new car loses ten percent of its value the instant you drive it off the lot,' or some such crap."

"It's true," Amy said.

"I really don't care." Clarabelle caressed the car's steering wheel, in no hurry to get out from behind it. "I worked hard for thirty years. I *should* have a new car once in my life. I deserve one."

Meg and Amy exchanged looks.

"Does Dad know?" Meg said.

Clarabelle smiled. "He will soon enough."

"Ooh," Meg said. "Ouch."

"He hasn't even called since he left," Clarabelle said. "Does he really think I'm going to sit home waiting around for him to come back? If he does, he's got another think coming. This girl's gone shopping!"

"Very responsible, Mom," Amy said. "Not."

Support them the best way possible.

"She can afford it," Meg said. Clarabelle had a decent pension and their house was long since paid off. Phillip might be cheap, but he was good with money. A new car wouldn't hurt anybody and it just might help her mother heal. "But, Mom—he rented a condo. I don't think he's coming back."

Clarabelle lowered her sunglasses and smiled coquettishly. "Does the color of the car match my eyes?"

"It does." Meg was glad to see her mother's eyes were no longer bloodshot. No tears today, at least not yet. "It's a very sexy car."

"I am woman. Hear me roar." Clarabelle handed a plate of brownies to Amy and finally got out of the car. "He wants to talk about second acts? Ha! Just wait till he sees mine!"

"Shit, the girls!" Amy briskly headed for the backyard. "They've been too quiet."

"I'm sure they're fine," Meg called after her. "Henry's with them."

"No, he's not. He was out here, remember? Then he went inside."

"I need to pay more attention to that boy," Meg said.

"Pshaw." Clarabelle stood in the driveway and admired her car. She lingered to show it off to David, who was pulling up, back from his grocery run. "How much trouble can he get in?"

"That's exactly my point." Meg went inside and quirked an ear, listening for Henry. Hearing nothing, she slipped off her clogs and made her way quietly to the TV room, thinking he'd be there, playing with the Wii. When he wasn't, she went to the spare bedroom that David and Amy used as an office and found him behind Amy's desk, in the midst of dialing the phone.

"Henry." He jumped and hung up. "What are you doing in here?"

"Nothing."

"Who were you calling?"

"No one."

"I saw you dialing, Henry."

"I was calling Ahmed." Meg's hackles went up when she saw the liar's blush explode across her son's neck and face. She walked toward him fast, her heart racing.

"I didn't know you had his number memorized," she said. "What is it?"

"It's . . . um . . ."

Meg held out her hand. "Give me the phone."

Reluctantly, he did. When Meg hit star 69, the partial number that came up had a 212 area code. He'd been calling Jonathan.

"Please don't be mad at me." Henry's lower lip quivered, and Meg was glad to see it. She *wanted* him to cry. Had she not just expressly asked him less than twenty-four hours ago not to go to Jonathan for any reason? She knew what he'd say: I never promised.

"Where are you getting his number from?" she said. "Tell me that, and I might just let you keep playing soccer for the rest of the season."

He dropped his gaze to the address book lying open on Amy's desk. Meg gasped and picked it up. There it was. Jonathan's name, address, cell and office numbers. The two address slots above it contained his outdated contact information, now crossed out.

Firecrackers exploded in Meg's brain and nothing made sense. No one from her family had been in touch with Jonathan since he left. *No one.* She peered at the entries. They were in Amy's handwriting, all right. But why? Why would her sister work against her like this?

Meg carried the address book to the kitchen and stood in the doorway as her mother regaled Amy with stories of her car-shopping experience. Amy listened gamely as she wiped off the counter.

"Excuse me." Meg held up the address book so Jonathan's contact information showed and made dagger eyes at her sister. "You want to tell me why you've got my ex-husband's contact information?"

Openmouthed, Amy looked from Meg to Clarabelle, then back to Meg. "I . . . I . . . I don't know. Just to keep track of him, I guess."

"Why, Amy? The man nearly destroyed me." Henry appeared beside Meg and tried to rest his forehead against her, but Meg sent him outside. When he walked away with his head hung low, Meg didn't feel remotely sorry for him.

Amy's eyes glistened. "I'm sorry. I just . . ." She shrugged. "I don't know."

"*Sorry*'s not good enough! *I don't know*'s not good enough! Henry called him, Amy! Do you have any idea of the damage this could do to my relationship with Ahmed? Or do you just not care? Can you not stand to see me happy when you're so miserable?"

"I'm not miserable!" Amy said.

"You act like you are!" Meg yelled and faced Clarabelle. "Are you in touch with him, too? Is my whole family going behind my back and maintaining friendly relations with the man who tried his very best to ruin my life?"

Clarabelle raised her palms in self-defense. "I hate the man," she said. "I wouldn't speak to him if he was on his deathbed."

"Well, thank you," Meg said. "It's nice to hear you say that."

"He was like a brother to me." Amy's tone was pleading. "He was the brother I never had and always wanted."

Meg's laugh was incredulous and spiteful. "And he was the husband *I* always wanted, and he couldn't keep his dick inside his pants! My own sister—my best friend! How could you do this to me? He's a cheater, Amy! When somebody cheats on someone you love and abandons her when she's pregnant, you don't forgive that. You don't speak to that person ever again."

"Ho, ho," Clarabelle said. "You're in for a rude awakening."

Meg glared at her mother. "What exactly the hell is that supposed to mean?"

"You can watch your language, missy," Clarabelle said.

"I will *not* watch my language," Meg snapped. "Not today."

"It's not like I'm in regular contact with him," Amy said. "It's just the occasional . . . you know . . . like, I sent him a condolence card last year when his mom died. That sort of thing."

Meg wanted to do physical harm. To the address book. To the salad Amy had so nicely tossed. Or to Amy herself. She could take the address book, and— "When's the last time you spoke to him?" she demanded.

Tears came to Amy's eyes. "Please don't ask me that."

"I'm asking, Amy."

Leaning against the counter, Amy's eyes sank closed. She gave an I'm-so-screwed laugh and shook her head from side to side like an idiotic metronome.

Finally, she looked directly at Meg, ready to accept her wrath. "Today," she said. "He called me this morning."

"So when you asked me if I was okay, you already knew I wasn't, didn't you?"

"That's right," Amy said. "He told me you sort of freaked out on him."

She'd freaked out on him? That was priceless.

"You suck," Meg said. "You people all suck."

"What did I do?" Clarabelle asked.

"You gave birth to *her*."

Meg left Henry in her mother's care and drove off. She had no destination in mind, nothing she could think to do. Her fury was all-consuming and she didn't want to be where anyone could find her. At the first stoplight, she turned the ringer off her phone and wondered how far she could drive before anyone really began to worry. It was noon-ish—she could make it to San Diego by six, or to Los Angeles by eight, or if she headed east she could be in Santa Fe before midnight.

She wouldn't really run away, of course. It was wishful thinking. Driving was therapeutic, just the act of motion, of owning your time. You could talk out loud to yourself for hours and no one would think you were crazy because no one would know. Your car was private, even as you drove in public.

The next best thing to hitting the open road was to drive the streets of Tucson. And so Meg did. She took Houghton Road north as far as she could, then Tanque Verde down to Grant, then Grant west to Sixth Avenue, Sixth over to Twenty-second, Twenty-second east to Swan and then back over to Grant, ending up at her father's new place.

He wasn't there, which confirmed the sort of day she was having. The condo he'd rented was in a newer complex of about a hundred units. Rather than call him to let him know she was there, Meg went to the pool area and pulled a lounge chair into the friendly November sun, keeping her father's front door in view. After so much driving, the lack of motion was welcome. Except for what looked to be a content old couple in the hot tub, Meg was alone. She stared at them and wondered how they'd managed to get it right, and then she flipped in her chair so she couldn't see them anymore, because who wanted to watch successful people when you were such a failure? *But you're not,* her inner voice whispered. *As of this moment, you haven't failed with Ahmed.*

But she would. Meg had an uncontrollable, physiological reaction every time she thought of seeing Jonathan: she experienced a choking anger. A yearning ache. A gaping shame. A heart-dropping fear. Had she clawed her way back from his betrayal only to have to face it all again? She was afraid, as well, of what he could do to her if he were so inclined. He could confuse her. Tempt her. Worst of all, he could want her.

Meg indulged in a downward spiral of self-pity, berating herself for the entire half hour it took her father to arrive. When he approached his condo, arms full of Target shopping bags, Meg rushed over, relieved.

"Magpie!" Phillip's great-to-see-you smile was the best part of Meg's day thus far. "Where's Henry?"

"With Mom."

"I feel like I'm off to college for the first time, buying all this stuff," Phillip said. "Come on in and see my new pad."

Meg felt a weird trepidation when she stepped inside his new place and looked around. She'd only ever known him to live at 2463 East Copper Trail, in the house she'd grown up in, with the faded furniture and yard-sale oil paintings. But he'd gone all out furnishing this place—or at least he'd gone all

Crate & Barreled out, which to Meg amounted to the same thing. Besides the well-chosen furniture, he had prints on the wall, faux plants on the tables and framed photos of his daughters and grandchildren. It didn't look like he was just moving in. It looked like he'd had this place for a while.

Meg wondered if her father had the decorating skills to pull off such a look on his own. She suspected not, although he must have been planning his move for ages. Then again, it didn't require much effort to walk up and down the aisles at Crate & Barrel and say, "I'll take one of that and two of those and that print off the wall? I'll take that, too." All it took was money, which he had. Or a girlfriend to do it for him.

"Has Sandi been here yet?" she asked, careful to keep her tone casual.

"I'm sure she'll pop over this week sometime." Phillip set his bags on his black rectangular four-person dining table and sat for a moment, exhausted from his shopping trip. "I'm only just up the road from the office. I thought about inviting you, Henry and Ahmed over for dinner this week, too, but I'm not ready to entertain quite yet. So can I treat you all to a nice lunch at the Arizona Inn sometime over the weekend?"

"Of course," Meg said. "You know that's my favorite place in town." He'd been taking her to the Arizona Inn for a fancy birthday lunch ever since she'd been a child. "How about on Thanksgiving itself?"

"I doubt we can get reservations anymore," he said. "Besides, you've got Amy's. I'm excused since I'm the black sheep of the family this year, but she'd be quite upset if you skipped her shindig. You know how she is about holidays."

He pulled himself up, rest break over. Meg watched as he tried to decide where things belonged—cleaning supplies under the kitchen sink, bath towels straight to the hallway washing machine, small throw rug immediately inside the front door.

"What are you doing for Thanksgiving, Dad?"

"I don't know yet," he said. "The residents here are having a potluck. I might join in on that."

Maybe he'd find his own little Loop Group. "I'm not exactly speaking to Amy at the moment," Meg said. "I sort of left a little while ago in a bit of a huff."

Her dad looked at her and frowned. "You two never fight."

"She's a traitor," Meg said. "Did you know she's been in touch with Jonathan all these years?"

Phillip's look was quizzical. "With your Jonathan?"

Meg's eyes filled with tears. "He's not my Jonathan. He's my ex."

He was her ex-Jonathan.

"Come sit on my new couch and tell your old man what's going on," Phillip said. Meg followed him to the couch and sat beside him, both of them putting their feet up on his new dark wood coffee table.

"Did you ever have to break bad news to someone and were tempted to delay it as long as you could because you knew the other person was going to be absolutely crushed by what you needed to say?" Meg asked.

Her father visibly paled. Then he cleared his throat. "This is all harder than I imagined it was going to be, and, Meg, I didn't want you to— Well, I wish you'd have—" He stopped himself with a jolt. "Wait. What were you going to say?"

"Jonathan called." Meg cringed. It felt like blasphemy to say the words out loud, and her dad looked as if he'd been sucker punched.

"Tell me he didn't."

"I wish I could," Meg said. "He's going to be in town for Thanksgiving this week and he wants to see me."

"You can't let him near Henry," Phillip said.

"He hasn't asked to see him," Meg said. "And of course I wouldn't let him. Henry's just too . . . well, he needs to be taken seriously, even though he's such a goof. Jonathan would mess with his head. He'd make Henry love him, you know? And then he'd leave him." She looked at her father in desperation. "I'm not a bad mom for wanting to keep him away from his father, am I?"

"You absolutely can't let him near Henry." Phillip searched her face. "And I don't think you should let him near you, either."

"Do you have any chocolate?" Meg asked. "I'm in desperate need of some."

Phillip pushed up from the couch, went to the cabinet next to the refrigerator, pulled out a handful of Hershey's dark chocolate Kisses and tossed a few to her. He unwrapped one for himself as he began to pace. "That man needs to be shot through his law-school-educated brain," he said.

"I wish." Meg felt a tiny bit better as soon as the chocolate was in her mouth. "Since when are you a fan of dark chocolate?"

"A little bit's good for you," he said. "I drink red wine now, too."

"I didn't even tell you the worst part," Meg said glumly.

"Henry was the one who initiated contact. Henry called him, if you can believe that. He got the number from Amy's address book."

Phillip stood dumbfounded. "Why would he do something so stupid? Doesn't he know how this could ruin things for the two of you and Ahmed?"

"Oh, Dad." Meg banged her head on the back of the couch a few times, welcoming the pain. "Please don't say that."

"Well, it could," he said. "Middle Eastern men are known to be jealous. They're like Latin men as far as their women are concerned."

"Ahmed's not your typical Middle Eastern guy," Meg said.

"That's what you keep saying, but you haven't actually tested him on something like this, have you? What does he know so far?"

"Nothing."

"Good," her dad said. "Don't tell him anything. I'm sure Jonathan went and sowed his wild oats for ten years and now has finally realized that the grass was not, in fact, greener any-where else. He's going to come here and try to win back the girl of his dreams. Just you watch. Don't fall for it, Meg. And don't let Ahmed get a whiff of what's going on. I guarantee he will not react well."

"I don't see how I can lie to my boyfriend," Meg said. "That's just fundamentally wrong."

"I'm not saying lie to him. I'm saying don't tell him."

"It's the same thing," Meg said.

Phillip shook his head in disagreement. "It's protecting yourself."

"It's keeping secrets."

"People have a right to their secrets," he insisted.

"I'm shocked you're suggesting this," Meg said. "I didn't think not telling him was even an option."

"It's the best option," her father said. "Besides, there's nothing to tell. You had a three-minute phone call with the guy and that's that. A three-minute phone call means nothing. It means less than nothing."

But Henry calling Jonathan did not mean nothing. It meant something huge—only Meg didn't know what.

*M*y *wedding gift to Jonathan was a Rolex watch that cost nearly as much as our wedding reception. At the time, I thought we'd agreed that he'd go into corporate law, and so the watch seemed like something he should have. (The watch makes the man, right?)*

For my wedding present, Jonathan got me a box.

I used to tell my girlfriends this as if it explained everything, as if from his gift alone I should have known it would never work out between us.

But the thing is, the box Jonathan gave me had meaning. I just didn't pay attention to it at the time.

The box was ornate. It had been designed in the early part of the twentieth century in a well-known artisan's shop in London. It was about eight square inches and on the top was an engraving of Pandora opening a box. In Greek mythology, Pandora is the world's first woman, sent by the gods to earth with a box containing all sorts of evils. According to the myth, Pandora opened the box out of curiosity, thereby releasing greed and lust and pettiness and deceit and ego and scorn and a thirst for vengeance into the world. (Women always get the blame, don't they?)

Jonathan explained this story to me and I think he sensed my displeasure with the gift because the voice he used became increasingly soft and soothing as he told it. There's another ver-

sion of the story, Meg *(Jonathan always did like to rewrite history)*.

In the version I like, *he'd said,* what got released weren't really evils at all, but gifts if only you'd look at them as such. And once they were gone, what was left in the box was hope.

That was the gift he'd wanted to give me—a legacy of hope.

After he left me, I threw the box in a garbage Dumpster along with all our wedding photos. Just recently, I did a little searching on the Internet and good old Wikipedia said this about Jonathan's version: It's meant to signify that "life is not hopeless, but each of us is hopelessly human."

I wish I'd saved the box. It would help me remember that what we consider bad in a relationship might in fact not be bad at all. Things like lust and fear and deceit might be invitations for us to go deeper—to see the one we love as he is instead of as we'd like him to be. Men aren't simpletons. They're very, very complex, and their souls are screaming for poetry.

For story time the next day, Meg chose *Jim's Lion* by Russell Hoban. *"Listen carefully, now,"* the story says. *". . . This is not kid stuff. . . . You've got all kinds of things in your head, everything you've ever seen or thought about, all in your head."*

It was the story of Jim, a boy who was in the hospital and frightened. A nurse told him to close his eyes and think of a place he loved and an animal would appear there who would find him and then lead him back from danger. Jim imagined a spot at the ocean he'd gone to with his family where they'd all been happy, and he imagined a lion, which he was afraid of at first and unsure if it was real. His nurse assured him it was. *"The real thing is always more than you're ready for,"* she said.

To help Jim face his fears, the nurse gave him a painted pebble—a don't-run stone—and after Jim clutched the don't-run stone in his hand and bravely held his ground with the lion, he grew strong enough for the operation he needed to live.

The ending was not *And they all lived happily ever after.* But things did get better for Jim. Meg had chosen the story especially for Marita, who was back in class and sat on Meg's right. An uncharacteristically somber Lucas was on Marita's other side and pressed his cross-legged knee into hers.

After story time, Meg gave her students smooth rocks the size of sand dollars to paint and keep as their own don't-run stones. At recess, she sat on a bench with Marita and shared a bunch of grapes. Marita swung her legs back and forth, which Meg took as a positive sign.

"How do you like staying with your aunt?" she said.

Marita stopped swinging her legs and leaned her head against the side of Meg's arm and sighed more wearily than a five-year-old should know how to.

"You've been asked a lot of questions by a lot of people in the last few days, haven't you?" Meg said. "I bet you're getting sick of them."

Marita nodded and silently watched as Antonio chased Lucas through the play structure. When he saw her watching him, Lucas darted over. "I'm the fastest runner in the class," he boasted.

Meg laughed. "And the most confident."

"I'm the most *everything*." He snapped his fingers in front of Marita's face. "Look at that," he said. "Can you do that? I could do it a million times if I wanted to, which I don't, because that would get boring." He snapped in her face a few more times until Meg playfully knocked his hand away.

"You try," he told Marita.

Marita attempted to snap but had a hard time coordinating her fingers.

"You've got to practice," Lucas said. "I practiced all day yesterday." He snapped a few more times. "Keep trying, and then one day you'll be able to do it, too."

"What did you two think of our story today?" Meg asked them.

"I liked it!" Lucas said. "If I had a finder, it would be a cheetah and I'd climb on his back and he'd run away from anything bad." He snapped in Meg's face. "What would *your* finder be?"

Meg brushed his hand away and thought of her father. "Mine would be a lion, like in the book. Quietly powerful, on the prowl to protect me. Just knowing he was out there somewhere nearby would make me feel safe, even if I still had to face the bad stuff on my own."

"You do, you know," Lucas said, just before he ran off. "That's what the story was about."

When Meg asked Marita what animal she'd choose for her finder, Marita closed her eyes and disappeared into her imagination for a long minute.

"My finder wouldn't be an animal," she said when she finally opened her eyes, which were the same color brown as Ahmed's. "My finder would be a Lucas. And my good place is here with you, Miss Meg. With you and with Lucas, too."

"I love that," Meg said.

Marita smiled shyly. "And I love you."

Meg's father had never steered her wrong before. That was what she kept coming back to, again and again. And even though keeping a secret from Ahmed didn't sit well with her, Meg finally accepted that her father might be right. She wasn't hiding a crime, after all, just a three-minute phone call.

Yet as she and Henry crossed the park to get to soccer practice, Meg was nervous, because even if keeping quiet about Jonathan's potential reappearance was in her best interests, it inherently went against what she wanted their relationship to be, which was one hundred percent honest in every respect. She kept trying to tell herself that a ninety-nine-percent honesty rate was still pretty darn good.

Ahmed greeted them both with a big smile and a buoyant hello. Henry said hi back and ran off to join the other boys, leaving the two of them alone.

"My dad wants to take us to lunch at the Arizona Inn sometime over the holiday weekend," Meg said. "Is there a particular day that works best for you?"

"Friday's bad, because I'm golfing in the morning. By the way, does your dad golf? We need a fourth."

"Why don't you invite me?" Meg asked. "What makes you think I'm not a golfer?"

"Do you golf, Meg?" Ahmed looked amused by the very idea of it.

"Why does that seem so funny to you?"

He stepped closer and tucked her hair behind her ear. She tingled from his touch. "Do you?"

"To be honest, the very thought of golf puts me to sleep," she said.

He laughed. "I thought that was probably the case. You don't seem like the golfing type. But it can be very calming, I'll have you know. Therapeutic. Contemplative. Life slows down on the golf course."

"I always thought people just went out on the golf course and got drunk," Meg said.

"I don't," he said. "I hang out with my friends, enjoy the landscape, smell the grass. . . ."

Meg beckoned him closer, then put her hand on his shoulder and whispered to him, "Do people ever have sex on golf courses?" She inhaled his exceptionally subtle aftershave and fell into the Pied Piper appeal of him: she'd follow this guy anywhere.

"People have sex everywhere," he whispered back. "Except us. I never realized how tricky it would be, plotting to have sex with a single mom."

She pulled back to look into his twinkling brown eyes. "Am I more than you bargained for?"

"You're worth every complication." Ahmed bestowed on her a kiss that was overly passionate for the setting—it was just this side of appropriate.

"I like outdoor sex," Meg offered. "Golf-course sex would be fine with me."

Ahmed laughed. "I'll keep that in mind, although there's always the getting caught factor to consider."

Meg shrugged flirtatiously. "The risk is part of the fun, right?"

"It'd make the papers if I got arrested for public indecency," Ahmed said.

"But there's nothing indecent about you," Meg teased. "You're a fine specimen."

"Why, thank you."

Just then Catherine approached. "Look at you two love-birds," she said. "You two are just the cutest."

Meg had been called *cute* and *perky* her entire life and thought the descriptions not only reduced her, but also completely lacked originality. Besides, Catherine had interrupted their wooing, so Meg narrowed her eyes and then did her best to ignore her.

"Anyway, my dad doesn't golf, either," she told Ahmed. "But if you ever want to teach Henry how to play, go for it."

Ahmed, who'd said a pleasant hello to Catherine, brightened at the idea. "I'll see if he's interested. Thanks."

"Calm and contemplative are two traits I'd love for him to work on," Meg said.

Ahmed grinned. "I can see where that might be beneficial."

He kissed her cheek, turned and headed onto the field, blowing his whistle to round up the boys. Meg sighed happily and for the remainder of practice tried to imagine how things would play out between them in bed. She'd bet there would be a lot of laughing. The first time, though, would have to be fast—*wham, bam*—because she had a lot to get out of her system—eight weeks' worth of built-up lust. She wasn't a prude and didn't quite understand how they'd been together this long with so little sexual satisfaction to show for it.

In the middle of Meg's quite pleasant daydreaming, Catherine sidled up. "Bradley has just *not* stopped talking about Henry," she said. "He talks about him nonstop! We really should arrange that playdate for the boys."

"We should." Meg smiled weakly, thinking, *We shouldn't.* She had enough stressors in her life at the moment without adding Catherine to the mix.

"Today's great for us," Catherine said. "How about after soccer? Henry could come home with us for dinner."

"On a school night?"

"This week?" Catherine waved off Meg's question. "Please. Teachers never really teach anything right before vacation."

"Um, yes, they do. You do know that I'm a teacher, don't you?" Meg was about to refuse on principle after the way Catherine had just insulted her profession, but then Ahmed ran by and flashed her that sexy smile of his and the contour of his thigh muscles was so very ripe for further exploration, and . . . "Having said that, I think Henry would love to spend some time with Bradley," she said. "I'll check with him after practice."

"Great!" Catherine beamed. "That would give you and the coach some much-appreciated time alone, I'm sure." She gave a sexually meaningful look in Ahmed's direction. "I know what *I'd* do if I got that man alone for any length of time."

Hey, Catherine, did you hear the one about thou shalt not covet thy fellow soccer mom's boyfriend? This woman was *seriously* inappropriate. Meg couldn't stand her, actually.

"Do you keep any guns in the house?" she asked out of spite.

"Of course not!" Catherine recoiled at the suggestion.

"Any rottweilers for pets?"

"Goodness, no!"

"Let your kids play Grand Theft Auto?"

"No, of course—"

"Watch R-rated movies? Associate with convicted felons? Suspected child molesters? Any no-good uncles wandering around in their boxer shorts?"

At that, Catherine narrowed her eyes, and Meg realized she'd gone too far. "Kidding," she said meekly. *Just wanted to get your mind off my boyfriend's sex life.*

At the end of soccer practice, Meg checked with Henry, who very much wanted to go to Bradley's, and then approached Ahmed. "Guess what. Henry's going to Bradley's house for dinner. He'll be there for several hours."

Ahmed's eyes sparked. "Whatever shall we do?"

Meg beamed X-rated thoughts in his direction and struck a blatantly transparent breast-swelling pose. "I have no idea."

Laughing at her, Ahmed glanced at his watch. "I do," he said. "Be at my house in an hour."

Forty minutes later, a freshly showered Meg stood naked in front of her closet with a glass of wine in her hand and considered her options. There weren't many, unfortunately. She was a single mom and a kindergarten teacher, not a seductress, and she'd already worn her sole little black dress on her first date with Ahmed.

Did she even have a decent-enough matching bra and panties? She had enough black underwear to outfit a widow's convention, but none of it was lacy or particularly lust-provoking, and while she didn't think Ahmed would mind, it struck her as pathetic that she had nothing worthy of true seduction. She suspected that each and every one of Jonathan's conquests while he'd been married to her had worn something other than all-cotton, not-even-push-up paraphernalia.

Meg sighed, and then it came to her. She'd go commando. It was most efficient, always a turn-on and perfectly solved the nothing-to-wear problem. As for outer garments, her lady-in-red dress with the built-in shelf bra would do just fine.

When Ahmed opened his front door, Meg almost lost her breath at the sight of him. He had on black jeans and wore a tucked-in rust-colored silky shirt, sleeves rolled up to three-quarters' length. Glancing at his forearms, Meg realized what it was about them that so turned her on. It was, first, the light tan color of his skin, a shade she'd envied her entire pale-skinned life. More than that, it was how, even at rest, the tendons on his forearms flexed, hinting that his entire body would be similarly muscled and efficient, with no wasteful flesh, only solid muscle and bone to press against. *Please let this happen tonight,* she thought. *Let me see if my forearm theory holds true.*

But as she stepped in and slipped off her sweater, Meg immediately noted the lack of romantic setup. Nothing looked any different than usual. The lights were bright, not a candle in sight. Ahmed even had a *TIME* magazine lying opened to an article about the bird flu—what kind of foreplay was this?

Meg scratched her head as she moved to take a seat on the couch. She made sure the hem of her dress, under which she wore nothing, was pulled down as far as possible. Two could play at this lack-of-foreplay game.

Ahmed sat two cushions over and casually stretched his arm over the back of the couch. "So, what's new?"

Meg was confused by his lackadaisical attitude—she would have thought him the romantic type (he hadn't even put on any blues music!)—until it occurred to her that maybe he'd somehow found out about Jonathan's phone call and was about to bust her for not telling him. "Nothing," she said. "Why do you ask?"

"Just making conversation." He said it lightly, but Meg sensed something more was going on.

"Are you mad at me about something?" Her heart pounded fearfully.

"I have yet to get mad at you," he said. "In fact, I can't imagine ever getting mad at you."

"Oh, come on," Meg said. "What if I stole money from you?"

He laughed. "I'd assume you needed it."

"What if I borrowed your nice Mercedes and wrecked it?"

He laughed again. "I'd assume it was an accident, and I'd be far more concerned about you than the car."

"You're so sweet," Meg said. "What if I lied to you?" She kept her voice light, but Ahmed's eyes lost their laughter.

"Lying would be bad," he conceded. "I've dated women who've lied, and it's pretty much a deal breaker for me."

Meg's mood deflated instantly. Ahmed peered at her and saw how her swallow came hard. "Is there something you should tell me, Meg?"

She thought of her father's advice not to tell him about Jonathan's call.

"I'm not sure," she said. "I have something I don't want to tell you, but it's something I don't want to *not* tell you, either, if that makes any sense."

Looking pained, he exhaled. "You should probably tell me."

"My ex-husband called me." She blurted it out and then squeezed her eyes shut. Ahmed waited to speak until she opened them.

"And?" he prompted.

"And nothing." Meg's heart pounded as if she were lying. *But she wasn't!* "He's coming to town and wants to get together, but I told him no. I've got absolutely no interest in seeing him."

"Okay, then," Ahmed said smoothly. There was just the slightest bit of edge in his jaw. "Is that all? Was there anything else?"

Wasn't that bad enough?

"That's all," Meg said. "Are you mad?"

"I don't see anything to be mad about, Meg," he said. "First off, honesty's good. It means you trust me. Second, he called you, not the other way around. And third, you don't want to see him. That's all good, as far as I'm concerned."

There was a tiny hint of unhappiness in his eyes, just enough to prove he was human and just enough to make Meg decide not to mention it had actually been Henry, not Jonathan, who'd initiated the contact.

He studied her intently. "Why does he want to see you?"

"I've got no idea." Meg's heart raced. "I don't even want to know, because it doesn't matter. I'm with you. These past months with you have been magical," she said. "My whole world's lighter and brighter and sparklier. I've had this new confidence ever since you came into our lives. I've stopped being so protective of my heart—I'm just putting it out there in a way I haven't in a long, long time. But that leaves me exposed. Does that make sense? I'm always waiting for something bad to happen to cancel out my happiness, as if I'm not entitled to it."

Ahmed took her hand. "I know that feeling, first from when my mom died and then from when I was sent away."

"So are we okay?" she asked.

"We're okay." But his eyes conveyed that maybe he wasn't, and his smile, meant to assure her, was heartbreakingly sad.

"Hey." Meg scooted over to get close to him and softly stroked his cheek. "This is why I didn't want to say anything. I didn't want to worry you."

"I love you, Meg," he said. "I can't help but worry."

Meg's heart surged. "You love me?"

"Can't you tell?"

"I can tell," she said. "It comes through in everything you do."

Ahmed, I'm going to reveal a secret. I have this thing about your forearms. Don't get me wrong—I like virtually every aspect of you—but the way the tendons in your forearms flex when you make even the smallest of movements . . . Well. It's quite the turn-on, because I'm reminded of your strength.

I have no doubt you'd lay down your life for me and Henry, but that's not the kind of strength I'm talking about. You're strong in how you think. How you reason. How you love. You're strong from the inside out.

Henry's got Violet. Marita's got Lucas. Who did you ever have? I wish I'd known you when we were children. I would have been the little girl who always made you smile.

I wish I'd been your first American teacher. I would have told you how smart you were. I wish I'd been your father. I would have told you how brave you were. I wish I'd been your mother. I would have told you how much you were loved. Whatever you missed in your life—whatever you needed and didn't get—I wish I could have given it to you.

I guess this is my way of saying: I love you, too.

"I thought we were going to have sex tonight," Meg said with a pout.

"Oh, we are," Ahmed said.

"Well?" Meg looked around the romantically lackluster room. "Our first time together is kind of a big deal. I don't need a candlelit dinner but . . . I don't know . . . something?"

"I would've liked to hire a private jet and flown us to Venice and wined and dined you and taken you on one of those gondola rides. . . ." He shrugged. "But there wasn't enough time to plan it."

"A single orchid would have been lovely." Meg picked up his *TIME* magazine and waved it as evidence. "I know the bird flu's a fascinating topic, but if I may be so bold, I'd like to think that having sex with me might prove fascinating for you, too. Worthy of some preliminary effort, anyway."

"Oh, Meg. You poor girl." He made a sympathetic face. "You're not asking for much, are you? A rose-petal trail to the bedroom. A fire in the fireplace. Just a little romance, right? I'm sorry. What a lousy boyfriend I've turned out to be."

"You're not lousy," she assured him. "You're wonderful. Just . . . surprisingly unromantic."

Ahmed stood and held out his hand to her. "Come with me a minute." He pulled her up, grabbed her sweater and helped her slip it back on, then led her to his back door. "Like I said, I wanted to take you to Venice, but I know we've got to pick up Henry by eight thirty."

Meg gasped when he opened the door. His entire walled-in backyard twinkled with candles in hurricane jars—there were fifty, at least. Overwrought Italian music was playing, the same sort that played at the Venetian in Vegas, and his three-tiered fountain gurgled in the background. His wide canvas hammock was equipped with cozy blankets to balance against the autumn chill, and a small table nearby was set with cheese, dried fruit, nuts, two wineglasses and a bottle of wine.

"The wine's a Bordeaux," he said. "Off theme, but I don't know my Italian wines very well and the guy at Fifty-eight Degrees was busy with another customer."

"This is awesome." Meg laughed and then socked him in the arm. "You had me completely fooled."

Ahmed rubbed his arm. "So you'll forgive me for pulling a fast one on you?"

"I *might* forgive you." When she put her arms around his neck, he slipped his around her waist and pressed her against him. "I haven't decided yet."

He gave her an oh so meaningful look. "I'll do anything to get back in your good graces."

"Anything? Really?" Meg meant for her voice to be teasing, but he'd begun kissing her neck, which was incredibly distracting. Her voice came out more as a whimper, instead, decidedly not the impression she wanted to give. When Ahmed looked at her uncertainly, she knew he was wondering if she was nervous, perhaps having second thoughts. Which was a ridiculous idea.

"Don't you be looking at me like that," she said.

He smiled. "How am I supposed to look at you?"

Meg kissed him with months' worth of pent-up longing. It was the kiss of a woman who was about to have sex after not having had it for a very long time, indeed. Ahmed responded with a soft groan and looked drunk with desire.

"Like that." Meg gave him a slow smile. "You're supposed to look at me exactly like that. How much time have we got left?"

"None to waste," Ahmed said.

Meg slipped her sweater off. "It's a good thing I'm naked under this dress, then."

His eyes widened. "Nothing under the dress?"

"Nothing."

"Prove it," he said.

Meg had to make a quick decision. She could be bold and whip off the dress and give him a memory he'd never forget. Or she could be her usual, slightly more inhibited self.

Her usual self won out.

"How about a glass of that wine?" she asked.

"Ah, yes." Ahmed turned graciously to uncork the bottle and pour them some, while Meg chastised herself. He'd been hoping for the brazen off-with-the-dress option, of course. And now what he'd always remember was how she hadn't done it. He'd remember how she'd wimped out.

Meg didn't want to be a wimp, not where Ahmed was concerned, so while his back was to her, she slipped out of the dress and stood naked except for her three-inch not-quite-spiked heels and shivered, from both the thrill of the moment and the chill in the air, as she waited for him to notice.

It didn't take but a moment. When he turned, completely unsuspecting, a wineglass in each hand, his breath caught at the sight of her. "Wow," he said. "I feel overdressed."

"You *are* overdressed," she said. "And it's lonely being naked alone."

"I'd hate for you to be lonely," he said.

"So come on over." Ahmed started over, keeping his eyes on hers. "You can shift your eyes downward if you want," she said. "In fact, I'll be offended if you don't. I might even put the dress back on."

"Please don't." He handed her a glass of wine and kissed her. The distance he left between them was an unpardonable tease.

"I'm cold," she said. "Warm me up."

He enfolded her in his arms, and the warmth of his body and the heat of his tongue were the perfect antidote to the chilly desert night. Meg shivered, and they'd only just begun.

"The blankets," she said. "Let's get under the blankets."

"Ah, but the moonlight."

"You cornball," she said. "Besides being cold, I've never been very good at having sex standing up."

He laughed. "You're so practical."

"I'm lustful," she reminded him. "And time is of the essence. And I *am* cold. It's November, you know."

Things moved quickly from there. Meg set their wineglasses on the table, lightly pushed him back onto the hammock and undressed him, starting with the buttons on his shirt and working her way downward, forgetting the cold and feeling more emboldened by the moment. Her forearm theory did hold true, as his naked body was darn near a work of art.

And all hers! Time really was of the essence, so once she'd undressed him, she straddled him, guided him inside her, pulled the blankets over them and intertwined her fingers with his as they made love.

Afterward, she whispered, "I'm keeping you, Ahmed Bourhani."

"You'd better," he whispered back. "Because it's lonely being naked alone."

Meg's father called early the next morning, waking her. "Can I come over?"

Meg yawned and dropped her head back on the pillow. It was six fifteen and her father was not an early riser. She sat up, worried. "What's going on, Dad? Are you okay?"

"I've got an idea I want to run by you," he said. "It can't wait."

"Can't you just tell me over the phone?" she said. "I've got school, you know."

"I know," Phillip said. "But it's a short week. You can take it a little easier Thanksgiving week, right?"

What was *with* these people?

"I'll get the coffee going," Meg said. "And just so you know, I have students for whom school is their happiest, safest place—the only place where everything works the way it's supposed to, and some of them are heading into a long weekend of chaos. So no, I can't take it easy this week."

While the coffee brewed, Meg brushed her teeth, stuck her hair up in a ponytail and threw on a long denim skirt and black sweater. She skipped a shower, as she'd taken a luxurious, dreamy, postsex bubble bath the previous night, after she'd picked Henry up from Bradley's and gotten him off to bed. Instead, she simply washed her face, whipped on some foundation and lipstick and was ready in less than ten minutes.

When her father tapped on the door, Meg opened it to find him pacing in front of it.

"Wow!" he said. "You look great."

She looked sexually satisfied—that was how she looked. She'd seen it herself.

"I've got a lot to be thankful for," Meg said. "Coffee's ready. Come on in."

Phillip stepped inside. "Henry's still sleeping?"

"Yep."

"How's he been acting since Sunday?" he asked. "Did he talk any more about Jonathan and why he called him?"

Things still weren't entirely back to normal between mother and son, and there was a careful tenderness on both their parts. Henry's behavior and Meg's anger had taken a toll, but not a fatal one. "I don't think he knows why he called him, but we're going to be just fine," she said. "I'm going to make sure that boy gets what he needs."

Which was herself and Ahmed, separately and together.

"And Amy?" her father said. "Have you talked to her yet?"

"Not yet." As Meg poured their coffee, her father climbed onto a stool at the breakfast bar.

"I've been thinking about that, too," he said. "And I need to say something you might not like hearing, which is that Jonathan was always good to your sister. Remember how he came home from college to take her to senior prom after that Roger schmuck broke her heart? And how he encouraged her to send off her poems to that literary magazine? He was decent to her, and he never made it seem like he was doing it just for you."

Meg remembered Amy's words: *He was the brother I never had and always wanted.*

"But still," Meg said. "She shouldn't have deceived me."

"Trust that she had her reasons for not telling you," Phillip implored her. "You're her hero. She looks up to you so much. I'm sure she was afraid of losing your approval. Of losing your love."

Meg put out her lower lip. "I hadn't thought of it like that."

"In the end, it's not your business, anyway," he said. "What happens between two people belongs to them alone. Like with your mother and me. While you're involved on the periphery, the breakdown of our marriage really isn't your issue."

"So you're not mad I didn't tell you about Mom's new car?" Meg asked.

Her father reddened.

"Oooh." Meg cringed. "Tell me you knew about the car."

"I know about the car," he said. "I just haven't figured out how she paid for it. I put the bulk of our money in an escrow account until we've got an agreement in place, and there wasn't enough left in our joint account to buy a car."

"Maybe she financed it," Meg said.

"Your mother hates owing anybody anything," Phillip said.

"Maybe the new and improved Clarabelle doesn't mind debt."

Phillip rolled his eyes. "Well, we both know that spouses and ex-spouses can be unpredictable. That's what brings me here, actually."

He looked at Henry's closed bedroom door and lowered his voice. "You need to go on the offensive with Jonathan or you're going to get blindsided by something really ugly," he said. "I have a gut feeling about this, Meg. There was nothing casual about his call. Life as you know it is about to change unless you're very careful here."

We need to meet, he'd said.

We have some unfinished business.

Come on, Meg.

Please.

In the brief instant during which Meg closed her eyes, she remembered the totality of what it had been like to be with Ahmed the previous night. How completely good and right it had been. Life as she knew it was getting better every day.

"How do we go on the offensive?" she asked.

"I know a good lawyer," Phillip said. "You and I should go see her today right after school. Jonathan could show up anywhere, at any time. You need to know your legal rights and be ready to throw them in his face if it comes to that."

Seeing a lawyer was about the last thing Meg wanted to do. She was a lover, not a fighter, and she'd always thought that all lawyers were good for was fighting.

But Jonathan was a lawyer, and if he was going to go after Henry, he'd use the law to do it.

"Okay," Meg agreed. "In my father I trust."

Nine hours later, Meg pulled into the parking lot of the north-side law offices of Lerner, Grimes, Kerrigan and Cleaver, PC with just minutes to spare. Violet's mother had agreed to watch Henry, so Meg had dropped him off there and then gotten delayed in Tucson's typically bad traffic. She'd been uptight on the drive over, but her heart softened at the sight of her father pacing in the parking lot, hands in his pockets like he'd wait for her forever if he had to. She parked the car and joined him.

"Ready?" he asked.

Meg kissed his cheek. "Thanks for being here," she said. "I know you've got a lot going on in your own life right now."

"I'm your dad," he said. "I'd do anything for you, Magpie."

"I sure wish Henry had a father like you."

"Henry's already got everything he needs—you," Phillip said. "Anything more would simply be icing on the cake."

That's Ahmed, Meg thought. *Icing.*

As soon as she thought of him, she felt guilty. He'd left a message on her cell phone that morning, and she hadn't called him back yet. She was glad she'd told him that Jonathan had called, but the sadness and worry she'd seen in his eyes had made her feel horrible. She'd decided to hold off revealing anything more until she had actual facts to share. This all might come to nothing. She only wanted to be prepared, and this way, she'd worry enough for them both. It was her burden to bear, not his.

Phillip held the door open for her and then stepped ahead to the receptionist. "Phillip Goodman and Meg Clark for Patricia Lerner, please."

The reception area was rich—rich as in sensory rich, with its mahogany-and-velvet chairs and its oil painting in a gilded frame above the honest-to-god *fireplace*, and rich as in . . . just rich. Three-hundred-dollar-an-hour rich. Meg bit her lip as she looked around. Phillip had offered to pay for the consultation, but Meg wouldn't let him. She was proud of the fact that she was sitting here at all and not crippled under a bathroom sink.

She wasn't a victim this time around, and that, in itself, was worth whatever cost she might incur.

Her dad gestured for her to sit and then took the chair opposite her. He crossed his legs, perfectly at home. He'd been here before, Meg could tell. "This woman is your divorce lawyer, isn't she, Dad?"

Phillip nodded.

"How'd you find her?" Meg asked.

"Sandi used her for her divorce." He checked his watch. "At five dollars a minute, she'd better not expect us to pay for the time we wait." He was the world's most impatient man when it came to waiting for people who billed for their time.

"I didn't realize Sandi was divorced," Meg said. "I thought she was still married to Bud."

"They divorced a few years back." Phillip stood and began to pace. "Now he's up in Montana, fly-fishing to his heart's content."

"How did I not know that?" Meg said.

Her father shrugged. "Now you do. *Here* she is." Phillip said it loud enough for the approaching woman to hear.

Some women just had their act together, and Patricia Lerner was one of them. Meg could tell it from her solid handshake alone. Dark-haired with a creamy complexion, she had a slight frame that disguised what Meg guessed was a lethal ability to come out victorious in any physical or intellectual confrontation. Just by looking at her, Meg got the feeling Patricia could shoot a gun, skin a deer, take down a bad guy with her bare hands and reduce a man to tears. She looked a little bloodthirsty, to be honest. Meg felt self-conscious as Patricia gave her the once-over. The suit Patricia wore probably cost more than Meg spent in an entire year on her own clothes. Meg supposed she might be exactly what they needed to scare off Jonathan.

"Come. Let's get to it." Patricia strode ahead into her office. As Meg and Phillip settled into the leather armchairs that faced Patricia's massive desk, Meg was awestruck by the view of the Catalina Mountains, which were in-your-face gorgeous in the late-afternoon sun.

For a moment, Meg was a senior back in high school, driving with Jonathan in his dad's old Studebaker. *I love how Tucson is surrounded by mountains,* she'd said. *They're so protective.* Jonathan looked over at her like she was crazy. *That's funny,* he replied without smiling. *I've always found them suffocating.*

"So." Patricia sat forward in her chair and tapped on her desk while looking pointedly at Meg. "Your father tells me that your ex-husband contacted you. What does he want?"

Meg brought her gaze from the mountains to Patricia's coldly capable green eyes. She never really trusted people with green eyes. She liked brown eyes. Ahmed eyes. And blue Henry eyes.

"We think possibly he wants my son." Meg looked to her father for help.

"He's been out of their lives for ten years," Phillip said. "He's the father of Meg's son, Henry, who's nine, but he's never been part of his life and has never paid child support."

"He paid it, like, three times," Meg corrected.

"We want to make sure his sudden appearance doesn't disrupt Henry's life. Or Meg's life, for that matter," Phillip said.

"So this ex-husband's a deadbeat," Patricia said.

"Yes," Phillip said.

"That's not quite fair, Dad," Meg said. "I never really went after him for the child support." Having him completely out of her life, she'd reasoned at the time, was in some ways better than being slapped in the face with the reminder of him every month.

"I hate deadbeats." Patricia's smile was ferocious. "I hate deadbeats and cheaters."

Beside Meg, her father coughed.

"Phillip?" Patricia said. "Can I get you some water?"

"I'm fine." He stood, went to a little serving tray and poured himself a glass of water. He drank it down, poured another and then brought one over to Meg. Nervous her hands would shake, she opted not to take a sip.

"I want to know if he has any legal right to see my son after all this time," Meg said. "I have full custody and he's never asked for visitation."

"You brought your divorce decree and child support order, yes?" Patricia looked at her expectantly.

Meg handed them over. That was another reason she'd almost arrived late. She kept both documents at the bottom of a box in her closet and she'd had to look through a few boxes until she'd found the right one.

Patricia scanned the papers. "What's been your contact with him thus far?"

"Well, for whatever ridiculous reason, my son called him, and since then, he called me at school last week and said he was going to be in town over Thanksgiving," Meg said. "He asked to see me. I told him no. Then he called me again last Saturday and again said he needed to see me."

"And before this?"

"Not since before our son was born."

"Really?" Patricia looked from Phillip to Meg. "Not a Christmas card? A quick visit while in town to see his family? He's never once laid eyes on his son?"

"It was for the best that he stayed gone." Phillip's voice had an edge to it. "He really pulled a number on Meg."

Patricia looked at Meg.

"He completely disappeared," Meg said. "Although I've just recently learned he's been in touch with my sister this whole time."

"We'd like him to stay gone," Phillip said. "Would an order of protection do the trick?"

Patricia leaned back in her chair and tapped her fingers idly on the desk as she thought. "Legally, he's got a right to reestablish a relationship with his son, if that's what he wants."

"How is that fair?" Meg asked.

"The law isn't always fair," Patricia said. "It's just always the law."

"But it's not in Henry's best interest," Meg said. "I really, honestly don't think it is."

"You're probably right." Patricia again skimmed the divorce decree and child-support order. "You do have some options if you're willing to play hardball."

"We're willing," Phillip said. "We'll do what it takes, won't we, Magpie?"

Meg thought of Henry and his messy-haired love. Of how Ahmed calmed him, and wanted to teach him to golf. Of the way Henry came to her classroom after school each day, loaded down with his backpack, having saved up his stories to tell her on the ride home. Of the Spanish-word insults he flung around with such glee. *No tienes cojones!*

Oh, yes, I do have balls, Henry Clark, Meg thought. *For you, I've got 'em.*

She agreed with her father: they'd do whatever it took to keep Henry whole.

Meg arrived home from the lawyer's office to find Ahmed sitting at her patio table, reading the newspaper. She felt immediately guilty, immediately skittish. He stood and kissed her cheek.

"You usually call me back right away," he said. "I thought maybe you regretted last night."

"You can't seriously think that," Meg said. "Last night was great."

His smile was a bit uncertain. "I thought I should check."

Meg took his hands. "You couldn't really have been worried."

"No," he said. "I guess not."

"I was with my dad," she said. "I went with him to see his divorce lawyer." It was the truth. Also sort of a lie, but not a complete one. "Want to stay for dinner? Does Henry know you're here?"

"Yes, to both," Ahmed said. "Henry's at Violet's watching PBS Kids. *Fetch!* or some such thing."

"Come on in," Meg said. "Let me figure out dinner. Oh! I know! We can make Persian food. I got a cookbook and all the ingredients we need for a rice dish and some sort of chicken entrée. I was going to bring it all over to your house as a surprise, but we could make it here. What do you think?"

"I think I'm a lucky man." He reached for her hand and kissed it.

"I'm the lucky one," she said. "Imagine if I'd fallen for a Scottish man. I'd be eating haggis!"

Using recipes from the cookbook Meg had bought at Antigone's on Fourth, *Persian Cooking for a Healthy Kitchen,* they made pistachio soup, chicken kebab, grilled tomatoes and a rice-lentil-and-rose-petal dish. Meg thought she'd never eaten a better dinner. Henry loved it, too, and Ahmed, usually a light eater, had three servings and told her he was in heaven.

Afterward, Henry took a shower and did his homework in his room. Meg puttered around the kitchen cleaning up, and Ahmed studied the framed pictures she had on the fireplace mantel, all of which were from their vacations at the ocean. He picked up a photo of her and Henry on Coronado Island, taken two years ago June, and studied it for a long time—long enough for Meg to sneak up and wrap her arms around him from behind. She and Henry had rented bikes that day, and each leaned against theirs. It had been toward the end of their week, and both were red-tan.

"His teeth!" Ahmed said. In the picture, Henry had two holes on the upper ridge of his mouth.

"He was the essence of childhood innocence," she said.

"I guess they grow fast, don't they?" He moved from her to replace the photo.

"Are you okay?" Meg said. "You seem sort of sad."

He shook his head and stepped closer. "Not sad."

"What, then?"

He looked at her for a long moment. "I wish you hadn't had to run off and get Henry last night."

Meg swallowed hard. "I wish I hadn't had to, either."

"I wish we lived together, so that when you left me, you'd always come right back," he said.

Meg smiled. "And I wish you'd make breakfast for us every day. You're a good pancake maker."

"I felt like we were a family that day," Ahmed said. "Did you feel it, too?"

Meg's breath caught. "I did. I always feel it when we're together."

Ahmed's hands hung at his sides, mere inches from her hips. She could almost *feel* them on her. She was about to make a move when there was a knock at the door. Henry ran from his bedroom and opened the door to find Violet outside.

"Can you come out?" she asked him.

Henry turned to Meg. "Can I, Mom? My homework's done."

"Sure," Meg said. She turned to Ahmed. "Do you want to have a drink by the pool?"

Ahmed agreed, and while Henry pulled a box of Popsicles from the freezer, Ahmed got Meg's six-pack of Corona from the refrigerator and cut a lime into slices, and they all headed down. Henry and Violet ran ahead.

"You'd miss this apartment complex if you moved, wouldn't you?" Ahmed asked.

Meg looked at him sideways. "What are you up to?"

"Just testing the waters," he said. "Listening for opposition and not hearing any."

Meg's breath came fast and she almost wanted to cry. *This is happening.* She stopped midstride, halfway to the pool, in nearly the same spot where they'd kissed that first time. "I wouldn't miss it so much," she said. "We could always come visit."

Ahmed grinned at her. "I was hoping you'd say that."

They passed half an hour of pleasant catching-up conversation with the Loop Group. In recent weeks, Kat had begun taking classes online for certification as a personal trainer. She and Ahmed found much to talk about, as he'd worked with a trainer for years at Precision Personal Training. Harley was contemplating getting another tattoo, and Meg tried to talk him out of it, but as far as Harley was concerned, the word *overkill* did not belong in the same sentence as *tattoo*.

Henry, taking a break from his card game with Violet on the other side of the pool, had just asked if he could get a tattoo one day, and Meg had just answered that yes, he could get an invisible tattoo anytime he wanted. He was trying to make sense of her joke when his eyes lit up. "There's Grandma!"

"Who's the hottie with her?" Kat said.

Meg squinted, but the man in question was a stranger to her. "Good question," she said. "I'll go find out."

As Henry ran to unlatch the pool gate, Meg downed the last of her beer and followed him. She waited as her mother hugged Henry; then she hugged her, too. "So, Mom, to what do we owe the pleasure?"

Clarabelle waved off any hint of occasion. "We were just out putting some miles on my new car. We stopped over at BeBe's and I thought since we were in the neighborhood . . ."

Meg eyed the man expectantly and waited for her mother to introduce them. "Meg, this is Andy," Clarabelle said. "He's an interior designer at Christopher's Fine Furniture and he's going to help me redecorate the house!"

"Dad's only been gone a few days," Meg said. "Don't you think maybe you should wait? And where are you getting all this money you're spending?"

"I'm fifty-five, Meg!" Clarabelle made gung-ho fists. "Life is short. I don't have a second to waste!"

"You're fifty-eight, Mom."

"Exactly my point!" Clarabelle looked over Meg's shoulder to the Loop Group table. "Is that a pitcher of drinks I see? And is that your handsome boyfriend?"

"It is on both counts," Meg said. "Would you like a margarita? We have that or Coronas."

Clarabelle looked at Andy, who gamely shrugged.

"Why not?" she said. "It is Tuesday night, after all."

"Exactly," Meg said.

Clarabelle greeted Kat and Harley and Ahmed and introduced them to Andy. As Meg poured their margaritas, the sound of opera wafted over to them. Clarabelle's face pinched in annoyance.

"This is the man who wanders around singing opera every night," she said to Andy, rolling her eyes. "I told you about him. Cuckoo!"

Meg looked helplessly at Ahmed. Opera Bob was one of her favorite people in the entire world, and of course she couldn't expect her mother to appreciate his beautiful soul—she'd never appreciated Phillip's, after all—but neither would she permit Clarabelle to mock Bob or trample on his artistry.

"It's a gift, Mom," she said. "We all appreciate Bob."

Ahmed smiled at her. "Another beer, Meg?"

"Yes, please." Thankful for him, she smiled back. Ahmed appreciated Opera Bob. Ahmed would never mock him.

"Andy said we could move a whole room of display furniture into the house to see how it looks before I make any final decisions," Clarabelle said. "Isn't that nice of him?"

"It's nothing short of amazing." Meg gave Andy the once-over. He looked like a decent person, but for all Meg knew, he preyed on older women who'd been recently dumped. For all she knew, it might be a very profitable niche. "Do you do this for everyone, or just for my mother?"

"Your mother's a very persuasive woman," Andy said.

Clarabelle laughed. "My house is decades out-of-date," she told the others. "My ex-husband never wanted to spend money on new furniture. As long as a sofa had half a spring, that was good enough for him. Meg's childhood bedroom *still* has that horrible green shag carpeting."

"He's not your ex-husband, Mom." Meg spoke through gritted teeth. "You're still very much married to him."

Clarabelle shook her head. "I'd say our marriage effectively ended the day he began his affair with that woman."

Meg slapped her hand on the table. "He's not having an affair!" As Clarabelle rolled her eyes, Meg turned to Ahmed. "He's not. She just can't see any other possible reason why he might have left her. Even though he told her exactly why."

"You've got your father on such a pedestal," Clarabelle said.

"Can I speak with you privately, please?" Meg could barely say the words without yelling. The others wisely stayed silent.

Opera Bob's serenade ended as Meg and Clarabelle walked to Meg's apartment.

"Oh, thank goodness," Clarabelle said. "I thought he'd never stop singing."

Meg turned on her mother the instant she'd shut the door behind her. "This is not okay. You're entitled to your anger," she said. "I know you're hurting—I've been where you are now. But you can't bash Dad like that, especially in front of Ahmed. It's important to me that he likes Dad, and he doesn't know him all that well yet, so your disparaging him just isn't very helpful."

"Your father is having an affair," Clarabelle said icily. "I smelled her perfume in his car. And this health kick! He's such a phony. He doesn't care about his health! He cares about getting laid!"

Meg tried to rein in her anger. "When you look for reasons to be suspicious, you'll always find them. Dad left you because you crushed his spirit. His words."

"He sat around like a bump on a log for thirty-five years." Clarabelle glared at her. "Crushing his spirit—that's ridiculous!"

"Couldn't you have gone to just one baseball game with him, Mom?"

"For thirty-five years, I asked your father to take me dancing," Clarabelle said. "*Thirty-five years.* And did he ever? No! Not once!"

"Tit for tat," Meg said. "Maybe if he'd taken you dancing, you would have gone to a baseball game, and maybe if you'd gone to a baseball game, he would have taken you dancing. But neither of you gave an inch, and now you've ended up alone."

"He's not alone," Clarabelle yelled. "He's with her."

"Who's *her*?"

"Sandi! That big-bosomed twit. That's what these men do. They ditch their wives for cheaper, sluttier women and then blame their wives to appease their guilt."

"But, Mom." Meg put her hand on her mother's arm to make her point. "That's not what happened here."

"This is what men do." Clarabelle extricated herself from Meg's grip. "By definition. They have affairs, and then they lie about them."

"Not all men, Mom."

Clarabelle shook her head. "You never saw the signs. Even when they were staring you right in the face, you never saw the signs."

When Ahmed and Henry arrived back at the apartment just then, Meg tried to see them both through Clarabelle's doubting eyes, her man and her man-to-be.

But she couldn't.

All she could see was their goodness.

Early Thanksgiving morning, Meg and Henry went for a hike with Ahmed at the Tanque Verde Ranch. Ahmed brought along three forks, whipped cream and a pumpkin pie he'd baked, and they ate it right from the pie plate, which Henry thought was the coolest thing in the world, and which Meg hoped might be the start of a nice tradition.

The rest of the day was not very celebratory. Meg spent most of it with Henry and her nieces, avoiding Amy and Clarabelle as much as possible. She dreaded what she had to do later: play hardball with Jonathan. She had to preempt him before he made his next move. Patricia Lerner had rightly counseled that he could show up anywhere—at their apartment, at school, at Amy's. If his goal was to build a relationship with Henry, he might show up where he knew Henry would also be.

To prevent that, Patricia had advised Meg to contact Jonathan and let him know that if he intended to seek visitation with Henry, she'd file court papers seeking back child support, roughly a hundred thousand dollars. If Jonathan didn't pay, he'd face jail time.

Meg knew it was the right strategy, but nonetheless it was a call she did not want to make. Yet that night, after she'd gotten Henry off to bed and after backing down several times, Meg dialed his cell phone number to completion.

"Hello?" Jonathan said.

"It's me," she said.

That was how they'd always greeted each other. *It's me.* As if there could never be anyone else.

His voice softened. "Hi there, me. I was just thinking about you."

Whoosh.

It was a funny thing about a voice and the time it could erase.

"Did you have a nice Thanksgiving?" he asked.

"Not particularly," she said. "You?"

"I did," he said. "Since I'm in the area, I took my old law school professor to dinner. Do you remember Professor Grimes?"

Meg was not about to make small talk with him. What did he think, that they were friends now? They had a shared history—that was all—which brought with it no obligations.

"You owe me in the neighborhood of a hundred thousand dollars in back child support," she said. "And I can have your ass thrown in jail if you refuse to pay it. If you intend to seek visitation with my son, I'll fight you every step of the way."

"Meg," Jonathan said. "Meg, Meg, Meg."

"Stop saying my name!" It was too intimate, coming from him.

"I always think of you in the fall," he said. "I'm not sure why."

Meg knew why and the thought made her heart beat recklessly. They'd been at their best in the fall, as they'd shared the start of new school years, new lockers, new sports teams, new coaches, new dorm rooms. Fall was all about stepping into the future, about moving forward, and for so many years, they'd moved forward together, into a future where they couldn't imagine being apart. She thought of him most strongly in the autumn, too, with each new class of kindergartners she welcomed, with each start-of-the-school-year shopping trip with Henry.

"I'm seeing someone," she said. "You should know we're very happy."

Jonathan chuckled. "I'm glad to hear it."

"I'm serious," Meg said.

"So am I," he said. "I'm not here to make trouble for you, Meg. I have no intention of disrupting your life, or Henry's. I know I don't have that right. I just . . ." His emotion was palpable as he stopped to take a deep breath. "You were a very important person in my life for a very long time, and I was horrible to you. I regret my behavior, and I'll regret it to my dying day, and I'm sorry. And that's why I keep calling. To tell you that."

Meg had fantasized about a moment like this, about Jonathan begging for a forgiveness she'd never, ever grant. She'd imagined all sorts of mercilessly clever responses, none of which suited what she was feeling at the moment, because what she was feeling was sad.

Inexorably,

gapingly,

weepingly,

convulsively

sad.

This was *Jonathan*. After all this time. *Her* Jonathan, calling for *her*.

Meg had to get off the phone. She had to hang up and crumple into a ball and hug her pillow and cry for the innocent, good-hearted girl she'd been. She knew she couldn't hold her tears back for very long. She'd say anything—*anything*—to get off the phone. So when Jonathan said he had something to give her and suggested they get together the next day, Meg said yes.

To Jonathan, she'd always said yes.

Meg sat on top of a picnic table at Himmel Park while she waited for Jonathan. She filled her lungs, held her breath to the count of eight and then released it. She did it again, and again, and again as she tried to talk herself into being calm.

But it was hard being calm while sitting in a park she'd been bringing Henry to since his birth, being in sight of the greatly feared-by-all-moms long slide, from which he'd once fallen and had to be rushed to the emergency room in fear of a concussion.

She'd been alone that day in her worry. Her fear of something bad happening to Henry never abated, never for one moment, and she knew part of it was pure motherhood—to *be* a mother was to be afraid—but part of it was also the abject knowledge that if something horrible *did* happen to Henry, no one would share the exact depth of her pain. It was the converse of how she felt sometimes as her heart filled with glory as she watched Henry run down a soccer field in this very same park and longed to have someone to turn to and say, *Look at our boy. Just look at him!*

Ahmed was there for her now, but Jonathan should have been there all along. He shouldn't have left her like he had, without even trying to work things out. Who knew? Maybe Meg would have stayed with him. Maybe she would have forgiven his infidelity, and maybe they would have gone on to have a happy marriage and more babies. Maybe it would have all worked out.

But he'd never even wanted to try.

When Jonathan emerged from the parking lot, sighted her and headed her way, Meg held herself absolutely still as she processed the sight of him. He now carried himself like his father, who'd died when they were in college. It was in the shoulders, mostly, how they curved forward just slightly, barely enough to cancel out the military-straight bearing their personalities likely would have preferred. Back in high school, the only time Meg had caught that posture on Jonathan was when he was weary after long runs. But now it seemed to have become part of him, this folding in on himself. He wore khaki pants and kept his hands in the pockets of a red jacket. He'd always looked good in red.

To reach her, he had to pass the long slide, plus the climbing tree, plus about a hundred yards of open space. Meg remained on top of the picnic table. She would not climb down, would not meet him halfway. She wouldn't put herself in a position where she might be easily reached for, easily hugged. This was the man who'd broken her heart and she wouldn't let herself forget it. This was the man who'd abandoned his son, who'd never even stuck around long enough to know what it was he was walking away from.

When Jonathan was a few feet from her, he stopped. As their eyes bridged the distance and the years, Meg realized how much she'd missed him. Hated him, yes—that, too, but he'd been such a big part of her life for so long.

Jonathan gave her his trademark smart-ass grin, reached into his jacket pocket, pulled out a pack of Watermelon Bubble Yum.

"Here." He tossed it to her. "I remember how you used to like it."

"*This* is what you wanted to give me? A pack of gum?" Meg laughed, both delighted and confused. "And here I thought you were going to hand me a check for all the back child support you owe me."

"You wouldn't really prefer *that* over a pack of gum, now, would you?" he asked.

Meg laughed again. She had to. This was Jonathan, after all, who was as familiar to her as her own reflection. But as seriousness took over, Meg looked for what about him was still there and what wasn't. He still had his face-defining cheekbones, and his eyes were still whip-snap blue like Henry's. But his hair wasn't as impressively thick as it used to be and his face had a smoggy, big-city pallor. He took her in similarly.

"You look like life's been treating you well," he said.

"I'd forgotten what your voice sounded like," she said. "Isn't that strange?"

"I'd forgotten yours, too," he said. "But it all came back in an instant. I have to tell you, my mind's been racing the past few weeks. So many memories, you know?"

"Oh, I know." Meg looked away from him for a moment, setting her gaze on the omnipresent military jets circling overhead. "Are you married?"

He shook his head. "I was, but that one didn't last long, either. I don't know how my parents managed to pull it off. I always thought I'd do it so much better than them."

"My parents are divorcing," she said. "That's my big news."

"Wow," Jonathan said. "That is big."

"It's long overdue," Meg said. "I'm sorry to hear about your mom's passing."

"Thank you." He gestured to the table. "May I?" When she nodded, Jonathan climbed up, keeping a respectful distance. He seemed to live inside himself now, and in his eyes there was a familiar loneliness that she'd completely forgotten. Even in their marriage, she'd often considered him lonely. He had things going on deep inside that he'd hoarded, a place inside himself where he used to go, leaving her behind and confused. It happened in an instant, sometimes. He'd left her even while he remained right beside her. How had she forgotten this, and where had he gone all those times?

"It must be strange, being an orphan," she said. "No safety net."

Jonathan looked past her to a group of kids about Henry's age who were playing kickball. "It sucks in so very many ways."

"Being a grown-up is shockingly hard sometimes, isn't it?"

Jonathan's smile was pained. Grim, almost. "You've just got to keep throwing your whole self in, right?"

"I can't believe you remember that!" He'd called it corny when she first started doing it with her kindergarten class.

"I remember everything, Meg."

His eyes hurt, they were so blue.

"Do you remember how you broke my heart?" she asked.

He nodded.

"So here we are," she said. "Ten years later. What was it like hearing from Henry?"

"Bizarre." Jonathan shook his head at the memory, still incredulous. "I cried for probably an hour afterward. Just wept. It hit me like a ton of bricks, that there's this kid out there, affiliated with me, and I don't know the first thing about him. He was so funny."

"I can't let you see him," Meg said. "You know that, right?"

"I understand," Jonathan said. "That's not why I'm here."

"He wouldn't tell me why he called you," Meg said. "He said if I wanted to know, I had to ask you myself."

Jonathan laughed. "You've got yourself a lively boy."

"I don't think I'd want him any other way," Meg said, smiling. "But calling him *lively* is putting it mildly."

They'd been sitting next to each other, looking out as much as at each other, but now Jonathan faced her directly. His eyes twinkled and he came alive. "So he calls me, and he goes, 'Hi, I'm Henry. Your son. And I've got a question for you.' Very businesslike. As if he had three minutes for me and not a second more." Meg laughed as he talked. Yep, that was her boy. "And I'm just standing there in the middle of my living room thinking, *Holy shit, is this for real? Is this really him? Is this really happening?* It was *crazy* weird."

"I bet," Meg said. "Like a bolt of lightning."

"Exactly." Jonathan nodded. "You know, you always sort of imagine something like this happening—some ghost from your past showing up, but—wow. That's all I can say. And his spunk just blew me away."

"Stop stalling and tell me what he wanted from you," she pressed him.

"Ah." Jonathan nodded and refocused his attention on the

moment rather than the memory. His voice lowered, became more solemn. "He'd like you to marry the guy you're seeing."

His name's Ahmed, Meg thought. But she didn't want to get into all the explanations with Jonathan.

"He needs to mind his own business," she said. "I can't believe he'd call you and tell you that."

Jonathan shrugged. "The way he sees it, it is his business. In effect, if he convinces you to marry the guy, he gets to pick his own dad—a specific, chosen father, as opposed to the lunk who happened to sire him."

But Ahmed hasn't even asked me, Meg thought. *Of course I'd say yes.*

"Why would Henry involve you?" Meg asked.

"Apparently you told him you weren't very good at being a wife," Jonathan said.

"Ah, yes." Meg remembered the conversation well. It was part of the what-would-happen-if-you-died talk they'd had. "I did tell him that."

" 'What does my mom need to do different so she can get it right this time?' " Jonathan said. "That was his question."

Of course.

Of course that was why he'd called Jonathan. Meg felt the familiar ache, the hole in her heart she couldn't fill, the question she couldn't quite answer. *Why is it so hard for you to get it right?* The question of a lifetime: what was wrong with her? Only Henry had the guts to go straight to the source.

"And?" Meg's voice wavered. "What'd you tell him?"

"He didn't want me to tell him anything," Jonathan said. "He was in a hurry to get off the phone. He asked me to promise I'd call you and tell you directly. And that's really why I'm here. I made him that promise, and I wanted to tell you in person."

Meg was glad she was sitting or her knees would have buckled. "Go ahead."

Jonathan smiled. "You say it like you're facing an executioner." He elbowed her. "You were a great wife, Meg. You didn't do anything wrong. I was the jerk."

You didn't do anything wrong. They were words she'd longed to hear, but upon hearing them she did not believe him.

"I must have done *something* wrong to make you want to hurt me so much."

He shook his head no.

"Come on," she said. "One thing."

Meg could see his chest pounding even through his jacket. Finally, he said, "I just . . . I couldn't breathe around you anymore."

"Funny." Meg felt sick to her stomach. "I couldn't breathe without you."

"I swear it wasn't you," he said again. "It was a physiological thing. Don't you remember that time I woke up in terror, having night sweats?"

"I remember." He'd dreamt he was being crushed by a massive slab of concrete after a building had collapsed on him, and people he'd known his whole life walked past on the sidewalk, noticing him and smiling and waving, willfully ignoring the fact that he needed help. He'd sobbed upon waking, so relieved his nightmare had ended.

"You had our lives all planned out," Jonathan said. "And you just assumed I'd go along, because, well, who *wouldn't* want a house in Sam Hughes and two-point-five kids and PTA meetings and brunch with your family on Sundays? I didn't even want kids—they never crossed my mind, except when you brought them up. I wanted adventure. Surprise. Some *grittiness* to my life, some New York City walking down a street, anything can happen feeling. The life you planned for us was too neat. Too perfect. Too *Good Housekeeping* magazine."

"But you knew that's what I wanted before you ever married me," she said.

"I loved you," Jonathan said, point of fact. "I fell in love with you before I even had my driver's license, and I thought love trumped everything. But it doesn't. Sometimes love isn't enough."

Meg sighed. "Oh, Jonathan."

"I'm sorry, Meg," he said. "I wish like hell I could've been the person you needed me to be."

Meg gave him a rueful smile. It was a funny thing about a voice. When it was a voice you knew well and it spoke the truth, you knew it.

As Meg drove away from the park, her head was jammed so full of competing emotions that her brain couldn't decide where to focus first. Jonathan wasn't the golden boy anymore, glowing with health and youthful invincibility.

He was alone.

He was going through life completely alone—no wife, no kids, no parents, no siblings. How could that possibly be a preferable way to live? Even if you did have a ton of friends and a fascinating career, how could that not be lonely sometimes, at least in the dead of night?

That was Ahmed's life, too, she thought. *Until you and Henry came along.*

They'd talked on, for nearly two hours. Jonathan had been a public defender for several years and he had some hilarious—and yes, gritty—stories to tell. She'd caught him up on the news surrounding her family and her job, and toward the end of their time together, she had finally offered some stories about Henry: how he loved the ocean. And soccer. And Violet, and Harry Potter. It had gone without saying that he loved Ahmed, too.

As they were saying goodbye, Jonathan had asked how serious her relationship was with Ahmed. *Pretty serious,* she'd replied.

Jonathan had looked at her as if he wished that wasn't the

case. *Lucky guy,* he'd said. He'd kissed her goodbye on the cheek and it was so familiar, his kiss, his smell, the way he said, *Okay, then,* afterward, as if now that he'd kissed her, he could face whatever came next.

In a way, seeing him had been anticlimactic—how could it not be, when she'd spent a decade anticipating it? There were no zingers tossed, no eyes flamed. There'd been just—them. Like it had always been when it was good between them. She'd been in no hurry. She would have been perfectly content to sit in the park with him for hours, saying nothing, just being with him.

Minutes away from the park, Meg got the shakes. Nervous, emotional shakes. Where had the ten lost years gone? How could it feel like it was just yesterday that they'd been together, but with the benefit of today's wisdom and experience? Life had knocked Jonathan down a few pegs. It had humbled him, and he came off as better for it. And what was she doing thinking nice thoughts about him after what he'd done to her?

She'd forgiven him, she realized, and with that realization Meg felt newly unburdened. And she had Henry to thank for it.

Henry, who'd made the call.

Henry, the coolest boy in the world.

What he'd done by contacting Jonathan was give her the ability to live their life motto: onward. Always onward.

And all she'd given him for it was grief.

Henry was playing a game on Sandi's computer when Meg arrived at her father's office to pick him up. Behind him, Sandi filed. "I can't believe my dad has you working the day after Thanksgiving," Meg said.

"Oh, I'm not officially working," Sandi said. "I just love days in the office when the phones are off. I get so much more done."

"Mom, I got to the highest level in Cube!" Henry said.

Meg leaned over Sandi's desk and kissed him. "Ga!" he said. "You made me mess up!"

Laughing, Meg held a Target bag out to him across the desk. "Maybe you'll forgive me once you see this."

Henry peeked in the bag and looked up at her. "No way."

"Yes, way."

"Is this for my birthday?"

Meg shook her head. "It's a just-because gift. Just because you're awesome. Just because you're exactly you."

"This is so cool! You're the best!" He pulled out the silver iPod, gawked at it, then ran around the desk and almost knocked Meg over with the force of his hug. Then he ran into Phillip's inner office. "Mom got me an iPod and it's not even for my birthday!"

Phillip came to his doorway and eyed her. "Your mom's day must have gone well."

"His mom's day went great." Meg couldn't say more, not with Henry around. "His mom is feeling like the world is hers for the taking. And the first thing I'm going to take is my son to dinner at his favorite restaurant."

Henry's mouth dropped open. "Chuck E. Cheese!"

Meg cringed. "I was thinking Macaroni Grill."

"Yes!" Henry said. "I love Macaroni Grill!"

"Then that's where I'm taking you."

First, she'd take Henry to dinner and later, after he'd fallen asleep, maybe she'd call Ahmed and invite him over. Sneak him in. Take him, too.

*O*nce upon a time over a Thanksgiving weekend, a handsome Iranian-American man named Ahmed and a blond, blue-eyed boy named Henry went to lunch at the Arizona Inn with Meg and Phillip.

The boy wore his best dress clothes and his high-top sneakers and sat at the table like a big kid. All of a sudden, he was *a big kid—a player, just like us, a player in the game of life.* When the grown-ups had tea after lunch, he did, too, sipping in rhythm with you, Ahmed sticking his pinky out, like you, setting his fragile porcelain teacup in its saucer with the softest of clinks. Like you, like you, like you.

Remember that?

You're a proper guy, conscious always of how you present yourself. And the Arizona Inn's a fancy place, where one speaks in a low voice and has to work to keep up with the politeness of the waitstaff. It's elegant. Hushed. Refined. Three things my boy is not.

And oh, that grand piano in the lounge! You can hardly blame a boy for sneaking over to play it. Dun, dun, dun, da-da-da-da-da-da-dun-dun-dun. "Heart and Soul," the beginner's joyful duet, played alone.

Even as he smiled the gracious smile that was part of his job description, the barkeep's eyes were unamused. A patron or two looked over to see if we'd rein that boy in, and inside myself, I cringed.

So smoothly you went to him, Ahmed, and slid onto the bench beside him. You had him begin again. A duet's meant for two, after all. Henry played the Heart part of the song, and you played the more complicated Soul.

Seeing you together like that, father and son no matter what any birth certificate said, made my father's eyes fill with tears. He's a keeper, Magpie, *he said, clamping his hand on mine.*

I told him I already knew you were a keeper.

Henry's got my heart, Ahmed—but you've got my soul.

One day the next week after school, Meg and Henry stopped at Whole Foods because it was their turn to bring fruit of the organic variety to soccer practice. Meg was still opposed to the organic fruit rule, both philosophically and practically.

Henry begged for the $4.99-a-pound plums and when Meg said no, he pleaded for the $3.99-a-pound grapes, to which she also said no. "We're getting bananas," she said. Bananas were three times cheaper than the grapes, and still ridiculously expensive in her opinion.

"Bradley hates bananas," Henry said.

"Boo-hoo for Bradley."

"Why can't we *ever* get what I want?" he complained.

"Henry." She fixed her best surely-you're-kidding look on him. "Did you forget about the very expensive iPod you just got?"

"Doh!" Henry gave himself a dope slap on the forehead. "Oh, yeah!"

Meg laughed. "It was not a cheap gift and I am not a rich

woman," she said. "And I'm not spending twenty bucks on fruit for a bunch of nine-year-olds. I'm just not."

"Can I at least get some Naked Juice?" Henry pointed to a refrigerated display. "I had it at Bradley's and it's really good."

"What's Naked Juice?"

"Oh my God, it's so good. It's got tons of fruit in it, like five or six pieces of fruit in one bottle, and it's sooooo good. Grandpa drinks it, too. I had some at his office. Please?"

"Bring me a bottle," she said. "Let me see it."

As Henry rushed off to get it, Meg counted out the requisite number of organic bananas. She'd noticed an old lady lingering near the peaches who'd seemed to be eavesdropping on her conversation with Henry. Now the woman leaned over to Meg and held out a peach to her.

"Smell this," she said.

Dutifully, Meg took the peach and raised it to her nose. Its pungency was remarkable. "This smells wonderful."

"I was remembering my mother," the old lady said. "She loved peaches but hated the fuzz, so I always had to peel her peaches for her. Peaches just aren't as fuzzy as they used to be, except for these organic ones. Only the organic ones smell like this anymore, either." She picked up another peach and held it to her nose. Meg was sure the old lady was back sixty years ago in her childhood kitchen with her long-dead mother, and she stifled the urge to cry.

"I used to refuse to eat apple peels," Meg said. "My dad bought this humongous apple peeler which my mother hated, and he attached it to the kitchen counter, and he'd peel my apples so the skin would wind around like a snake and dangle in one long, curvy string. It was the neatest thing."

"Is your father still alive?" the woman asked.

"He is," Meg said.

"Then treasure him." The woman gingerly put the peach she was holding back onto the display. "I never did much care for peaches, myself."

Henry bounded back. "Here it is, Mom. Can we get it?"

Meg wrinkled her nose as she examined the bottle. "It's green, Henry."

"Grandpa says green stuff's really healthy," he said. "It's superfood."

"And you think that just because you're a super kid you should have superfood?"

"Ma-om!"

"Yes, you can get the Naked Juice. Go get one for Ahmed, too, because he's a super soccer coach."

Henry headed off, and Meg tore off a plastic Baggie. She'd decided to buy a few peaches.

"He's a beautiful boy," the woman said.

"Thank you," Meg said. "He's got his father's eyes."

Meg was astounded when she said it, despite the fact that it was absolutely true.

Soccer practice had turned into one of Meg's favorite ways to pass the time because it gave her ninety unobstructed minutes to ogle Ahmed. The more intimately she knew his body, the more tantalizing she found him. He was so darn ogle-worthy it wasn't funny.

In the car on the way home after practice, Meg smelled the distinct odor of manufactured watermelon. She glanced in the rearview mirror and saw Henry pop a piece of the gum Jonathan had given her into his mouth.

"Where'd you get that?" she said.

"From your purse."

"You know you're not supposed to go in my purse without asking, Henry."

He grinned at her. "Can I have a piece of gum?"

"No, you may not."

"You need to get better about sharing, Mom." He blew a bubble at her, which exploded on his nose.

"Serves you right," she said. "Not to brag, but I'm probably the best bubble-gum blower in all of Tucson."

"Not for long," Henry said.

By the time they arrived at the apartment complex, Henry had three pieces of gum in his mouth and couldn't even chew with his mouth closed. As they passed the manager's office, Harley was just locking up.

"Hey, Meg," he said. "Perfect timing. You've got a delivery in the office."

"I do? Who's it from?"

"New York."

Jonathan. Meg could feel her breath escaping.

"New York's not a person," Henry pointed out.

"Henry, why don't you run along and see if you can find Violet? I'll be at the Loop Group table in just a minute."

Henry looked at her for a long moment and she could tell he was deciding whether to cut her a break. Her face must have been pale, or tense, or frightened, because Harley studied her with interest and then told Henry to be off.

When Harley tried to give her the envelope, Meg recog-

nized Jonathan's handwriting and wouldn't take it. "This will
be the demand for visitation he swore he didn't want." After
swearing Harley to secrecy, Meg told him about Jonathan's
visit. "I was a total pushover, all because he gave me a pack of
bubble gum."

She asked Harley to open the envelope for her and braced
herself as he slit it open and pulled out the card inside. She
tried to extrapolate from his expression what sort of reaction
its contents warranted, but Harley kept his face neutral as he
scanned it.

"Well?" she said. "How bad is it going to get for me?"

Harley looked up and gave her a broad grin. "Happy birthday," he said. "Happy Thanksgiving, Merry Christmas and
Happy Hanukkah, all rolled into one."

Meg's heart thundered. "What're you talking about?"

Harley roared with laughter and then read the card out
loud. "'Dear Meg, It was great seeing you. You're as beautiful
as ever. Since you didn't like the gum—Regards, Jonathan.'"

"I don't get it," Meg said.

Harley laughed again. "He sent you a check, Meg. For a
hundred thousand dollars." He separated the check that was
paper-clipped to the card and waved it at her. "You're rich!"

Feeling the room spin, Meg leaned against his desk. "Please
don't joke."

"It's no joke." Harley read from the check. "'Pay to the
order of . . . Meg Clark, one hundred thousand dollars.' Here.
See for yourself."

He thrust the check at her. Meg counted. One, two, three,
four, *five* zeros after the one.

She stared at Harley, then at the check, then at Harley again.

One

Hundred

Thousand

Dollars

Signed, Jonathan Clark.

RE: Services rendered.

Jonathan had scrawled the note at an angle, casually, as if in a hurry. As if a hundred thousand dollars meant nothing to him.

"This is what he owes me in back child support," she said. "Where would a public defender get his hands on this kind of money?" As soon as she said it, Meg knew. It was from his inheritance.

"Who cares?" Harley said. "Just deposit it before he changes his mind and puts a stop payment on it."

A hundred thousand dollars was crazy money. It was run-away-to-Paris money. Get-big-screen-TVs-for-every-room money. It was buy-a-house money. It was money in the bank. A safety net. Breathing room.

Meg called Jonathan that night after Henry was asleep. She took a blanket out to the patio, wrapped herself in it and called him. His hello was sleepy.

"Did I call too late?" Meg said. It was after midnight in New York. "You used to be such the night owl."

"I'd just gone to bed," he said.

"Is that check for real?" she asked.

Jonathan chuckled. "It's for real."

"Are you trying to buy your way back into my life?"

"That's not why I sent it, Meg," he said. "I sent it because I owe you."

"You're trying to cancel out in the span of a week all the years you did me wrong," she said.

"I'm trying to rewrite history."

"But you can't do that."

"Yes, you can," Jonathan said. "People do it all the time."

She tried to imagine him at that moment, in an apartment in a big city, alone in the darkness under the covers, lying flat on his back in his bed, talking to her on the phone. He'd be naked, since he'd always slept in the nude. *It's lonely being naked alone.*

"You know what hurt the most?" Meg said. "How you never called me. Not even once. It made me feel like I wasn't worth anything. I was carrying our baby, and you couldn't have cared less."

"I thought about you nearly every hour of every day for years," Jonathan said. "I swear it's true."

"Bullshit."

"I knew the exact minute Henry was born," he told her. "I was in Central Park and there were these kids on a swing. They kept going higher and higher, red coats, big smiles, and they'd caught my eye, and all of a sudden, I felt this warmth in my heart. I don't know how else to describe it. I just knew he'd been born. I called your sister later that day, and sure enough, I'd finally put some good out into this godforsaken world with the birth of our son."

"It doesn't do me a bit of good to hear this now," Meg said. "And it should have been me you called that day, not my sister."

"I thought your father would kill me."

"What am I supposed to do with a hundred thousand dollars?" she asked.

"Pretty much anything you want."

"But the same holds true for you," Meg said. "This is life-changing money."

"I did what I wanted with the money," Jonathan said. "I gave it to you."

"As part of your feeble attempt to rewrite history?"

"That's right." It was good to hear him laugh. "Although I was going for heroic."

"Heroic's a stretch." Meg smiled into the darkness beyond her patio. "But it's a start. I'll give you that."

Meg hid the card and check in her kitchen junk drawer underneath the "Mothering the Fatherless Boy" article her mother had given her. Hidden yet handy, she could examine it as often as she wanted. *A hundred thousand dollars.* With that kind of money, a person could right a lot of wrongs.

Meg began with Amy. Ever since she'd blown up at her for still being in touch with Jonathan, things had been eggshell-tiptoey between them. Amy had worked so hard to prepare her usual excellent Thanksgiving dinner. Meg hadn't been very appreciative and she'd felt bad ever since. Jonathan *had* always been exceptionally kind to Amy—because of his urging, she'd gotten her first of eventually three poems published in *The Sun.*

So Meg made reservations for the two of them at the Elizabeth Arden Red Door Spa at the Westin La Paloma. Amy found a babysitter and met her there. Meg had offered Ahmed a multitude of sexual favors in exchange for watching Henry for a little while before and a little while after soccer practice. He assured her the favors were appreciated but not necessary.

When Meg arrived at the Westin, Amy was already there and she threw her arms around Meg. "I don't deserve this treat. I haven't been a very good sister. I'm sorry for going behind your back and being in touch with Jonathan all these years."

"I'm the one who's sorry," Meg said. "As Dad says, it's really none of my business if you and Jonathan are still on friendly terms."

"It's really none of *Dad's* business," Amy said. "But whatever."

"Are you ready?" Meg kept up her spirit of enthusiasm as she looked at the bright red door through which they would walk. Tall and wide, the door alone made her feel out of her league. Plus, she didn't especially like people waiting on her, but perhaps, like dark chocolate, it was an acquired taste. "Should we go pick our pampering?" she asked.

"This isn't cheap," Amy warned.

"Maybe I came into a little money," Meg said.

"Well?" As Amy waited expectantly, Meg imagined in a flash what she'd experience in reality if she told Amy about the money: her heart would quicken at the sharing of her secret. *You'll never believe it,* she'd say. *But you can't tell anyone.* Amy's eyes would widen. She'd squeal. Clutch her. Congratulate her. Tell her how lucky she was. Say, *See, he's not such a bad guy.*

Which perhaps was true. But even if Jonathan was no longer her bad guy, Ahmed *was* still her good guy, and she hadn't as yet been able to bring herself to tell him she'd seen Jonathan. He'd been sad and worried that night she'd told him about Jonathan's call, and while she was relieved she'd told him about it, she had to believe that her seeing Jonathan would bother Ahmed—especially being told after the fact, *especially* after he'd told her how important truthfulness was, *especially* since the secret meeting was followed up by an outrageously large check. Every hour that went by, Meg felt as if she was lying by not telling him and resolved again that she'd tell him . . . but still, the hours ticked on by and still he didn't know. So now she was lying to herself, too.

But Meg decided that until she told Ahmed, she wouldn't tell anyone else.

"Maybe I'll tell you another time," Meg said to Amy. "For now let's treat ourselves well."

Faking bravery, she pulled open the poppy red door. As she approached the receptionist, she felt like a kid tiptoeing behind the altar at church. This was not a place where she belonged. The lobby furniture alone probably cost more than the hundred thousand dollars she'd been given.

After they checked in, they took the menu of spa options to a red leather couch and huddled together, examining it. *Abhyanga*—what the heck was that? *Shiatsu? Reiki?* These were not words from Meg's world. *Craniosacral* must have something to do with the head—a fifty-minute head massage? No, thanks. And if she wanted hot stones on her body, couldn't she just lie down on a hiking trail somewhere in the desert?

"Is anything jumping out at you?" she asked Amy.

"The Signature Stress Melter Ritual's got my name all over it," Amy said. "But it takes almost two hours, so it wouldn't leave time for anything else." She made a boo-hoo face.

"You wanted a facial and a hand-toe thing, too, didn't you?" Meg said.

"A mani-pedi, you mean?"

"Whatever," Meg said. "I guess I failed spa talk one-oh-one in college." She bit her lip as she looked around the plush lobby. "I hate it when places don't list prices."

"Let's ask," Amy said.

Meg shook her head, knowing the prices would start her on her usual downward spiral. For this money, she could buy every student in her class a new pair of shoes . . . or five days of college for Henry . . . or immunizations for all of Africa. No, it was better not to know.

"For once, I want to make a decision about something that isn't based on money," she said. "Or my lack of it, which is more often the case. Whatever it costs, we deserve it."

"I think that's a really bad idea." Amy went to the reception desk and looked over the price list. After studying it, she said something to the receptionist and sat back down next to Meg. "You know what I'd really like? A piece of chocolate raspberry mousse cake."

Meg looked around for the cafe. "I didn't realize they served food here."

"They don't, you goof," Amy said. "I'm talking about at AJ's."

Ah, AJ's Fine Foods, for fine, rich people. "I don't think we're going to have time to go there, too," Meg said.

"I mean I'd rather do that than this." Amy put her hand on Meg's knee. "I'm really touched you brought me here, but this isn't me. It's just not how I'd ever choose to relax. I'd rather take a nap. Or even better, I'd rather have coffee and dessert—with my sister and without my kids. Would you mind horribly if we did that instead?"

Mind? Heck, no. No arm-twisting necessary. "That's fine with me," Meg said. "As long as you're not saying it just because of the cost."

"I'm not," Amy promised. "Every time we're at AJ's, I let the girls pick whatever dessert they want—anything—and I always say, *Make sure you get what you really, really want, because Mommy's not sharing.* And then they pick a chocolate-chip cookie or some stupid thing, and before I've even taken the first bite of my chocolate raspberry mousse cake, they poke their fingers in it to lick the frosting. It drives me crazy! Can't I have *anything* all to myself? Just a friggin' piece of cake—is that asking for too much?"

She had actual tears in her eyes.

"You poor, put-upon, stay-at-home mom," Meg teased. "Don't be so selfish."

"When did selfishness become such a crime?" Amy asked. "That's what I want to know."

If selfishness was a crime, then the desserts they got were truly sinful. They sat in front of the fireplace on the patio at AJ's. Amy, of course, got the cake, while Meg got cheesecake.

"I'm so totally in heaven right now." Amy held a forkful out to Meg. "Want a bite?"

"After your sob story back there? No way!" Meg said.

"This is different," Amy said. "I *want* to share with you."

"No, thanks." Meg held up a forkful of her cheesecake. "I'm pretty happy myself."

"I swear, this cake is food for my soul," Amy said. "Why do we not do this sort of thing more often?"

"Because each slice has about a million calories?" Meg suggested.

Amy's face fell. "Meg? I need a new life."

"Maybe you could start a business baking personalized, individual chocolate raspberry mousse cakes for stressed-out moms who don't want to share," Meg suggested.

Amy rolled her eyes. "Funny."

"You don't need a new life," Meg said. "You just need small changes to the life you already have. The simple things in life are actually the finer things in life. For instance, when's the last time you wrote any poetry?"

"Poetry. Right," Amy said. "I could scribble it on the walls with the girls' crayons in my spare time. Oh, wait. I forgot. I don't have any spare time."

"So cynical," Meg said. "I thought chocolate was supposed to kick-start happy hormones."

Amy laughed. "I'm such an ingrate, aren't I? How's this—I look forward to indulging in the writing of poetry after my beautiful girls are out of the house."

"But you won't be the same person then as you are now," Meg said. "And who you are now's important, too."

"Good point," Amy said through a mouthful of cake. It really *did* look heavenly. Meg decided she'd get one to go and share it with Henry. She could certainly afford it. "I could at least write *bad* poetry now, and then make it better once I have the time."

"There's the spirit! And maybe you *should* write it on the walls in crayon, because what the hell, they're only walls."

Amy's mouth dropped open, but she had a gleam in her eyes. "I couldn't do that. It's naughty."

"It's appropriate naughtiness," Meg said. "Do it in the laundry room. Whoever goes in there besides you?"

"I'm going to," Amy said. "*Appropriate naughtiness.* That'll be the title of my first poem, which I shall dedicate to you."

"Here, here." Meg raised her coffee cup in a toast. "To appropriate naughtiness."

"To appropriate naughtiness," Amy agreed. "Speaking of which, can I ask whatever happened between you and Jonathan?"

If only I understood it myself, Meg thought. But she explained as best she could about her visit to the lawyer, about how she'd called him on Thanksgiving and seen him the day after. She told Amy about the powerful rush of feelings his visit had stirred in her, how they'd spoken on the phone since his visit and how she'd dreamed of him the previous night. The only thing Meg left out was the check.

"What does Ahmed think of all this?" Amy asked.

Meg cringed. "Beyond the first phone call, he doesn't know anything about anything."

"Good," Amy said. "It's none of his business."

"How can you say that?" Meg said. "This is someone I'm hoping to spend the rest of my life with!"

"Trust me, he doesn't want to know," Amy said. "Even if he thinks he does, he doesn't. Did I ever tell you Peter Flynn called me last year?"

"Ooh, sexy Peter Flynn," Meg said. "He was hot."

Amy reddened. "Did you know I slept with him in high school?"

"What! No! You didn't!"

He'd been one of Catalina High's resident bad boys. He'd had too-long hair, sung in a hateful punk band, and probably been stoned or worse throughout most of high school. But none of that negated the fact that he was the hottest guy in Amy's class.

"We were at this football game, and he was with his friends

and I was with mine and he leaned over and goes, *Hey, let's get out of here.*" Amy buried her face in her hands and laughed at the memory. "I was shocked he even knew who I was!"

"So you just *had* to sleep with him," Meg said.

"Hello, I *wanted* to sleep with him." Amy giggled. "He introduced me to the pleasure of the one-night stand."

"Amy!"

"Do you want to hear my story or not?"

"Of course I do!"

"So Peter Flynn called me last year out of the blue—he'd Googled me or something—and like an idiot, I told David."

"Did you blush and giggle when you told David, too? Like you are right now?"

"No, but it brought up all these ridiculous questions about my past. Men don't want you to have a past. They want to believe your life started the moment you met them. And if you're smart, you let them. *Oh, I've never loved like this before. I never even knew what love* was *before I met you.* That's what they want to hear."

"Ahmed's not like that," Meg said.

Amy shrugged. "So tell him."

"You think I should?"

"Hell, no," Amy said. "There *is* a line with these things, Meg, which unfortunately isn't always obvious until it's been crossed. My advice? Cease and desist with Jonathan right now, because if you haven't already crossed the line, you're darn close to it."

Meg traded some watching-the-kids time with Violet's mother later in the week and took Ahmed on a surprise date to Seven Cups, a Chinese tea shop on Sixth Street. She'd read in *Tucson Green Magazine* that it was the premier Chinese tea supplier in the world—right there! Six blocks from her house and it was the best in the world! And even though Ahmed was Persian and not Chinese, Meg thought he might enjoy some world-class tea. Besides, it was the thought that counted, and for that, Meg hoped to score major good-girlfriend points.

They went at the end of what had been a stressful workday for Ahmed, and the moment they entered the small tea shop, the world outside fell away. Soft Eastern music invited them in, and the lights in the shop were dimmed. Meg watched how Ahmed's face relaxed into calmness, like Henry's did after a nice backrub.

"Have you been here before?" Meg spoke in a quiet voice, as did virtually everyone in the shop. In the back there was a fish tank, which Henry would love—maybe they'd bring him along next time.

Ahmed shook his head. "I've noticed it as I've driven by, but I've never stopped in before."

The retail part of the store was in the front and the tables in the back, and as they waited, unsure whether they should seat themselves, Meg slipped her hand into Ahmed's and kissed his cheek. "Maybe if there were sidewalks out front, more people would walk by, notice it and stop to visit. Oh, wait. The RTA'll take care of that. I keep forgetting."

He grinned at her. "You're not going to let that drop, are you?"

"Nope," she said happily.

As he put his arm around her shoulders and squeezed her to him, an Asian woman approached and escorted them to a middle table, leaving them to study the tea menu.

"What do you recommend?" Meg asked Ahmed.

"Sadly, I usually drink Lipton's Earl Grey tea," he said. "Iranians drink a lot of tea, but I don't know that our tea palates are very refined. It's more the ritual that's important."

"Just what is the ritual?"

"You'll see," Ahmed said. "For me, the very act of preparing a cup of tea for myself often changes the course of my day. It's very calming."

Meg chose a yellow tea, since she'd never heard of it before, and she ordered it in a glass rather than a pot. Ahmed ordered black tea in a pot.

They were served and their conversation meandered quietly as they waited for their tea to steep and cool. It was a skill, Meg thought as she watched how Ahmed filled the requisite wait time with a gentle story here and a funny comment there. There was a real art to his conversation that Meg hadn't noticed before. She could feel herself being led by him, drawn into the expansively cozy mood he was establishing.

"You *are* different when you have tea." Meg twisted her

glass gently, watching the tea leaves float downward. "It's as if this moment is in your blood and you're coming home to it."

He smiled at the observation. "In Iran, nothing of importance is discussed until several cups of tea have been consumed."

They chatted and enjoyed their tea, and when a fiftyish American man approached their table and asked how they liked the tea, Ahmed asked if he was the owner. He was, and introduced himself.

"Austin Hodge." He shook first Ahmed's hand and then Meg's as they introduced themselves.

He correctly guessed that Ahmed was from Iran and asked him questions that indicated he was more familiar with the country than the average American was. "I'm fascinated by Iran," he said when Meg pointed this out. "Probably because I've always wanted to go there." He told of the one tea-growing region in Iran and asked Ahmed if he had read any Rumi and told him a Sufi story he knew. His manner was gracious and giving and he stood with his fingers linked in a unique yin-yang position, which Meg found delightful and immediately imitated, finding it established her firmly in the moment and made her feel at peace.

"He was so cool," Meg said after Austin Hodge left.

"It's nice to find people who actually know something about Persian culture," Ahmed said. "You don't see that every day. He knows more than I do about Rumi and Hafez and Sufiism."

"Do you study Persian history?" Meg asked, making a mental note for future gift-giving opportunities.

"You know," Ahmed said, "I have studied it a bit, but I've come to realize I'm not all that interested in the glories of the past. The Persian Empire. Cyrus the Great. The rugs, the poetry. Give me the modern writers and artists and filmmakers any day. Creativity's thriving in Iran, in spite of the repressive government."

"Maybe because of it," Meg suggested.

"I have a few books that I bet the owner of this place would find interesting," Ahmed said. "I should drop them off."

"I'd like to read them, too," Meg said.

"You would? Essays and short stories and poetry by Iranian writers?"

"Sure," she said. "Or maybe you could read them to me. I think I'd like that best of—"

She was interrupted by her cell phone, which brayed out rudely in the hushed tea shop. She quickly reached to silence it.

"It's my dad," she said. "I'd better take this." Meg was sure she was violating all sorts of tea-taking protocol by answering the phone. "Sorry," she beseeched Ahmed. "He's just going through a tough time right now."

"Go ahead," Ahmed said.

"How's my favorite father today?" Meg said by way of greeting. "I'm having a lovely tea date with Ahmed, so I can't talk long. What's up?"

"You're with Ahmed?" Phillip asked. "Did he tell you we met for lunch today?"

"No, he didn't tell me you met for lunch today." Meg eyed Ahmed, but he gave no indication he'd even heard what she'd said, even though he must have. "Did you invite him or did he invite you?"

"He invited me," Phillip said.

Meg gasped as a crazy thought came to her: maybe Ahmed

had asked her dad for permission to marry her! He was the type to honor such a custom. She couldn't tell if she was right by looking at Ahmed, though, because his expression remained frustratingly neutral.

"What'd you talk about?" she asked her dad. She was probably off base anyway.

"Oh, this and that." Phillip cleared her throat. "I'm sorry to bother you," he said, "but I was hoping you could go to the house and get my baseball-card collection. I left it in the hall closet."

Her father's baseball-card collection was probably as valuable to him as either of his daughters, and that was only a slight exaggeration. "I can't believe you didn't take it with you."

"It completely slipped my mind," he said.

"That's understandable considering the circumstances," Meg said. "But you can't really think Mom would do anything to it, do you? She knows how much it means to you."

"'Hell hath no fury like a woman scorned,'" he said.

"But she's the one who scorned you," Meg said. "She's been scorning you for longer than I've been alive. Sure, I'll get it. I'll head out in a few minutes."

Meg agreed to stop by the house on her way home, and Phillip would come over to pick up the card collection after the UA baseball team practice. After Meg hung up, she looked expectantly at Ahmed. "Well?" she asked. "We've been sitting here for over an hour making small talk. Were you planning to tell me about your lunch date with my father?"

"I had lunch with your father today," Ahmed said.

Meg laughed. "Really? What a surprise! Did you talk about anything interesting?"

"Not about anything I can tell you at the moment," Ahmed said. Meg waited for a teasing smile, or a hint of dampened excitement, but he was impossible to read.

"That's it?" she prompted. "That's all you're going to say about it?"

"Yep."

Meg sipped her tea, disconcerted. Ahmed's engaging and unguarded mood had soured with her father's phone call, and it was her fault. "Again, I'm sorry for answering my phone," she said. "It was rude of me. I shouldn't have."

Ahmed reached for her hand across the table. "I like that you're there for your father, no matter what. It's a great quality and one of the things I love about you the most."

Meg sensed his sadness. "I know you'd like to be there for your dad, too. I wish he'd let you."

"Fathers feel they have to be heroes in their kids' eyes," he said. "But I'd take a flawed father who loves me over a nonexistent father any day of the week. Wouldn't you?"

His look was intense with conviction, and as Meg looked into the brown eyes she loved so much, she saw the heart of the boy he'd been. She saw Henry's heart, too, and it occurred to her that without knowing it, Ahmed was speaking for Henry as well as for himself: a flawed father was better than no father at all, as long as that father loved his child the best he could. The implications of Meg's realization were huge, but they could not be denied.

"I think maybe yes," she agreed. "As long as there's love amidst the flaws."

Meg pulled up to her parents' house—make that her mother's house—and looked at it from the curb for a long moment. It was a weird feeling, to think how a house could end up being more permanent than the family who lived in it.

At the front door, she punched the bell and listened to the familiar ding-*ding*-ding and waited for her mother's footsteps. When she didn't hear them, Meg rang the bell again. Still nothing, but she could see her mother's new convertible in the garage, so Meg walked around to the backyard to see if maybe Clarabelle was there.

When she wasn't, Meg's gut kicked out a warning: something wasn't right. She walked back around to the front, and as she did, she flipped open her cell phone and speed-dialed her mother. Through the closed windows, she heard the phone ring inside, but no one answered.

Meg's heart quickened. She rang the doorbell insistently and redialed her mother's number. When the answering machine came on, she began a frantic are-you-all-right tirade of a message. Only then did her mother pick up. "Meg?"

"Mom! Where *are* you? Are you okay? I've been ringing the doorbell for ten minutes now! Are you *there*? Are you inside?"

There was no mistaking the exasperation in her mother's

voice. "Well, of course I'm inside, Meg. This isn't a cell phone, you know."

"Open the door," Meg said. "Let me in."

There was silence on Clarabelle's end.

"Mom?"

"I really wish you'd call before stopping over," Clarabelle said. "I'm busy right now."

"Doing what, watching *Wheel of Fortune*?" Meg said. "Open the door or I'm going to break it down."

Clarabelle harrumphed, and from the change in her breathing, Meg could tell she was coming to let her in, berating her the entire way: who talks to their mother this way? Why don't people respect privacy these days? Why do people think just because someone's home they're required to answer their door?

Wa-wah-wa-wah-wa-wah-wa.

It was like those Charlie Brown cartoons: the instant Clarabelle kicked into her holier-than-thou, rhetorical-question bullshit, Meg stopped listening. But Clarabelle sure got Meg's attention back in a hurry when she opened the front door.

Her mother—her *mother*, hello!—stood before Meg in strappy high heels and a gorgeous, elegant, deep blue silk— Meg didn't even know the word for it—dressing gown—was that what it was called? Rich-lady lingerie?

Clarabelle's hair was mussed and something about her was clearly out of sorts. Her lips looked not bruised but a bit puffy and her makeup, while not exactly wrong, was not exactly right, either. It looked like it had sort of been schmeared around in the throes of . . . Meg was dumbfounded. She'd never seen her mother like this, but there was no denying it:

Clarabelle looked like she'd just had great sex. Meg stared at her mother and tried to shake off the thought, tried to come up with an alternative explanation. "Were you asleep?"

"Of course not," Clarabelle said. "It's only six o'clock."

"Then why are you dressed like that?"

Clarabelle raised her chin haughtily. "If you must know, I'm entertaining a gentleman caller."

"A *what*?"

Clarabelle enunciated her words this time, even though they'd been perfectly clear before. "A gentleman caller."

"You're getting *laid*?"

"Must you be so crude?"

Talk about crude! Clarabelle was still a married woman!

"I'd be willing to bet a hundred thousand dollars it's not Dad in there," Meg said.

Clarabelle rolled her eyes. "Your father—now there's a losing bet," she said. "All he ever did was age me, sitting around watching baseball on ESPN all the time. I feel like I've gained back ten years of my life since he's been gone. Maybe twenty!"

"But . . . but . . . ," Meg sputtered. "Who have you been having sex with?"

Clarabelle looked for a moment like she wasn't going to answer. Meg raised her eyebrows to let her know she'd wait as long as it took.

"If you must know, it's the furniture salesman," Clarabelle said. "Andy."

"Tell me you're joking," Meg said. "He's my age!"

Clarabelle's eyes twinkled. "Two years younger, actually."

That made him thirty-two, to Clarabelle's fifty-eight. Or to her forever fifty-five, as she preferred to call it. She was such the Demi Moore. "This is *not* appropriate naughtiness, Mother," she said.

Clarabelle scoffed. "I've been appropriate my whole married life, and excuse me for saying so, but naughty's far more fun!"

"Mother!" Meg couldn't help but laugh. This was girlfriend talk, not mother-daughter talk.

"Oh, come on, Meg," Clarabelle said. "He's here, he's willing. He's more than able. I'm climbing back in the saddle, so to speak."

Meg shuddered at the image. "Fine," she said. "But you should do it with someone closer to your own age."

Clarabelle put her hands on her hips. "Now that's just stupid talk. Think about it. A man Andy's age doesn't need little blue pills to make the magic happen. Andy does triathlons. You know what that means, right?"

"It means he does triathlons," Meg said.

"It means he's got stamina that doesn't come from a pharmacy," Clarabelle said. "*Goodness*, he's got stamina! How is that not better than being with a man my age?"

Meg laughed again. "You may have a point there." But she quickly turned serious again. "I don't want to see you getting hurt."

"I'm not climbing Mount Everest, Meg. I'm just having sex." Clarabelle glanced to her closed bedroom door. "Men date younger women all the time."

"But it won't last," Meg said. "You know that, right?"

"Don't worry about me," Clarabelle said. "My eyes are wide-open—except when they're closed. I'm just having a little fun recapturing my youth, after a long time of life not being very fun."

"You don't feel . . . I don't know . . . ?"

"Foolish?" Clarabelle supplied the word Meg didn't want to say. "No, not at all. I refuse to. Sometimes I look in the mirror and I see the wrinkles and the age spots and the thinning hair and the saggy jowl, and I think, *Who is that woman?* Because it's not me. Inside, I'm the same as I was in my early twenties. Or maybe I'm back to who I was and wanted to be after a lifetime of trying to be what society pushed me to be, which was a proper, boring, aging woman. I'm not robbing the cradle," she said defiantly. "If anyone is, he is."

"But you're still married, Mom," Meg reminded her. "Who's supposed to tell Dad?"

Clarabelle waved her off and inched the door closed. "Believe me, he's so busy with his girlfriend that he won't notice, and if he does, he won't mind a bit . . . although Sandi's hardly a triathlete, come to think of it. Now thanks for stopping by, but—"

Sandi? Not again. Her mother was delusional. Meg stuck her foot in the doorframe. "I need to get something," she said. "Can I come in? It'll only take a minute."

Clarabelle gave her a pinched-nose reply. "I don't think so." She tried to close the door, but again Meg stopped her.

"I promised Dad that I'd pick something up for him. It's in the hall closet, and I'll only be a second, I promise. Then you can get back to your triathlete."

Clarabelle narrowed her eyes. "What is it you want to get for him?"

"His baseball-card collection."

Clarabelle rolled her eyes. "Of course. The sun rises and sets on that baseball-card collection. You wait here. I'll get it."

Meg poked her head inside, both to keep an eye on her mother and to check out the progress on her redecorating project. The living room was completely cleared out, and the absence of ugly furniture was itself a great improvement. There was a fresh coat of cream paint on the walls, and the crap-brown carpet had been removed to reveal gleaming hardwood floors. Meg shook her head to see such beauty underneath. Their house—their home, their family—could have been glorious if only they'd attended to it, kept up with the changing times, but there'd been no progress, no growth, no reinvention. While Meg looked around, Clarabelle pulled a manila envelope from one of the closet shelves and brought it to her.

"This isn't it," Meg said. "It's in all those binders and shoe boxes, remember?"

"Oh, I remember," Clarabelle said. "This is all that's left. I sold the rest."

When Meg gasped, Clarabelle shrugged, unrepentant.

"How else was I supposed to pay for my new car?" she asked. "And the furniture I've got on order? But don't worry. I didn't sell his favorite player. I saved all the Pete Rose ones because your father's a cheater, just like him."

"I don't know how to tell him," Meg said to Ahmed later that night. They were on her patio, watching the sunset and drinking wine. After leaving the tea shop, Ahmed had come back to her apartment to collect Henry while Meg went to her mother's house. Henry was now inside playing Monopoly with Violet.

"I mean, beyond the fact that she wasted no time getting herself a boy toy, Dad loved those baseball cards," Meg said. "How do you tell a man you love something that you know is going to break his heart?"

"Very carefully," Ahmed said.

"My dad had thousands of baseball cards, probably every single one produced from the fifties through the seventies." From the envelope Clarabelle had given her, Meg pulled out eight career-spanning Pete Rose cards—all that were left.

"Were the cards she sold really worth enough for her to buy a car?" Ahmed asked.

"I doubt it," Meg said. "I'm sure she just did it for spite. She knew how much they meant to him. You should have seen him. He had all the greats—Hank Aaron, Robin Yount, Ted Williams, Willie Mays. He knew all their stats, all their stories. But Pete Rose was his favorite. Pete Rose was his guy."

"What was so special about him?" Ahmed said.

"My dad just identified with him for some reason," she

said. "I'll never forget the night Pete Rose broke the record for most hits. All four of us watched the game together in the den. It's actually one of my favorite memories of the whole family together. We were all so excited, mostly because it was great to see my dad so happy."

She remembered the moment with clarity even after all these years. "Dad grabbed Mom and twirled her around and kissed her with total passion," she said. "My sister and I acted like we were completely grossed out, but really, it was nice to see."

Meg stared at the fresh-faced Pete Rose card on top and sighed. "And then he got caught cheating."

"How'd he cheat?"

"He was a big gambler," Meg said. "He bet on baseball— even on games where he was manager. He says he never bet against his team, but to this day, no one other than him knows for sure. My dad says it's easier to influence a loss than to make a win happen."

"Do you think that, too?" Ahmed studied her closely.

With a sigh, she sifted through the Pete Rose cards again. His eyes had hardened as the years went by. In his later pictures, he seemed jaded, broken. Life had taken its toll.

"I remember the day the accusations broke," she said. "It was horrible. My father looked like he'd lost his best friend. He just sat disbelieving as he watched the report on the nightly news. He went for a walk by himself afterward, which he almost never did, and when he came home, he complained of a headache and was the first one in bed. I think his heart broke a little that day. For sure, the world seemed less kind."

Ahmed studied her closely, and even as Meg wondered why, she was thinking of her mother in her rich-lady lingerie and the accusations she'd made against Meg's father. She was thinking of her father's new office furniture and his newfound focus on his health and how Bud was fly-fishing in Montana now. She was thinking how clearly conflicted her dad seemed lately.

"Oh my God," she said, with sudden realization. "My father's having an affair."

Ahmed reached for her hand and Meg was glad for it. Without it she'd go in search of a sink to crawl under, or a drain that could wash her away. She looked in desperation at Ahmed, her calm-souled boyfriend in whom still waters ran deep. At Ahmed, who'd just a short while ago gotten her to agree that a flawed father was better than no father at all. "You knew, didn't you?"

"He told me at lunch today," Ahmed admitted.

"But why?" Meg asked. "Why would he tell you and not me?"

"He's afraid you'll never speak to him again," Ahmed said. "He knows how you feel about cheating. He does want to tell you, but he doesn't know how."

Meg felt sick. "How long has it been going on?"

"Several years," Ahmed said.

Which came first? Meg wondered. Had he had the affair, and any others before it, because her mom was so grumpy, or did she become grumpy because of the affairs?

Meg looked again at the Pete Rose cards. What an asshole he'd turned out to be.

"He's basically been lying to me for years," she said.

"He loves you, though."

"Love's not enough," Meg said, remembering Jonathan's words from the park that day.

"I disagree," Ahmed said. "Love is enough, if you decide it is."

As Meg climbed the ramp of the Frank Sancet Stadium at the University of Arizona campus, she carried the manila envelope that contained her father's Pete Rose cards.

He was there for a casual practice, and Meg knew that while the stadium would be nearly empty, he'd still be sitting in his season-ticket spot.

For the first time in Meg's memory, he wasn't alone.

Sandi was with him, wearing a bright red sweater and a U of A baseball hat over her black beehived hair. Phillip's arm was around her and clearly had been for years.

Observing them from behind, Meg trembled in the chilly December air. A blanket was spread across their respective laps—Sandi's contribution, Meg was sure, since she'd never seen her father cozied up at a baseball event before.

Meg watched them for a long time. She'd witnessed first-hand the years of belittlement, the decades of disappointment in her parents' marriage. She knew that for many, many years her father had forgone compassion, the human touch, peace in his own home. The office had been his refuge, so it was no surprise that he'd sought comfort there. He was not gregarious, not a charmer, not a seducer or a letch. He was an everyman who pushed his out-of-date glasses back up on his aging face and who smoothed his hands over his ever-thinning graying hair.

With Sandi, he wouldn't be lonely.

Meg took a seat in the back bleachers. Her father and Sandi looked like any old married couple on one of their better days. Sandi laughed at something her father said, then adjusted the blanket so they were better covered. They were nerds, in the sweetest sense of the word. They'd take good care of each other.

But a father wasn't supposed to lie to his daughter, especially if his reasons weren't noble. Especially when he went around spouting platitudes like *If you want to know how a man feels about you, don't listen to a word he says. Instead, watch what he does. . . .* She'd listened with an open heart to everything he'd ever told her, and he'd turned out to be a liar.

Meg pulled her cell phone from her jean jacket, dialed her dad's number and watched him retrieve his phone from his pocket with his left hand while keeping his right arm around his mistress.

"Hi, Meg!" His eyes were on home plate, but Meg nonetheless saw his smile in profile. "How'd the supersecret mission go? Did you get the baseball cards?"

"Hey, Dad." Fighting to maintain a neutral tone, she cleared her throat. "There's something I need to ask you. Mom keeps saying you're having an affair, and I just want to ask you flat out: are you seeing Sandi?"

Phillip removed his arm from Sandi's shoulders and straightened in his seat. When Sandi looked at him, he made an oh-shit-we're-busted face at her.

And then he lied. "No," he said. "I'm not seeing anybody."

The stadium around Meg swirled and blurred; even Sandi for a moment wasn't clearly visible. A pinpoint of light was on

Phillip alone, the single lightbulb swinging in the interrogation room.

Even when they were staring you right in the face, you never saw the signs.

"You know you could tell me if you were." Meg kept her voice even. "I might actually be okay with it. In fact, it would be important to me that you told me the truth."

"I think your mother's seeing someone," he said. Sandi frowned at him.

"She is," Meg confirmed. "She's seeing a very decent thirty-two-year-old athlete. I'm asking about *you*, Dad. About you and Sandi."

When her father stood, Meg's heart quickened. If he turned, he'd see her. But he didn't. He stretched and reached for Sandi's hand. "It's a lonely world, Magpie."

"I know it is, Dad," she said. "I've been alone for a long time myself. And I know that even though you were with Mom, you were alone, too. I understand your loneliness."

So tell me. Tell the truth and I'll respect you in the morning.

"Dad?" Meg prompted.

"Sandi and I are very good friends," he said. "And I think there's a good chance we will date in the future. She's the kind of woman I can see myself being happy with."

Jonathan's leaving her had been the most painful experience of Meg's life, bar none. But watching her father smile at Sandi, thinking he was pulling a fast one on his daughter as she sat right behind him and watched him do it, ranked a very close second. Meg was fading. Evaporating. She gripped the edge of the bleacher, having no one anymore to keep her grounded.

As Ahmed had said, lying was a deal breaker.

"Is there anything else you should tell me?" Meg could hardly hear her own voice—that was how weak it came out. "Now's the time, Dad."

He sat back down next to Sandi. "Not that I can think of, Magpie. Were you able to get my baseball-card collection out of the house?"

The cocky son of a bitch had his arm back around Sandi. And it had been there for years, no matter what lie he was feeding Meg now.

"I think it's time you stopped calling me *Magpie*," she said. "I'm not a little kid anymore."

As the silence on the other end of the line screamed at her, Meg slipped down the back steps to the ground level of the stadium. She couldn't stand having her father in her sight, in her heart, in her life anymore.

Meg tossed into a trash can the envelope that contained the remainder of her father's only legacy from a hobby he'd loved for a lifetime.

"The baseball cards are gone," she said. "Every last one is gone."

When Meg arrived back home, the complex was readying itself for bed. Now that the sun had set, the pool's underwater lights glowed, beckoning the swimmer who'd break the smooth surface. The lawn sprinklers spurted, and curtains were drawn, shielding those inside from the world that had gone dark on them. Occasional laugh tracks punctured the otherwise still night.

When Meg caught sight of Ahmed on her patio, some of the brittleness left her heart. He'd stayed behind to keep an eye on Henry and Violet, who were into their third hour of Monopoly.

Ahmed—her protector, her lion. It wasn't true that she had no one anymore to keep her grounded. She had him. She rested her hand on his shoulder as she passed him to take a seat.

"I gave him the opportunity to come clean with me," she said. "He chose not to."

She tried to strike a match to light her vanilla-scented tabletop candle, but the flame sputtered and she had to strike a second one. That one never sparked. The third, however, flared cooperatively, and after she lit the candle, Meg turned to Ahmed to take in his luminescence. He was beautiful by candlelight. Beautiful by any light, actually.

He looked far away, though. His right elbow rested on the table, his index finger pressed against his lower lip, as if he were rubbing away dead skin or the remnants of a kiss.

"Ahmed?" His eyes were dark. Haunted, almost. "Ahmed?" she said again.

He studied her for a long moment. Then from his lap he pulled out the envelope from Jonathan, inside of which was the card and the check.

"Oh shit." As Meg sank back in her chair, a meteor shot straight out of the sky and fell on her. Meg knew it would hurt like hell in the morning. He must have come across the envelope in her junk drawer, probably while in the midst of doing something nice for her son.

Dear Meg, it was great seeing you.

Ahmed's expression was noncommittal. "You've got one chance to explain this."

You're as beautiful as ever.

What could she say—*it's not what you think?*

Meg tried to take his hand.

"Don't," he said.

Meg picked up the book of matches, flipped the cover open, then tucked it closed again. Ahmed raised an eyebrow, and Meg knew he wasn't going to make things easy for her. "Can I just say, first, that besides Henry, you are the most important person in my life?"

"And yet . . . ," Ahmed said.

"And yet," she agreed lamely.

When Ahmed's eyes sank closed, Meg suspected what was going on behind them—a litany of their love, a parade of memories stored that were now resurfacing, unbidden, unwanted, seen in the new context of her betrayal. She knew, because she'd been there herself minutes before and a decade ago.

Fear coursed through her. "It's not what you think."

"You don't know what I think," he said.

"You think I lied," she said. "I told you I wasn't going to see him and then I saw him. But I swear, when I told you I wasn't going to see him, I didn't intend to. It sort of happened after the fact."

"And you conveniently forgot to mention it?"

"Ask me anything, Ahmed," she said desperately. "I'll answer with complete honesty."

When Ahmed held out the envelope, Meg accepted it, wishing Jonathan had never sent the check. She didn't need the hundred thousand dollars. She needed Ahmed.

"What does he mean about the gum?" he asked.

Of all the rotten, stinking, crappy luck.

Meg could have kicked the ground. Words did not exist to explain about the gum.

"He sent me this money because it's what he owes me in back child support. He was in town over Thanksgiving and I met him at a park." Meg rushed her words. "My dad and I went to see a lawyer for advice on how to handle things, because I was concerned Jonathan might want visitation with Henry, and . . . well . . ." She stopped and gulped for air. "My father told me not to tell you, and I took his advice. I'm sorry. I regret it profusely."

"Your father's judgment's not the greatest," Ahmed said. "That much we know. But I asked about the gum."

Men don't want you to have a past, Amy had said. *They want to believe your life started the moment you met them. And if you're smart, you let them.*

She and Jonathan had been dating for only a few weeks the first time he asked her for a piece of gum. They were in the stairwell at school, shoved behind a propped-open doorway that led to the second floor, stealing a few minutes of puppy love before going to their shared geometry class. That day she wore a short plaid skirt with knee-highs, stupidly fashionable, and chomped on her gum. He stepped close to her, pressing her backward with his very nearness. Once she was cornered, captured, he asked for a piece.

In Ahmed's backyard, there had been that moment when Meg, after a moment of trepidation, stripped out of her red dress and stood naked before him. Naked in the moonlight, shivering with love. As Meg thought back now, that was their secret handshake, hers and Ahmed's, being as bold as the moment called for. Being as bold in the moment as they could possibly be.

In the hallway of Catalina High, when Jonathan trapped her in the corner and asked for a piece of gum, she'd brought his mouth to hers and with her tongue pushed to him the piece of watermelon-flavored Bubble Yum she'd been chewing.

That's so gross, he'd said, laughing.

You didn't ask for a new *piece.* She'd been as coquettish as her fifteen-year-old virgin self could be.

Here, he said. *Take it back.*

Their first inside joke, their secret handshake—they'd passed used gum back and forth for years.

Meg couldn't do it.

She couldn't look Ahmed in his brokenhearted eyes and tell him about the gum. It was her memory, and it was private. She'd no sooner tell Ahmed about the gum than she'd tell Jonathan what had happened in Ahmed's backyard that night.

"I've got no idea what possessed him to mention the gum," she said smoothly. "It was a silly thing, and it meant nothing."

"You're such a liar." Disgusted, Ahmed pushed back from the table. "You're hoodwinked by this guy all over again. You can't hide it. It's all over your face. You've got this wistful yearning in your eyes for what I'm sure is your rosy-eyed view of a marriage that probably wasn't all that great in the first place."

"You weren't there," Meg said. "You don't know what my marriage was like."

"Do you, Meg?" Ahmed glared at her. "He was a jerk. He left you high and dry. He's not all of a sudden a great guy just because he gave you the money that he's owed you for ten years! A decent person would've provided for his son all along."

"I know that," Meg said.

"I don't think you do. He's trying to buy his way back into your life, and you don't see it."

"I didn't tell you because I didn't want to worry you," she said.

"Well, you succeeded," he said. "I skipped worry and went straight to anger. Your not telling me that you saw him is the same as flat-out lying about it. And as I said very clearly, lying's a deal breaker for me. I won't be in a relationship with someone I can't trust."

"You can trust me," she begged. "I'm never going to see him again."

"See him all you want."

"Please, Ahmed," she pleaded. "I thought we were in this forever! I thought you were going to ask me to marry you!"

Ahmed stood to leave. Meg stood, too. "I don't even know who you are," he said, "except a person who lies to me."

"Jonathan and I had unfinished business." She looked at him imploringly. "That's all it was. I saw him at a park. We wished each other well. He made good on his child-support payments. He doesn't want me back. He knows about you. The gum was just some stupid joke back from when we were in high school. *Please,* Ahmed."

She wondered why she always felt compelled to say *please.* It never worked. Ahmed looked away from her, to the curtained kitchen window. Inside was a boy who loved him very much, a boy he'd seemed to be willing to accept as his own. He looked at her, pained. "You say he doesn't want you back, as if that's supposed to matter. What if he did? What if he does the next time?"

"There's not going to be a next time," Meg said. "I promise."

"Were you ever planning to tell me you saw him?" Ahmed asked. "Were you ever planning to tell me about this massive check he gave you?"

She knew that the truth—that she hadn't exactly decided how or if to tell him—would not go over well.

"Jonathan's not a threat to you," she said. "Yes, I have complicated feelings where he's concerned, but he's my yesterday. Ahmed, you're my forever."

"One small problem, Meg," he said.

"What's that?"

"Besides the fact that what you just said is sappier than hell at a time when you need to be very plainspoken?"

Geez. So much for wooing him back with words.

"Yes," she said weakly. "Besides that."

He leaned close to emphasize his point. "I don't trust a word that comes out of your mouth anymore."

"That's not a small problem," she said in a very small voice.

"You're right," Ahmed agreed. "But you know how it is. Sometimes it's just easier to lie."

As he walked off, Meg closed her eyes so she wouldn't have to watch him go, so she could pretend she wasn't being left, yet again, by the man she loved.

Jonathan knows me in a way no one else ever can, because he knew me back when I was an innocent, back before my heart formed its aching black holes. Even as it was him who damaged me, the fact remains: he knew me before I was damaged, and not many people in this world do.

When he gave me the hundred thousand dollars, I accused him of trying to rewrite history, to cancel out all the bad he'd done with this one act of good. I told him it was impossible. I told him you can't rewrite history.

But I've changed my mind.

I think we can.

We can decide any day of the week to get over ourselves. To look at a situation in a new light. To let something go or hold someone close. To stand and fight or to slink away in shame.

In any case, Can a person rewrite history? *is the wrong question to ask, because no matter the answer, it still deals with the past. Here's the better question: in the moment that matters, who are you going to be?*

The next morning was coffee-shop day. Soccer day. Henry's clear-cut, hanging-out-with-Ahmed day, and Henry had no idea that Ahmed had walked out of Meg's life and possibly his, too. Meg had yet to figure out the riddle: how did you tell a person something that you knew was going to break his heart?

Very carefully was the answer Ahmed had given, and she knew he was right. The grown-up heart was tougher than she'd given it credit for. It endured attacks. Got cut open, stitched back together. Got shocked into obedience. Could be forced to keep beating even as it gave up the fight.

Meg could handle her father falling in love with Sandi. She could handle, now, ten years later, the fact that Jonathan had cheated on her and then left. Ahmed could have handled Jonathan's reappearance. In fact, Meg knew now they likely would have come through the experience better for it. In trying to protect Ahmed, she'd hurt him, because in trying to protect him, she hadn't honored the capacity and strength of his heart.

She'd been a wreck after he'd left. She'd begged off movie night with Henry and instead invited Violet to spend the evening. The two kids continued their Monopoly marathon while Meg lay in her darkened room and tortured herself with recriminations and cried more tears than she would've thought she had in her. One sole hopeful thought got her through the hours: it couldn't really, actually, in true fact, be over between them. Such a punishment in no way fit the crime, and Meg clung to the hope that after Ahmed cooled off, he'd see that, too.

Besides, they were still alive.

For that reason alone, it wasn't over. Their love was forever.

They'd whispered in the crevices of the night about babies they might sneak into the world. Licked each other's lovemaking sweat. Talked of growing old together.

Their love wasn't ended. It had just begun.

But at dawn, she was alone.

When she and Henry arrived at LuLu's, LuLu was behind the counter, arranging the pastry display. She smiled broadly at Henry and watched Meg with increasing worry, confirming what she already knew—she looked haggard. Puffy-eyed. Pathetic.

"Where's your boyfriend, *chica*?" LuLu asked.

Meg made big don't-ask eyes at her.

"He's running errands," Henry said. "We probably won't see him until soccer."

Meg ran her hand through the uncombed hair of her sweet son, who still believed what she told him to believe, who still believed in her. "You want cocoa today or cider, baby boy?"

"Cider," Henry said. "And stop calling me *baby boy*."

"But you'll always be my baby." Henry pulled away from her tangled caress.

"And you?" LuLu said. "The usual? *Pobrecita*, you don't look so good today." She drew a mug of coffee and passed it across the counter to Meg. "Coffee's on the house."

LuLu's small kindness threatened to plunge Meg right over the edge. It was hard to be there without Ahmed—he was part of them now, and his absence was palpable. His absence was throbbing, actually. Meg thanked LuLu for the free coffee, paid for their scones and cider and braced herself as they rounded the corner to the seating area, hoping against hope that he'd be there. That he'd come to his senses and seen the symbolism in beginning again where it had all begun before, in this lovely little coffee shop.

But he wasn't there, as she'd known he wouldn't be. She'd just let hope get the best of her yet again.

"Let's sit over here today, Henry." With a hand on Henry's shoulder, Meg guided him to a darker corner table by the swinging kitchen door.

He resisted. "But that's our spot. We always sit there."

"Let's dare to be different," Meg said. "Change is good."

"Whatever." Henry tossed the chess set on the table.

Meg took a seat. "We need to talk," she said. "It's going to be a somewhat difficult discussion."

Henry looked at her blamefully, as though he knew already she'd done something wrong. Stubbornly, he lifted the lid off the chess box and began to set up a game.

"Ahmed and I had a fight last night," Meg said. "It was bad, and he's pretty mad."

"You're a poet and you don't even know it," Henry said without a hint of a smile. "I'm white. I go first." He moved a middle white pawn forward two spaces, then looked at her. "What'd you do?"

How do you *not* break a boy's heart?

By telling as much of the truth as you possibly can, Meg decided, and what you hold back, you do out of consideration, not cowardice. That was the only way Meg knew to keep a heart intact when the information to share might be upsetting.

"Remember when you called you-know-who in New York?" she asked him. "Your father, Jonathan?"

Henry's eyes were wary beyond his years. "Yeah?"

"Well, he came to town last week and I met him at the park," Meg said. "I didn't tell Ahmed."

"You should have told me!"

"*Shhh,*" Meg said. "Keep your voice down. I didn't want to tell you. I didn't want to tell anybody. Grandpa's the only one who knew."

Henry's look was scolding. "That's a bad secret."

Meg sighed. "I know."

"And Ahmed found out and got mad at you," Henry guessed.

"That's right," Meg said. "How'd you know?"

"Easy," Henry said. "That's what happens to me every time there's something I don't tell you. Don't worry. He won't stay mad forever. *You* never do. Go. It's your turn."

Meg laughed, appreciative for his sweet nine-year-old perspective. She made a quick move, a side pawn forward one. "Sometimes grown-ups aren't so quick to forgive one another as they are to forgive kids."

"He's gonna forgive you," Henry said. "You know how I know?" Arms folded and hands crossed, he leaned forward across the chessboard. "He's going to ask you to marry him."

He nodded knowingly, gloating. "I saw the ring. He took me out to dinner to ask me if it was okay. I said it was, of course. Duh! And Ahmed said maybe I can go to Sam Hughes for fifth grade if it's okay with you. By then I'll be old enough to stay by myself until you get home, and that way, I could be on the chess team and in orchestra and I'd still get to see Violet every day. So can I?"

Meg choked on nothing and coughed emptily. "Excuse me." She slapped her chest and coughed more to buy herself some time, to keep herself from falling so far she wouldn't be able to get herself back up. Ahmed with the creamy-coffee eyes and smooth patrician skin *had*, in fact, wanted to marry her. Meg wished she could pull some stunt, like getting really sick and having to be hospitalized, to make him rush to her side, to be reminded how much he loved her. Maybe she could cough herself to near-death.

"I didn't know you wanted to join the orchestra," she finally said.

"Well, I do." Henry took a sip of his cider, the chess game long since forgotten. "What was it like? Seeing him, I mean. My real father."

His real father. As if he had any other.

Meg gulped her coffee. "Weird," she said. "Very weird."

"Did he ask about me?"

Meg's heart quickened. Here it was, coming back around, what had frightened her in the first place, introducing this powerful element into their lives and not knowing how it would affect her most-beloved boy. Henry would remember whatever answer she gave for the rest of his life, and while it may or may not be true that we find ourselves in the broken pieces of our heart, she didn't want her boy broken. Period. Life would break him soon enough, and she'd be there for him when it did, but for as long as she could, she'd shield him. Because that was what you did with the ones you loved—you shielded them if you could and comforted them if you couldn't.

Which, she realized, was what her father had been doing for her when he continued on the previous night with his lie.

And so Meg lied to Henry, because damned if it wasn't the

right thing to do. The truth was, Jonathan hadn't asked much about Henry at all. She'd been the one who'd offered information about him.

"He wanted to know everything about you," she said. "Your favorite classes at school. What position you play in soccer. What sort of books you like to read. He probably asked a hundred questions about you."

"He knows we're with Ahmed, right?"

"He knows," Meg said. "And he told me you called him to find out what I did wrong with him so I wouldn't make the same mistakes with Ahmed. That was very sweet of you, Henry."

"That's why you bought me the iPod, isn't it?" Henry asked. "As a thank-you?"

Meg shook her head, although he wasn't entirely wrong. "I bought it because you're my favorite boy in the whole world."

Henry basked for a moment before he asked, "So? What did you do wrong?"

Meg straightened. "As a matter of fact, he told me I did nothing wrong."

"Good," Henry said. "Ahmed should like hearing that."

When Ahmed missed the soccer game that afternoon, with Catherine of all people filling in as coach (how was *that* not a slap in the face on Ahmed's part?), Meg called him—several times—always getting his voice mail. After her fourth call, her anger started to build. Couldn't he even pick up the phone if only to tell her not to call anymore?

All day he ignored them.

Meg and Henry spent the evening down at the pool with the Loop Group and Violet. Meg tried to get into the expected spirit of frivolity, but with her phone in front of her, taunting her with its silence, the evening was interminable. Several times, she was tempted to leave Henry in someone's care and drive over to Ahmed's just to see where his head was at—to see if there was a chance for them. But each time, she talked herself out of it, because what if he'd decided it was, truly, over forever between them? If that were the case, she preferred not to know quite yet.

When they arrived at Amy's the next day for brunch, Clarabelle was already there, accompanied by Andy. Both chatted with David as he grilled chicken and corn. As Henry ran off to find his cousins, Meg waved a greeting and then tracked down Amy, who was in the kitchen and smiling for a change.

"Come on," Meg complained to Amy, gesturing to Andy

and Clarabelle out the window. "Bringing her boy toy to brunch?"

Amy laughed. "I think they're cute. And they're not being lovey-dovey or gross about anything."

"It doesn't bother you that she's seeing someone your age?" Meg asked.

Amy shrugged. "Live and let live. They're two consenting adults." She finished sprinkling pine nuts on the salad and took the bowl to the table. "I think the only thing we need to be careful of is that no one takes advantage of her. Takes her money or anything. Not him, necessarily, but I'm sure there'll be others."

"This is surreal, thinking about our parents dating," Meg said, shaking her head. She paused and then added casually, "How upset would you be if Dad dated someone?"

"When will you stop blinding yourself to the obvious?" Amy gave her an exasperated look. "He *is* dating someone. He's dating Sandi."

Meg gasped. "How'd you find out?"

"Mom's known for years," Amy said. "And she hasn't exactly been quiet about it."

"She's suspected," Meg said, "but that didn't mean it was true. Although it is, by the way. And why am I always the last to know these things?"

"Because you're Meg," Amy said. "You see what you want to see. You want everyone happy and *Leave It to Beaver* all the time. Come here. I've got something to show you."

She led Meg to the laundry room, flung open the door, and swept her arm out. "Voilà! My new poetry room. What do you think?"

Meg looked around the room in wonder. What had been a boring, functional room now had soft yellow walls with Magic-Markered poetry scribbled all over them.

"I love it!" Meg said. "Good for you."

"David painted it for me," Amy said. "And he's also going to come home early from work one day a week so I can take a poetry class at the Poetry Center on campus."

"That's awesome," Meg said.

"He's cooler than I've been giving him credit for," Amy said.

Meg felt sudden nostalgia for their nonspa, dessert-at-AJ's outing as she looked at the laundry room walls. "Was it really just two days ago that we had this discussion? Life was so much easier back then."

"You've been having a rough weekend?" Amy asked.

Meg leaned against the washer, crossed her arms and updated Amy about everything: how she'd seen their father with Sandi. How he'd lied. Finally, how she'd gone back home and Ahmed had found the card and check—now that Ahmed knew about them, there was no point keeping them a secret from Amy anymore.

Amy hugged her. "He'll come to his senses. He'd be a fool to let you go."

"That's what I keep telling myself," Meg said. "But every minute I don't hear from him, it's harder to believe." She approached a wall and examined the writing on it. "Can I read one?"

"Read this one," Amy said. "I'm calling it 'Sailboat.' It starts here. I haven't written the 'Appropriate Naughtiness' one yet."
Each line of "Sailboat" was written in a different color, not in

straight poem form, but rather like graffiti on a bathroom stall door. Meg read it out loud.

> *From a distance the sailboat is enviable.*
> *Not lonely.*
> *From a distance you can't tell it's bloated, taking on water,*
>   *slowly drowning from the weight of itself.*
> *You can't tell it's already failed, its conclusion inevitable but*
>   *unknown to all but the captain*
> *Who curses himself*
> *For not knowing how*
> *To ask*
> *For help.*

Meg turned to her sister. "Are you really this sad?"

"I'm not sad at all," Amy said. "I'm just honoring my dark side. You should try it sometime."

I had a dream last night that the sun didn't come up," Henry said the next morning at breakfast. He was slouched over his cereal bowl and they were officially into day three without having heard from Ahmed. Meg, too, had been having ugly dreams. She'd had the same nightmare two nights in a row and no matter how many times she forced herself awake, she kept going back to it.

"I don't think you have to worry," Meg said. "The sun's too stubborn to stop rising."

"The sun *doesn't* rise," Henry said. "We rotate. Can't you get anything right?"

"Hey," Meg said. "Unnecessary roughness."

"I want to drive by Ahmed's on the way to school," Henry said. "There's something I need to tell him."

"We're giving him time, remember?" She said it wearily, as she'd said it numerous times already. They'd left messages, both of them, and she'd finally turned off her phone's ringer the previous afternoon because its lack of ringing was starting to seriously piss her off. "You can tell him at soccer practice tomorrow."

"He might not go to soccer practice tomorrow." Henry glared at her like it would be her fault if Ahmed didn't show up.

Meg pretty much just went through the motions at school that day. She picked *Green Eggs and Ham* for the story of the week and had her students work on painting place mats during Messy Monday art period.

At lunchtime, Lucas fell off the monkey bars and broke his left arm. He'd been hanging upside down, knees tucked under the bar, twisting and talking to Marita, who was watching him from below, when he slipped. Meg saw it happen and couldn't get to him fast enough to ease his fall. His parents picked him up to take to the hospital for an X-ray and then to set his arm. The incident left Meg shaken. He might have broken his neck if he'd fallen the wrong way. Had he subconsciously known there was a right way to fall or did he just get lucky? Because it was Lucas, the boy who danced to Mozart, she suspected it was the former. Lucas was a boy who made his own luck.

At the end of the day, Marita lingered at the doorway after the other students left. "Miss Meg?" she asked. "Will Lucas be okay?"

Meg trailed her fingers down Marita's long black hair. She exempted herself from the not-touching rules where Marita was concerned. The girl had lost her mother and needed comforting, so damn the rules. "He's going to be just fine," she said. "He'll be back at school in a few days and we'll all get to write on his cast."

"Will you see him before he comes back?" Marita asked.

"I think so," Meg said. "I'll probably stop by his house for a visit tomorrow."

Marita took Meg's hand and pressed something cool and

smooth and round into it. It was her don't-run stone. "Will you give this to him?"

Meg's eyes brimmed. "You're sure? Don't you need it yourself?"

Marita shook her head no.

"I'm okay now," she said. "Lucas needs it more."

When Henry asked if he could go to Violet's after school that day, Meg was glad to let him go. She straightened up the apartment and then rewarded herself with a bubble bath, complete with lit candles, a Norah Jones CD and an extra helping of raspberry bubbles. The only thing missing was a chilled glass of white wine, which she would have had if it had only been after five o'clock. Instead, she sipped cold water from a wineglass and tried with great determination not to think about Ahmed, realizing only after she was in the tub that Norah Jones was probably a pretty bad choice of music. She needed something more like Bon Jovi's "You Give Love a Bad Name."

Really, how *dared* he not call them back?

She stayed in the tub until she was good and pruned, and then slipped into the fancy yoga outfit her mom had given her for her birthday the previous year, thinking as she put it on, as she did every time she put it on, that she should give yoga another chance. She'd taken a yoga-for-pregnant-moms class while pregnant with Henry, but she'd dropped out after crying her way through the first two classes because the instructor wouldn't shut up about the importance of a peaceful womb when she was in midst of her post-Jonathan breakdown.

Just as Meg slipped her hair into a ponytail, she heard a tap at the door and opened it to find Violet outside. "Can Henry come out?"

"He's already out." Meg's confusion staved off panic. "He's playing with you."

"No, he's not," Violet said. "I just got home. I was at musical theater."

Meg's heart rat-a-tat-tatted and her mind raced. How long had he been gone . . . had he come back in while she was in the tub . . . where else could he be . . . ?

"Hold on," Meg said. "Let me check his room." She turned. "Henry? Henry!" She was at his door within seconds. Not there. *Damn it.* Meg grabbed her cell phone on the way out the door. "I'm sure he's with Harley, helping him do something or other. Have you seen Harley since you've been home? Come on, hurry. Help me look for him."

Meg scanned the pool area and laundry room and clubhouse, but Henry wasn't there. He wasn't in the office, either. No one was. Harley had left a note taped to the door, *Gone Fishing*, which was code for off-site. Nor was Henry on anyone's patio or balcony. And he wasn't allowed in anyone's apartment without her explicit permission, and all the residents knew it.

"Where would he be?" Meg asked Violet. "Do you guys have any hiding places or anything?"

"Not really," Violet said reluctantly.

"What do you mean, not really? You either do or you don't. Come on, Violet. This is important."

"Well, we sort of have one place."

"Have you checked there yet?" Violent shook her head. "Okay, take me there. Fast!"

Meg scrambled along with Violet to an unsightly stand of evergreen bushes behind the manager's office and followed her into them. Meg looked around in wonder. It wasn't a sort-of hangout, as Violet had implied. It was a well-stocked fort. An old tablecloth of Meg's was spread on the ground. There were a cooler and flashlights and a suitcase, which Meg flipped open. Inside, she recognized, among other things, the black journal she'd given Henry for his last birthday. When she lifted it out, a picture of Jonathan fell from it into the dirt.

Meg picked it up, amazed. It was from when he was in college and had flown back from New York to take Amy to her junior prom. He'd been a good guy. Meg had taken the picture and then stayed home and watched a movie with her dad while Jonathan and Amy had gone to the prom and the postprom parties. "Where'd Henry get this? His aunt's house?"

"I think so," Violet said.

"You don't know where he is, do you?" Meg asked Violet in a stern voice. "This is very serious."

Violet shook her head and looked as worried as Meg felt.

"I've got to call the police." When Meg flipped her phone open to call, she saw she had a voice mail from Ahmed— Ahmed! He'd help, no matter how mad he was at her. She speed-dialed his number.

"Henry's missing," she said as soon as he answered. "I think he might have run away." The alternative—that he'd been taken—was too horrible to say out loud. "I know you're mad at me," she said, "but I need you to help me find him."

"He's right here, Meg." Ahmed's voice was cool. "I left a message telling you that about two minutes ago. I found him waiting on my front steps when I got home from work."

"Oh, thank God. I'm going to kill him." Meg sank to the ground in relief. What sort of mother took a bubble bath while her son went missing? "Was he running away?"

"He says he wants to talk to me, man-to-man," Ahmed said.

"If you had called him back, he wouldn't have ventured out by himself to find you," Meg said accusatorily. "He could have gotten hit by a car. Or stolen! *Horrible* things could have happened. Child molesters roam these streets—you know that! There's danger everywhere! When he calls you, you need to call him back. You're mad at me, not him. You still need to look out for him, no matter how you feel about me."

"You're right," he said. "I'll do better in the future."

"Why *didn't* you call him back?"

"I figured you'd answer."

His reply was annoyingly matter-of-fact.

"Nice," Meg said. "Real nice. I never would have thought you had a mean streak."

"And I never would have thought you'd lie," he countered. "Do you want me to drop him off after we talk?"

"Don't do me any favors," Meg said. "I'm coming over."

She hung up the phone. "He's okay," she told Violet.

Violet obviously knew it, since she'd been privy to Meg's side of the conversation, but Meg wanted to say it out loud, to scream it from the mountaintops—*Henry's fine, just fine!*

Now that the danger had passed, Meg lingered, curious to check out the fort more thoroughly. They had a wind-up emergency radio, a book on insects, and a magnifying glass. Inside the cooler were juice boxes, candy bars and a bag of pretzels. "How long have you had this place?"

"I don't know." Violet shrugged. "A long time."

"I'm taking a candy bar." Meg took out a Twix, Henry's favorite, feeling entitled after what he'd just put her through. "Who bought this food for you guys?"

"Harley."

"Harley knows about your fort?"

Violet nodded. "That's why he doesn't have anyone trim the bushes."

"Another secret," Meg said. "The number of secrets being kept around this place is really remarkable."

She slipped the picture of Jonathan and Amy back into Henry's journal, and put the journal back in the suitcase, resisting the temptation to read it. Had Violet not been there, she might have. It was obvious Henry had more on his mind regarding Jonathan than he'd ever let on to her.

"Does Henry talk about his dad a lot?" she asked Violet.

"You mean his real dad or Ahmed?"

Meg gritted her teeth. "His real dad."

"Sometimes," Violet said. "But he talks about Ahmed a whole lot more."

On the four-minute drive to Ahmed's house, Meg ate the Twix candy bar and sent up a prayer of thanks that Henry was okay. She also asked for guidance on how to reach Ahmed's heart in a way that would open it to her again, but unfortunately no insights had arrived by the time she pulled up to his property.

She sprang up the walkway, eager to set her eyes on Henry and see for herself that he was safe, but when she landed at the front door, which was open, she stopped herself because she saw Henry and Ahmed deep in conversation and was taken back again to that very first day they'd met, and to so many days since then, remembering their heads tilted toward each other, the man and her man-to-be, keeping good counsel. Today, they had mugs of tea set out before them on the coffee table with a little tray of sugar cubes between them.

On the couch, Henry's back was to her. Ahmed, in his work clothes but with his tie loosened, leaned forward in the armchair as he listened intently to Henry. Ahmed saw and didn't acknowledge Meg, but neither did he alert Henry to her presence. His expression was one of affectionate absorption, and as he allowed Meg to eavesdrop, she understood why.

"And so you should be mad at me, not her," Henry said. "She was supermad—screaming mad—when she found out I called him. She almost drove off and left me at the park! I know I shouldn't've done it, but it was the only way I could think of to get her to marry you."

Ahmed raised an eyebrow. "If and when people marry needs to be up to them only. You can't meddle in your mom's life like that. It's not fair to her."

Thank you, Ahmed.

"But she thought she was bad at being married, and she was wrong," Henry said. "Now she knows she's not. If I hadn't've called him, she still wouldn't know that."

Ahmed sipped his tea, slowing down the momentum of the conversation. Henry, too, sipped his tea after popping a sugar cube into his mouth to suck on while he drank it—the Persian way of taking tea.

"What was it like, talking to your dad?" Ahmed asked.

Henry shrugged. "It wasn't like anything." He reached to the plate of sugar cubes, took several and began tossing them in the air. Meg rolled her eyes. Ahmed watched him for a few moments and then asked him to stop.

"This is important." Ahmed spoke in a low, conversational tone. "He's your father. Were you nervous? Angry? You know that my dad wasn't around for me when I was growing up, either. I used to get real mad about that sometimes. Sad sometimes, too."

Henry shrugged again. "I wasn't mad or sad."

But from behind, Meg saw Henry sniffle and wipe his nose.

"I just felt bad, because he didn't ask me anything about myself," he said. "Not one single, stupid thing, like what my favorite food was or did I have a best friend. That sort of thing. I think, you know, he should have asked."

"He was probably very surprised to hear from you," Ahmed said. "He was probably so surprised he could hardly think straight."

"Yeah," Henry agreed. "My mom said he asked a ton of questions about me when she saw him."

"How did you feel about her seeing him like that?" Ahmed asked. "Did you know she was going to?"

Nosy, Meg thought. *None of your business.*

Henry shook his head. "I didn't even know he was here until yesterday."

"How do you feel about your mom not telling you?" Ahmed eyed Meg in the doorway. She narrowed her eyes at him.

"I didn't care," Henry said.

"It didn't bother you that she kept such a big secret from you?" Ahmed said. "Because it bothered me a lot that she kept it from me."

"She didn't do it to hurt you," Henry said. "She did it not to hurt you."

Yeah, Meg thought. *Take that.*

"But I am hurt," Ahmed said.

Get over it, Meg thought irritably.

"She's sorry," Henry said. "She's really, really sorry. She wants to marry you and for us to live here and for you to be my dad. That's what she wants, and I do, too. I want you to be my dad. Like we talked about."

Ahmed glanced at Meg, then back to Henry.

"It's really hard to get marriages right," he said, his voice thick with emotion. "Most people don't, and it's an awful feeling when a marriage fails, and that feeling doesn't go away for a really long time. So you've got to be a hundred percent sure before you marry someone. You've got to have one hundred percent trust, and your mom and I don't have that anymore."

"She didn't lie," Henry said. "What she did was not an actual, true lie. She just kept a secret."

"There's this thing called a lie by omission that applies here," Ahmed said.

"Please," Henry pleaded. "I'll do anything."

Meg couldn't stand by anymore. Henry's desperation reminded her too much of herself back when Jonathan had left. She'd had no pride, no depth to which she wouldn't sink to make him stay.

"Enough, Henry," she said from the doorway, stepping inside. "You can't bully someone into loving you."

"I love him," Ahmed snapped at her. "Don't you dare suggest otherwise."

"You be quiet," Meg said. "I've had quite enough of your pity party."

"Mom!" Henry ran to her and threw his arms around her waist and squeezed her. He was her desperate little cobra, sobbing profusely. Meg kissed his forehead and tried to comfort him and whispered what felt like lies about how everything would be okay.

Ahmed joined them near the door. "Don't ever suggest that I don't love him." His voice had lost its snappishness, but Meg's anger toward him had not abated.

"One fight," she said, disgusted. "One stupid fight and you walk? Is that the best you can do?"

"I didn't walk because of the fight and you know it," he said.

"You're so afraid of being left that you leave first—is that it?" Meg asked. "*Man.* Here I thought you were my lion, but you're just a scaredy-cat. You've got that whole fear-of-abandonment thing going on."

"No, Meg, *you've* got that whole fear-of-abandonment thing going on," Ahmed said. "I'd appreciate it if you didn't project your own screwed-up issues onto me. I've always survived being left. Sometimes it's the best thing that can happen, even though it might not be obvious at the time."

Such the rationalizer. Such the quitter.

"But that's not the case here," Meg said. "It would be a mistake for you to let this end. You love me, Ahmed! I dare you to say you don't, and if you do say it, you're the real liar around here."

"Sometimes love's not enough," he said. "Didn't you just say that the other day?"

"I was wrong!" Meg tried to rein in her emotions. "You were the smart one," she continued calmly. "You said that yes, love is enough if you decide it is. Remember?"

"I remember." His eyes glistened.

"Maybe my decision to see Jonathan without telling you was a bad one," she said. "Maybe not. I still don't really know. But right, wrong or indifferent, it was *my* decision to make and I stand by it because I made it out of love. That's the important point: *I made it out of love.* Do you believe that?"

Ahmed looked positively miserable. He went back to the living room proper and took a seat in his armchair. "I think you made it out of fear."

"There was some fear involved," Meg admitted. "But it came from a place of love, too."

She went to him, knelt before him and put her hand on his knee.

"Listen," she said. "It can be very hard to stop being mad at a person after you've been mad at them for a long time. I know this. I was mad at Jonathan for ten years. Anger is what killed my parents' relationship. Let's not make the same mistake. I know you're deeply, deeply disappointed in me, but we have something really special here, Ahmed. We have something precious."

Ahmed's eyes were muddy, troubled waters, and Meg wished she could pull him to her and comfort him, but she sensed he wouldn't let her—yet.

"I'll leave you now," she said gently. "I'll leave you to think. But you've got to know that our relationship was never in danger by my seeing him. Jonathan can't ruin what you and I have. Only you and I can do that, and I, for my part, am not going to. You're the best thing that's come my way in a very long time, and I treasure you, and I will always treasure you."

Ahmed, fighting tears, gave Meg the saddest smile she'd ever seen, and she wanted to say the words a million times.

"I treasure you, Ahmed," she repeated. "I treasure everything about you. I just hope that even in your anger you can see that you treasure me and Henry, too. Because we're keepers."

"Wow," Henry said as they drove away. "You were awesome back there. You were even better than me."

Meg scoffed. "I was way better than you."

"Not way better," Henry said. "Just a little bit."

Meg looked at him in the rearview mirror. "I don't know if giving him more time is going to work, Henry. He might not change his mind—but it's worth a shot, right?"

"Um, yeah!"

"Okay," she said. "So I need to talk to Grandpa now."

"Is he mad at you, too?"

"As a matter of fact, I'm mad at him."

"Because of Sandi?" he asked.

I don't friggin' believe this, Meg thought. *My nine-year-old son figures these things out before I do.* She looked at Henry in the rearview mirror. "What do you know about him and Sandi?"

"They like each other," Henry said. "It's totally obvious."

"It wasn't obvious to me," she said.

"A lot of things aren't," he said. "Grandma says it's because you insist on seeing the best in people."

Well.

"I don't think that's such a bad way to be," she said.

"Me neither. I think we're happier this way." Henry sang one of his favorite kindergarten songs, with embellishments he'd learned at camp. "'Stay on the sunny side, always on the sunny side, stay on the sunny side of life—yee haw! You'll feel no pain as we're driving you insane. Stay on the sunny side of life. Tell a joke!'

"Hey, Mom," he said. "Why did Tigger stick his head in the toilet?"

Meg grinned. "I have no idea."

"He was looking for Pooh."

She groaned. "That's disgusting!"

"It's supposed to be!" Henry said. "That's the whole point!"

When they arrived at Phillip's office, Sandi was behind her desk, reading a Harlequin romance. *She needs a new hairstyle,* Meg thought uncharitably. *That one's forty years past its prime.*

"Hi, Sandi," she said.

"Hi, you two! Your father's not expecting you, is he?" Meg could tell Sandi was trying to assess her mood without letting on.

"Is he here?"

"He is." Sandi scanned her phone's display. Meg was sure she was looking for a way to warn her father.

"I'll just surprise him," Meg said. "We seem to be all about surprises lately."

"Go get him, Mom," Henry said. As Meg headed to her father's door, she heard Henry say to Sandi, "You should have seen her with Ahmed. She was awesome."

When Meg entered her father's office, he startled back in his chair. "Meg! I was just about to leave here and come see you."

Her anger spiked upon seeing him. "About what, Dad? The price of tea in China?"

Phillip gestured. "Have a seat."

When she remained standing, he came around his desk and led her to the couch. He gave her a long, intense look. "I have a confession," he said. "I lied when you asked if I was seeing Sandi. I am, in fact, seeing her, and I've been seeing her for a long time."

"I know you're seeing her. Ahmed told me," Meg said icily. "Plus, I was sitting ten feet behind you at the stadium the other day when you were on the phone assuring me that you *weren't* seeing her. It made me sick, Dad, that you'd lie to me like that."

Phillip sat back, stunned. "I don't know what to say."

"How about you're sorry?"

"I am sorry," he said.

Meg crossed her arms. "I'm disappointed in your lack of respect for Mom. I know you two aren't right for each other and I believe one hundred percent that you'll both be happier apart. But there's a right way and a wrong way to go about things, and what you did was selfish, and what's more, you took the coward's way out by beginning an affair while you were still with Mom. I don't like that my father's a coward."

Phillip looked devastated. "Do you remember that time I took you fishing at Silverbell Lake when you were about seven?"

"Vaguely," Meg said.

"You cried when you found out we had to put hooks through the worms." He smiled at the memory. "And then you cried when you saw the hook in the fish's mouth. You always were a very sensitive soul."

Meg shrugged. "The idea of sport fishing still bothers me."

"I never fished after that day," he said.

"Really?" Meg thought back. "I guess I never knew that."

He squinted at her through his glasses. "You make me want to be a better person, Meg. You always have. I'm sorry I let you down."

Meg's heart softened as Ahmed's words came back to her: *I'd take a flawed father who loves me over a nonexistent father any day of the week . . . Wouldn't you?*

He'd known, when he'd said it.

He'd already known this moment would come.

Yes, she'd said. *As long as there's love amidst the flaws.*

The peach-lady's voice from Whole Foods came back to her, too: *Is your father still alive? Then treasure him.*

Meg looked at her flawed father—at the balding, aging man before her in the out-of-date glasses—and she knew without question that he loved her, and that therefore, they could work through anything.

"Let's make a deal," she said. "Let's hold each other to a very high standard going forward."

"Yes," he agreed. "Let's not lack courage, you and me."

Meg did something she'd never done before: she took two personal days off from work. She dropped Henry off in the morning and picked him up afterward, and in between, she withdrew into herself.

The first day, she had coffee alone at LuLu's and did some journaling. Afterward, she went for a seven-mile hike in Sabino Canyon, and when she was about three miles into it, surrounded by a forest of saguaros, she began to tremble uncontrollably. She'd put up a good front for Henry and Ahmed, but it was strategic bravado. Here in nature, the truth burst through: she was terrified of losing Ahmed.

Their love had felt fated. She'd asked Ahmed once—pestered him, actually—why he'd gone to LuLu's that first day. Why *that* coffee shop on *that* day at *that* time? *It's not for us to question,* he'd said. *Only to appreciate.*

But really. How did a person come into your life seemingly out of nowhere and turn out to be exactly what your soul needed?

And how could he later be inclined to leave?

And how—how—could you make him stay?

Meg trembled three miles into her hike because after poking at the questions from every which way, she realized she already knew the answer to the last one.

You couldn't. There was nothing you could do to make a person stay if he was inclined to leave.

She walked to the top of the canyon road, found a boulder to sit on, took a few deep breaths and called Ahmed. He, good heart that he was, picked right up. "How are you today, Meg?"

Meg took his friendly tone as a good sign. "I'm doing well," she said. "I'm playing hooky from school and wanted to know if you're free for a lunch date."

"Ah, I'm not," he said. "I've got a committee meeting over the lunch hour."

"How about coffee afterward?" she asked. "Or you could come over to my place for tea, wink, wink. Henry's not home."

"I'm booked, Meg," he said. "All afternoon. I'm sorry."

"I'm not going to quit asking," she said.

"I don't want you to."

Hope fluttered in Meg's heart. "Just how mad are you?"

"Not very." Ahmed's voice was generous. "I appreciate your persistence quite a bit, actually."

"It's that hokey-pokey thing," she said. "You just gotta keep putting your whole self in."

Meg took in the beautiful fractured canyon, so green, so brown, with the sky so blue in the background. She wondered how a person would have felt to be sitting on this same boulder back when the earthquake struck Mexico those centuries ago and rippled upward, tearing open the earth to create these canyon crevices. Scared, she'd bet. But still. It would have been unforgettable, had you survived it. It would have been a story for the ages.

Go there, she thought.

"I heard you bought me a ring," she said.

He sighed. "I did, indeed, buy you a ring. I can't believe Henry told you. He promised he wouldn't."

"For future reference, you can't count on Henry to keep a secret," Meg said, "no matter how much he swears he'll keep it."

"Well, so much for the surprise," Ahmed said cheerfully.

Go there, go there, go there.

"I think maybe we should take the ring off the table for the time being," Meg said.

"I think maybe we shouldn't," Ahmed said.

Meg swallowed hard. He wasn't making this easy on her. "I think we should focus on right now instead of on forever."

"But I'm a forever kind of guy," he said. "And I want to have babies with you."

Meg smiled at that. "I'm changing by the minute," she warned. "I'm not the same person I was yesterday, and who I am today won't be who I am tomorrow."

"We'll change together," he said. "Love is what you become together, right?"

Birds chirped. The sun shone. The cactus in front of Meg was hundreds of years old and would live for hundreds more.

Somewhere in the world, church bells were ringing and the water was pure and men were shaking hands and meaning it.

In other words, there was hope.

I keep having nightmares about Henry being swallowed by the ocean. We go every summer, the two of us, to a stretch of beach in front of the Hotel del Coronado, a resort that until recently we couldn't afford. We buy five-dollar ice-cream cones at the resort's Moo Time ice-cream joint and feel rich indeed as we make our way to the sand.

Henry with his saltwater hair leaps, runs and spins his way up and down the shoreline like an excited puppy. The ocean infiltrates his soul. Possesses him. Me, it scares, because while it allows you to play, to swim, to use it for pleasure, it's unsentimental. No matter how much you love it, it doesn't love you back.

Gently rough, roughly gentle, its foamy waves tease and chase your ankles, but when you go deeper, they whip you. Even close to shore, where it should be safe, the ocean floor pulls out from under you, slides you along, moves you away from where you began. You can't stay in one place no matter how hard you try.

In my nightmare, I am there, in water up to my knees, inhaling the thick fish-salt air and stretching my arms wide, letting the day embrace me, thinking all's well. And all is well. Around me, birds squall and children shriek and Henry is right there, shimmering in the sun, loving his life as the waves crack against his back. For Henry, getting knocked over is the fun part. Time and again, he comes up laughing. There's no place he loves more than the ocean.

I can see him. He's right there.

And then in my nightmare, he's gone.

And the unflinching ocean doesn't miss a beat. It just goes on and on relentlessly.

It was time to deposit the check.

That was Meg's only real goal for her second personal day off from school. She'd put off depositing it for a variety of reasons, mostly psychological, and while she felt she'd addressed those as well as she ever would, one remained: she couldn't get over the strangeness of actually having money. She couldn't imagine handing the check to a bank teller who probably made twelve dollars an hour and say, *I'd like to deposit this check, please.* Would they even *take* her money, or would they think she was a forger, a fake? What did a person do after they'd deposited a check for a hundred thousand dollars? You had to buy *something*, didn't you—something more than a four-dollar Frappuccino or a fifty-dollar pair of flip-flops? The problem, which wasn't really a problem, was that her needs were few, her pleasures simple.

As she was dusting the photo of her and Henry at the ocean, Meg hit upon one way she could spend some of the money. She'd have to check with her father, but she was pretty sure she wouldn't owe taxes on child support, so if she deposited the entire check and let the interest accrue, she could fund a week at the Hotel del Coronado every summer on the interest alone. Ha! They could even order room service. And if Henry was willing and things worked out, maybe they'd invite Ahmed to join them, maybe for a few days and maybe for forever.

That decided, a newly energetic Meg turned up the radio,

92.9 The Mountain, Jennie and Blake in the Morning, finished her cleaning, and jumped in the shower, eager now to get
to the bank. When she stepped out, her cell phone was ringing.
Worried it might be the school calling about Henry, she ran,
wrapped in her towel and still dripping, to the kitchen
counter, where she'd left her phone.

Jonathan's number stared up at her.

"Hello?" She clutched the towel around her tightly, as if he
could see her.

"How are you, Meg?" She smiled at his voice, even as she
wasn't exactly happy to hear it.

"I'm doing great." She turned down the radio. "The birds
are chirping in my world. What's up?"

"You're just on my mind today, that's all."

Meg couldn't help herself. "Why am I on your mind
today?"

"Probably because I'm standing right outside your door,"
he said.

"No, you're not." Stupidly, Meg went to it, unlatched the
chain and flung open the door.

Sure enough, there he was.

"Oh," she said into the phone. "I guess you are right outside my door." She stood dripping before him, dressed in only
a towel. They simultaneously hung up their phones.

"Well, hello!" His eyes popped as he hammed up the
awkwardness of the moment. "It's been a while since you
welcomed me in such a manner."

Meg laughed. They'd gone through a sex-as-soon-as-you-
get-home phase at one point, one of their better phases. "I
suppose I should invite you in."

She stepped back to allow him entry, feeling naked in just the towel. She *was* naked in just the towel.

"Henry's not here, I take it?" Jonathan asked.

"He's at school."

He entered and glanced around, then peered at her. "And why aren't you?"

"Personal day," Meg said.

"But you never take personal days."

"I'm a changed woman," she said.

Jonathan had one particular smile that came out in moments that had the potential of turning a certain way, like when an argument was ready to escalate or when they reconnected at a party where they'd been separated. It always stopped the traffic in her heart. It was a hey-wouldn't-you-rather-go-have-great-sex smile. The smile had always, always worked on her.

And he was smiling it now, and all that was between them was a towel held up with a shaky, perhaps disloyal hand.

Ahmed, Meg reminded herself.

Yes, there was Ahmed to consider. If he showed up right then, he would not be happy. She could imagine the look in his eyes. They'd be dark, hardened. Like the flat surface of a lake that had just sunk a boat with no apologies to offer or accept.

Yes, there was Ahmed to consider.

"Knock it off with that smile," Meg told him.

Laughing, Jonathan knocked it off.

"I'm going to go change," she told him.

"I'll stay here."

The smart-ass. "Damn straight, you will!" she said.

She locked her bedroom door behind her, kept the towel clutched about herself, bent over at the waist and gave a long, silent scream. What was this all about? Who'd asked for this—had *she* given permission for such a moment to be happening?

No, she had not.

And yet here it was, happening nonetheless.

This was Jonathan. The guy who'd left her. The guy who, by coming back a few weeks ago to tell her in person something he could easily have told her over the phone, had nearly ruined things between her and Ahmed.

Not true, she told herself. He'd had nothing to do with that. She'd been the cause of the rift, the creator of the void.

Straightening, Meg threw on an old, unflattering pair of jeans and the baggiest sweatshirt she could find, slapped on some foundation, and twisted her hair into a ponytail. The brightness in her eyes she couldn't dull, but she would not dress up for him.

When she came back out, he was sitting at her dining room table. Not being a believer in feng shui, he sat with his back to the door, his customary position. He gave her a once-over and said, "You don't look a day over thirty-four."

Meg grinned at him. "That's because you're not around to age me. Coffee?"

"Please."

She got him a cup, refreshed hers, and joined him at the table. "I'm surprised I didn't come in to find you looking at the photos on the mantel. Aren't you curious about your son?"

Without taking his eyes from hers, Jonathan lifted his coffee cup, blew on it, then took a sip and set it down. "You two vacation in Coronado, I see."

"I guess that answers that question," she said.

His eyes gleamed with memory. "Do you stay at that same crappy hotel we stayed at?"

Meg laughed. The summer after their senior year, before he'd gone away to college, they'd driven all night to see daybreak at the ocean. "They tore that place down years ago," she said. "We stay at an equally crappy one a few blocks down. I think this summer we're going to stay at the Hotel Del. I came into a little money recently."

Jonathan gave her a pleased smile. "The check's no good unless you cash it."

"It's on my list of things to do today," she said. "Which reminds me, are you going to start sending monthly child-support payments? Because you really should."

"I will." He nodded. "And I'll even go so far as to say you should file an order with the court to amend the paperwork, because the payments should be based on what I make now as opposed to what I made when I was just out of law school."

"Okay," Meg said, rattled by his decency. "I will."

"You don't have any pictures of your boyfriend up there on the mantel," he pointed out.

"No," she said. "I don't."

Jonathan examined the blackness of his coffee before meeting her gaze again. "You think you'll end up marrying him?"

His tone was even, neutral, but Meg felt a weight behind his words. She took a slow, deliberate sip of coffee, keeping her eyes on his. "For me, it's not about the ring."

"You have changed," he said. "But then, I already knew that."

"Why'd you come?" Meg asked.

There was pain in Jonathan's flaming blue eyes and he didn't need to say anything. Meg knew exactly why he'd come.

"Don't," she said. "Don't do this."

"I'm not doing anything," he assured her. "I'm just . . ." He stopped to sigh, to summon the right words.

"I'm with Ahmed now," Meg said.

It came out weak.

It felt like a lie.

He nodded. "I'd rather you were with me, instead."

Meg sank her face in her hands, a peekaboo baby, wishing that since she couldn't see him, he couldn't see her. With her fingertips, she caressed her forehead, traced her fingers over her eyebrows, soothed herself. Ahmed's hands had done the same thing. Jonathan's, too, many times more.

She was with Ahmed now, it was true.

But it was also true that in the most secret corner of her heart, Meg had dreamed of this moment for years—ever since Jonathan had left her.

"You left me," she said after she'd collected herself. "How could I ever think you wouldn't leave me again?"

"I'm a different person now," he said. "I'm ready to be the husband you deserve, and the father Henry needs."

Isn't that what men always said?

"I'm with Ahmed," Meg said. "Firmly. And forever, I hope."

"But—"

"But nothing," Meg said. "You can't just come back after all this time and think you can pick up where you left off."

"I don't want to pick up where we left off," he said. "I want to start over."

Meg shook her head. "We don't need you."

Jonathan reached and took her hand. "But I need you."

Wow, Meg thought. *Just . . . wow.*

Sadness overwhelmed her as she looked at their intertwined fingers. She was holding hands with *Jonathan Clark,* the first boy she'd ever loved, the first man she'd ever hated.

"You were the first person outside my family to think I was something special," she said. "That means something very profound."

"I still think you're something special," he said.

Meg slipped her hand from his. "We don't share the same values, Jonathan. You said it yourself at the park. I *am* still the same person I was back then. I still want the same things. I'm only different in that I'm far, far stronger. I'm older and wiser and a little beat-up by life but better for it, I hope. You forced me to be strong when you left me."

"The fact that you fell apart after I left has haunted me all these years."

"You call it falling apart," Meg said. "I call it surviving."

"See?" He smiled. "You *can* rewrite history. You just have to look at old things in a new way. Take what's useful, leave what's not."

Meg studied him, the man who'd given her Henry. Part of her would always love him. But his desire was selfish.

"I can see why you'd want to be with us," she said. "All the hard work's been done. We've put years into becoming who we are, and now you want a ready-made wife and son. Ahmed's all about what he can add to our lives, and you've always been someone who takes, takes, takes."

"I want to add to your life, too."

"My answer's no, Jonathan."

She got up and walked away from him to let him collect himself, and from the fireplace mantel she picked up her favorite photo from Coronado. Henry's baby teeth had fallen out and his adult ones had grown in. He'd be losing his molars soon, and then he'd shoot up tall and his voice would deepen. Everything about him would change, yet in his mind his father never would. He'd always be just a face in an old photograph. The guy who came to town once but neglected to see him.

I'd take a flawed father who loves me over a nonexistent father any day of the week.

Ahmed—a man she loved, a man whose judgment she trusted—was right. Meg went back to the dining room table and handed Jonathan the photograph. He studied it, memorizing it.

"I was thinking of taking Henry to Rincon Market after school for a snack," she said. "Do you want to meet us there? Would you like to meet Henry?"

"You'd really let me meet him?" His eyes widened with surprise, then softened with gratitude.

"Sure," Meg said. "Today's a gift, right?"

"Won't he hate me?" he asked. "I've been an absent parent, and I hurt his mom."

"All fathers are flawed," Meg said. "This happens to be a very good time for Henry to learn that."

Rincon Market, five hours later, the Sam Hughes neighborhood hangout, with a small section for grocery items but a killer bakery and café. Henry sat at a table with Jonathan and Meg and ate two bananas, a peach and an apple as he peppered Jonathan with questions about his life. Did he ever get lost in such a big city as New York? How cool was it to ride the subway? In his job, did he ever help bad guys get away with stuff? Had he ever been in Times Square on New Year's Eve to see the ball drop, and did he know Donald Trump?

Jonathan loved the questions and gave great answers. Yes, he did sometimes get lost, but it wasn't scary because he just waved down a cab and so far he'd always been able to find his way back. Riding the subway was *very* cool. Sometimes bad guys did get away with stuff, but often they got exactly what they deserved. Yes, he'd seen the ball drop in Times Square on New Year's Eve, and while he didn't know Donald Trump, he had met the mayor.

At that, Henry's eyes popped.

"Me, too!" he said. "I went to lunch with the mayor, me and Ahmed!"

As they talked, Meg studied the two of them and marveled at the way their mannerisms mirrored each other's. Both quirked their heads to the right when intrigued by a question. Both used their eyes to underscore a point. Both presented themselves as quick-witted while disguising their serious intent: each wanted the other to like him, desperately. Meg could see it because she knew them both so well.

Jonathan questioned Henry as well. What was his favorite subject in school? Had he read *The Mysterious Benedict Society*? Besides Harry, Ron and Hermione, who was his favorite character in Harry Potter? Did he have a best friend? Were girls good or gross?

Henry grew more animated with each answer he gave. His favorite subject was none, because he didn't like his teacher or his school, but next year, if Meg and Ahmed got married, he was going to Sam Hughes, where he could play on the chess team and join the orchestra. He'd never heard of *The Mysterious Benedict Society* and, anyway, he liked movies more than books. Snape was his favorite other Harry Potter character, because Snape loved Harry's mom so much that he died to protect her son. Violet was his best friend. And girls were good, not gross. *My mom's a girl,* he said. *And so's Violet. Both good.*

"Have you kissed her yet?" Jonathan asked, glancing at Meg.

"Who, Violet? Or my mom?"

Jonathan looked at Meg to indicate *I see we've got a smart-ass on our hands.* Meg's look signaled back *He inherited it from you.*

"Violet," Jonathan said. "I'd hope you kiss your mom many times each day."

"Of course I've kissed Violet," Henry said.

This was news to Meg. When and where and how often and had there been tongue involved? All questions for another time. Or not. Some questions were better left unasked, she decided.

"Can I give you some advice?" Jonathan said. "Be good to her. Be as good to her as you can possibly be, and try not to break her heart."

Henry nodded, very seriously. "I'm really going to try to get it right."

It was then—as Meg and Jonathan locked eyes, as Meg came full circle in her forgiveness and in her appreciation of the absolute rightness of the moment—that Ahmed walked into the market.

Henry saw him first. "Mom." He grabbed her arm. "There's Ahmed."

When Meg had picked Henry up from school and told him on the drive over that they'd be meeting Jonathan at Rincon, Henry had asked if Ahmed knew. *Don't worry about Ahmed,* Meg had said. *You leave him to me.* To which Henry had replied, *Yeah, but remember what he said about a lie by that other thing.*

A lie by omission, Meg had said. *Yes, I'm quite familiar with the term. You just enjoy this moment, and I'll deal with Ahmed later.*

A match lit inside Meg when Ahmed, having just stepped through the market's automatic doors, glanced idly around. She stood to intercept him.

"Henry, you stay here." She made her voice low and dead serious. "If there's ever a time for you to do what I say, this is it. Got it?"

He nodded. "Got it."

Jonathan's eyes were cool. "Let me know if you need me," he said. "I've got your back."

Just then, Ahmed caught sight of them. He looked from

Meg to Jonathan to Henry, and then back to Jonathan again. The same blue eyes, same blond hair that curled at the ends, the same little forward curve of the shoulders. There was no mistaking they were father and son.

As Meg walked to Ahmed, his body was fighter-tense.

His fists were clenched.

His eyes were the flat surface of one very pissed-off lake.

This time when Ahmed turned and left her, Meg didn't just close her eyes.

She went after him.

She caught up to him outside the market. "Ahmed!" She grabbed his arm. "Don't be this way."

He jerked his arm back. There was a half second in which he nearly raised a hand to her in anger, but it turned into a point of accusation. "I have *one* question."

He trapped her with his eyes, cornered her inescapably. Spewed hate. Meg found herself gripped with anger.

"If you've got a question, just ask it," she said. "You don't need to announce you've got one."

When Ahmed dropped his mouth open, astounded by her flippancy, it angered Meg more. "Well?" she said. "Ask your question."

"Were you planning to tell me?" He narrowed his eyes at her. "Or did you think I wouldn't find out you two were seeing him?"

Meg narrowed her eyes back. "That's actually two questions."

Ahmed's eyes widened. He had a bomb triggered, ready to detonate, and Meg could tell her taunts were not helping in his struggle to restrain himself. *Good,* she thought. It was about time he unleashed himself. Time he lived raw, which Meg was coming to think was the only worthwhile way to live.

"Maybe you should check your voice mail once in a while,"

she said. "What were you doing that was so important you couldn't call me back? I've been leaving you messages for five hours. I'm going through something important here, and you flaked on me. You let me down, Ahmed. I expect better from you."

He blanched. Physically stumbled backward. "You left . . . ?" He shook everything, everything, out of his head. "I left my phone in my locker at the racquet club again." He looked devastated. "You left a message?"

"About twenty." Meg pulled her cell phone from her pocket and displayed the screen that showed the calls she'd made that day. It was littered with Ahmed's name. She held the phone out to him. "Call your voice mail. Pick up your messages. You'll see."

He didn't take the phone. "Oh God. Shit, Meg. I'm so sorry." He covered his face with his hands and rubbed hard, as if to peel away his hateful thoughts. "I shouldn't have doubted you. I should *not* have doubted you."

"No," Meg said. "You shouldn't have. We both know Henry can't keep a secret. Do you think I'd leave my fate in the hands of a nine-year-old and expect him not to blab to you that he'd met his father? I'm not trying to hide anything."

There was an empty table to Ahmed's left and he slipped into a seat, weakened. Depleted. Meg slid into the seat across from him. "I'm sorry," he said. "I'm so, so sorry."

"Apology accepted," Meg said instantly. "Now buckle up. Jonathan came to town to ask me to get back together with him. To give it another shot. To see if we could get it right the second time around."

Could this day get any worse? was the question Meg saw in Ahmed's eyes. She smiled to reassure him: it would only get better, as long as they were willing to work for it.

"What did you tell him?" His face was a mixture of reluctance and hope.

"I told him that he's my yesterday and you're my forever," she said.

Delighted, Ahmed reached to hold her hand. "For some reason, it sounds so much less sappy this time around."

"I thought so, too."

They fell into their teenage, dopey-grinning snow-globe bubble of love, and Meg knew everything would be okay between them—for now, and hopefully for a heck of a long time beyond now. For forever, if such a thing were possible.

The moment was broken by Henry, who flung himself at Ahmed and hugged him, and by Jonathan, who stood back and watched. Meg went to him.

"I've got to catch my flight," he said.

Meg nodded at the man she used to love, at the man her boy would grow to love. "You'd like to stay in touch with Henry, I take it?"

Jonathan burst forth with the same smile she'd fallen in love with all those years ago. "He's an awesome kid. You've done a remarkable job with him, Meg."

Ahmed stood and joined them, a tricky feat with a nine-year-old boy smothering him with love. Jonathan extended his hand.

"Jonathan Clark," he said. "Next time I'm in town, I'd like to buy you a cup of coffee. We have a few people in common and we should probably get to know each other."

Ahmed shook Jonathan's hand, and here, in this small corner of the world if nowhere else, men were shaking hands and meaning it.

"I'd like that," he said. "I know a great little coffee shop we could go to."

"He fell in love there," Henry said. "With my mom."

Meg woke in terror that night from the same horrible nightmare, the one in which Henry disappeared into the ocean. *When will it stop?* she wondered, and knew the answer—never. This particular nightmare would go away, but life would bring others. The best you could hope for was to have someone in your life who knew you—who really, really knew you and loved you in all your complexity and in spite of all your flaws. Someone who'd support you so you wouldn't be alone as you struggled to survive your nightmares.

She got up and made herself a cup of warm milk and honey, and then she called Ahmed, even though it was three o'clock in the morning.

"I keep having these nightmares," she said when he answered.

"Do you want me to come over?" he asked.

"I don't think so," Meg said. "I just wanted to hear your voice. To know I'm not alone in the world tonight."

She told him about the nightmare, and then she told him more about Jonathan's visit. She told him how she'd finally deposited the hundred-thousand-dollar check from Jonathan and how she was going to buy back her father's baseball-card collection from a dealer in town. She'd tracked him down earlier that day, and the collection was mostly intact, with the exception of a few cards he'd sold online. He'd been confident he could find some Pete Rose cards for her, too.

"I want to buy a present for you, too," she said. "I just don't know what. Tickets to Venice?"

"Don't buy me anything," he said. "Write me a letter, instead."

"Really?" Meg was delighted by the request. Letter writing was such a lost art. "You want me to write you a love letter?"

"Write anything you want," he urged her. "Tell me a story. Tell me what's in your heart and on your mind. Make it the letter of a lifetime, and sprinkle it with your fairy dust."

After they hung up, Meg pulled out her rose-colored linen stationery from her little secretary desk and the nicest pen she could find and made herself a cup of tea and dimmed the lights and set herself up at the dining room table.

Before she began, she checked on Henry and found him smiling in his sleep. She straightened his covers to protect him from the night chill and kissed his forehead and whispered an I love you, hoping he'd hear it all the way into his dreams.

Back at the dining room table, she lit a candle. She sat, blew on her tea, and wondered how to start.

Write anything you want, he'd said.

Meg thought of her mother and her father and their broken-down marriage, of furniture salesmen and women with beehive hairdos. She thought of Lucas and Marita—the comfort he'd brought her and the don't-run stone she'd passed onto him. She thought of Henry and Violet and the secret place they went to. She thought of their kiss, and of Jonathan's advice to Henry: *Be as good to her as you can possibly be.* She thought of

Amy and David and chocolate raspberry mousse cake and scribbling poetry on laundry room walls and of honoring one's dark side. She thought of Amy's advice: *Men don't want you to have a past. They want to believe your life started the moment you met them.*

In a way, Meg felt her life *had* begun—again—the moment she met Ahmed at LuLu's that one Saturday morning. But she did have a past, and it was something to be honored, not denied.

It took Meg a long while to come up with her opening line—beginnings could be so hard. As could middles. As could endings.

Sometimes it seemed that *everything* was so hard.

But just because something was hard didn't mean it wasn't worthwhile. Easy was for wimps, not for people like them.

Dear Ahmed, she finally began. And then she smiled. *It's easy to look at men and think they're idiots.*

Photo by Lance Fairchild Photography

Laura Fitzgerald is also the author of *Veil of Roses* (Bantam, January 2007). A native of Wisconsin, she lives in Arizona with her husband, who is of Iranian descent, and their two children. Her favorite part of being an author is interacting with readers and attending book clubs by phone and in person. She can be reached through her Web site at www.laurafitzgerald.com.

One True

THEORY

of

LOVE

LAURA FITZGERALD

A CONVERSATION WITH LAURA FITZGERALD

Q. Tell us how you came to write One True Theory of Love.

A. Second chances can be times of great reinvention, or they can be total hell, and they don't bring with them the guarantee of a happy ending. At its heart, *One True Theory of Love* is a story about second chances and the courage they require.

I got the idea for the novel when I was in Wisconsin visiting book club members who'd read my first novel, *Veil of Roses.* As I got to know the women over the course of a few hours, I was struck by how many were in the midst of major life changes: divorces, new relationships, retirements, job switches, kids finally out of the house, deaths of loved ones. People can respond to such changes passively or actively, and those who experience them actively ultimately ask themselves: *Well, who am I going to be now?*

That becomes the central question Meg faces as she decides whether or not to pursue a relationship with Ahmed.

Q. One True Theory of Love *can be described as a romance, but it's unlike most romances in that the focus isn't just on the couple but also on the other people who have a stake in the success or failure of the relationship. Why did you choose to explore the romance from this different perspective?*

A. I guess because Ahmed isn't the goal for Meg. Instead, he's her reward—if and only if she can become the bold and openhearted person she truly wants to be. To do that, she needs to honor her past, deal with her fears and insecurities, value the complexity of other people as well as herself, and finally—no small feat—she must summon the courage to take a leap of faith, knowing she may or may not get her happy ending.

Meg has so much at stake. First, her self-concept. She doesn't want to let herself down. At the same time, she's a fiercely protective single mom who has created for her son, Henry, what is in many ways an admirably safe and happy world. She's well aware that he will one day judge her by the choices she makes regarding Ahmed, and she wants to be sure she's making the right choices for the right reasons.

Since pretty much everyone in the story is in the midst of seizing or denying or needing a second chance, how they all go about it enables Meg to use them as a barometer for how she should face her own second chance.

Q. The novel also explores the impact of the protagonist's previous marriage on her newly evolving romance. What about that idea intrigued you?

A. As do most of us, Meg wants to avoid making the same mistakes in her future that she made in her past. She was sucker punched by her first husband's betrayal, which was particularly difficult for her because she'd let her entire self-image be defined by who she was in relation to him rather than who she was as a person in her own right. When we meet her, she's happy, healthy, and strong—but it's been ten years since her marriage fell apart and she still doesn't have a sense of her role in that failure. If she can't figure that out, how can she know she won't screw it up again?

Q. Your first novel, Veil of Roses, *also featured a character with an Iranian background, the protagonist, Tamila. Surely that's not a coincidence?*

A. In its earliest version, *One True Theory of Love* was actually an international-espionage thriller, in which Ahmed (now the main character's love interest) was drawn into a U.S.-Iran conflict against his will.

It was quite a departure from *Veil of Roses* in every regard, and ultimately it became clear—again, as I met with readers—that what they appreciated most about *Veil of Roses* was that it was a quick, lighthearted read that also had some emotional heft to it. It went down easy but wasn't frivolous. To make my next book similar, I decided to change it radically.

The story's gone through more drafts than I care to remember, and pretty much all that's stayed from that first one is Ahmed, a basically good guy who happened to have been born in Iran. I'm pretty sure I've written my last Iranian character . . . unless this turns out to be a prequel to my international-espionage thriller!

I should also mention that my husband is Iranian-American, which I'm sure played a part in my choosing to write about Iranians.

Q. One True Theory of Love *is your second novel. Did you suffer from the dreaded "sophomore slump"?*

A. I didn't experience "sophomore slump"—thankfully. I love the story and characters, so every day spent writing it was both a pleasure and a challenge. I wasn't always sure of the ending, but I knew it would be a satisfying one, and that helped me write through the parts where the characters suffered. Storytelling really is both an art and a craft, and when I ran into problems, I referred back to my knowledge of the craft and usually found what I needed there.

The hardest part about writing this book was telling the story in a simple manner while honoring the complexity of the characters.

Q. *What do you hope to write in the future?*

A. Time will tell what my next book will be. I'm very intrigued by mother-daughter stories and the changing nature of such relationships, especially in moments of challenge, so that will likely be a part of my future writing. Also, I think I'll always be interested in stories of reinvention—women whose lives change radically (whether they'd prefer it or not).

Besides writing more women's fiction, I plan to spend the next few years writing books for teenage girls (YA fiction) and some middle-grade fiction. Middle-grade fiction interests me because no one loves a good story more than a child. I'm very impressed with the quality of some of the writing for this age group and want to contribute to it. A good story is such a gift to give a child.

In my YA fiction, I'll be exploring the same sort of questions I do in my adult fiction: how do you define happiness, and what are you willing to do in order to live a happy and fulfilling life? In the moments that really matter, how do you act courageously, in a way that honors who you want to become? It can be quite difficult being a teenager today, and I think good fiction provides not only solace and support, but also an escape from the pressures found in the real world.

Q. What writers do you most admire and enjoy? Are there any who have had a particular influence on your work?

A. I appreciate any writer who keeps me turning the pages, and if I can find one who makes me feel something—who makes me laugh or gets me choked up or just gets me in the gut—they go on my must-buy list. Jonathan Tropper's writing is laugh-out-loud funny and I particularly appreciate how he very deftly turns a humorous moment into a heartfelt one. Elizabeth Berg is a writer I go to when I want to feel good about the world and when I need to be reminded of the power of kindness. Her stories have a ton of heart. Both Tropper and Berg have given me many hours of pleasure in the last few years.

Other fiction writers whose work I admire include Kent Haruf, Richard Russo, and Dennis McFarland. For nonfiction, I enjoy Tracy Kidder and Frank McCourt. Bill Carter's

Fools Rush In is the book I'd grab in a fire if I could save only one.

Q. *Are you in a reading group? What's that experience been like for you? What have you read in the last year that you just loved?*

A. I'm in a book club with about twelve of the coolest women I know, and our meetings keep getting rowdier and more provocative as the years go on. Some book clubs are quite focused on analyzing the books they read, but we're much more interested in the drinking and eating that goes along with our book discussions. The books we read often spark topics of conversation, but as much as anything are just an excuse for us all to get together once a month. A recent book that generated a good discussion is *The Female Brain* by Louann Brizendine. We also found much to discuss in Jon Krakauer's *Under the Banner of Heaven*.

I'm also in a mother-daughter book club with my ten-year-old daughter, and I treasure how books bring us together and provide us with ways to discuss the increasing complexities of her life.

Q. *What do you hope readers will take away from* One True Theory of Love?

A. I simply hope readers close the book feeling their time has been well spent, in whatever way they define that. If they are looking for a fun read, I hope they find it. If they are looking for comfort or an escape from the real world or for a book that makes them think—I hope they find it.

QUESTIONS FOR DISCUSSION

✖

1. What's your reaction to the novel? Did you enjoy it? Were you emotionally engaged? What aspects did you like best and which least?

2. Do you agree with the first line of the novel: "It's easy to look at men and think they're idiots"?

3. What do you think are Meg's greatest strengths as a character? What are her weaknesses?

4. Jonathan blindsided Meg by leaving their marriage when she'd learned she was pregnant. Was he just a louse, or are there hints about Meg's own failures in the marriage? When he reenters Meg's life, has he changed?

5. The author explores the impact of an old relationship on a newly developing one. Draw from your own experience to discuss some other ways in which new relationships are shaped and constrained, and made better or worse, by previous relationships.

6. Meg learns that her father, whom she relies on for advice and guidance, has been misrepresenting himself with a major lie. Compare Meg's view of her father versus the reality, and discuss possible reasons for his behavior. Have you known men (or women!) who have behaved similarly?

7. Meg prides herself on her close relationship with her son, Henry. Do you think she's a good mother? Is there anything about her parenting that you would either emulate or do differently?

8. Meg's mother, Clarabelle, is making changes in her life now that her marriage is over. What do you think of those changes? What kind of mother do you think she was to Meg and Amy? What kind of wife was she to Phillip?

9. Do you agree that Ahmed is a pretty terrific guy? How do you see his and Meg's relationship evolving after the book ends?

10. Do you have a theory of life similar to Meg's Hokey-Pokey Theory of Life? Has it served you well?